YOU CAN TRUST ME

MIRANDA RIJKS

Published by Inkubator Books
www.inkubatorbooks.com

Copyright © 2025 by Miranda Rijks

ISBN (eBook): 978-1-83756-590-0
ISBN (Paperback): 978-1-83756-591-7
ISBN (Hardback): 978-1-83756-592-4

Miranda Rijks has asserted her right to be identified as the author of this work.

YOU CAN TRUST ME is a work of fiction. People, places, events, and situations are the product of the author's imagination. Any resemblance to actual persons, living or dead is entirely coincidental.

No part of this book may be reproduced, stored in any retrieval system, or transmitted by any means without the prior written permission of the publisher.

PROLOGUE
TWENTY-FIVE YEARS AGO

The little bell rings. Again. I'm upstairs trying to concentrate. Computer Studies is my favourite subject and I'm going to be a programmer when I leave school. It's cool, because mostly it's the boys who are good at it. The only girls in the class are Karin and me and she looks like the back end of a bus.

The bell chimes again. *I'm not her slave, although she acts as if I am.*

I shove the earphones over my head but still that little tinkling sound rings through. Slamming down the lid of the laptop (stolen, because how the hell am I meant to afford a laptop?), I stomp down the stairs.

'Can you make me a cuppa, love?' Mum wheezes. The sound of her breathing makes me want to scream. The kitchen is filthy because she can't haul herself up to clean it and I've got better things to do. I fill the kettle up with water and switch it on. How I hate this place. Every evening I hear the couple next door screaming at each other and then having loud make-up sex that goes on for hours and hours. It's gross. I can't carry on living here in this minuscule box, with its paper-thin walls and mould-ridden ceilings. Mum only leaves her chair in front of the television when she needs to use the brown, water-stained bathroom, and then it's up to me to help her. I should be out with my friends, having the time of my life. Instead, I'm her carer.

And I've had enough.

I rinse out a dirty mug and plop a teabag inside. When the kettle has boiled, I pour in the hot water and then open the fridge. We're practically out of milk and I can't be bothered to go out again to get some. Besides, I used the grocery money on a packet of cigarettes. I tip the dregs of the milk carton into the mug and carry it back out to Mum.

Her wheezing is really bad today. That awful high-pitched whistle that makes me want to scream every time she exhales.

'Here you go,' I say, handing her the mug, knowing that it's too hot for her stiff fingers to hold.

'Can't you put it down for me?' she asks.

I plonk it on the side table and some of the hot liquid slurps over the top.

'For heaven's sake,' she mutters. She glances over at it. 'You know I like it milky. Put some more milk in it.'

It's been like this day after day, week after week, month after month. Do this. Do that. This isn't good enough. Can't you try harder. Be kind.

'We haven't got any more milk.'

'Well, go and get some,' she wheezes. 'You need to think ahead.' *Wheeze.* 'Plan.' *Wheeze.* 'Look at what's in the fridge and make sure you don't run out.' *Wheeze and whistle.*

I know it's not much, the moans and the criticism. Not today. But when it's incessant, and it *is* incessant, sometimes you get to a tipping point. And suddenly I can't take it anymore.

Every muscle in my body tenses and a shroud covers my eyes. I need to scream. To feel pain. To make it stop. I grab the cushion on the sofa, the ugly, green cushion that's got a wine stain right in the centre, and stride towards Mum.

'What are you doing, love?' she asks. Except I don't register her words.

'Put that cushion down. It's my favourite.'

It's as if Mum is talking to me from miles away, through thick brick walls, her words sounding like faint gibberish. As for me, my body is being controlled by some weird force, making me do this. Making me shove the cushion into Mum's face.

She struggles. Of course she does. But I'm young and strong and fit, and she's got emphysema and is flabby and overweight, and so ugly in every way. I hold it firmer and firmer over her face while her limbs twitch like crazy. I push harder, holding it there for three minutes, five minutes, for what seems like forever. And then her body just collapses in on itself and everything goes limp.

Eventually, I pull the cushion away from her face. She's completely still, flopped over like an obese rag doll. Her eyes are glazed and shocked-looking, but she's not seeing me. At last, she doesn't see me.

I stare at her and all I feel is relief. So much relief.

As I gather up my things and leave the pokey flat, there is a sense of euphoria. I'm free. I don't have to answer to anyone, to be nagged at, to be ground down, day after day.

My life is my own to do whatever I want. Now I know how easy it is to kill, I feel an overwhelming confidence that my future will be full of great things. I close the front door to this horrible flat, locking it behind me, and then I dance down the stairs, do a fist pump and step outside into the bright sunlight. Into my golden future.

CHAPTER ONE

AMELIA

I look around the room at the women lying flat on their yoga mats, eyes closed, breathing deeply. This is my favourite moment, the time when I appreciate the stillness. I feel euphoric, knowing I've enabled them to make a profound difference to their health and wellbeing. I would like to stay in this moment of tranquillity, except I can already see the shadows of people congregating on the other side of the opaque glass door. Our time is up.

'Thank you for being part of this practice today. Remember you can call upon this sensation of calm even in the busiest moments, and peace is always within reach.' I bring my hands up to my chest in the prayer pose and bow my head. 'Namaste.'

The ladies in my class are always in a hurry to leave, despite the peacefulness of the meditation they've just experienced. Mats are quickly rolled up, expensive athletic-wear hoodies tugged back on, and the chatter in the room becomes increasingly loud. Some wave their thanks at me, others just hurry out. I don't mind. My classes are consistently full, twenty women jammed into this square room, and that's the only thing that matters. Every day, I pinch myself that I'm being paid to do a job I love.

I think back to my humble beginnings; the bedroom I shared with my sister in our tiny, terraced house where Mum and Dad worked all hours to pay for our school uniforms and one big present a year. A house where there wouldn't have been enough space to roll out a yoga mat. I worked hard at school in the hope that I could live somewhere bigger when I grew up. When I completed my yoga teacher training last year and told Mum, she fell silent and then asked, 'Why on earth would you be doing some happy-clappy thing like that?' I didn't even try to explain. Mum understood the jobs I had in my twenties and thirties. Achieving good grades in the sciences, I trained in pharmacy and worked my way up the ranks until I became a senior hospital pharmacist, responsible for managing drug distribution and getting involved with medication safety initiatives. Weird as it sounds to some people, I enjoyed the mountains of paperwork and compliance, and in the latter years, spent much time attending conferences all over the world.

Mum never told me to my face that she was proud of my single-minded ambition, that she secretly applauded my rapid promotions. But before he died, my dad let it slip from time to time. I earned enough money to pay for my parents to renovate their house and even expand it, except they declined, of course. And then I met Hudson and everything changed. My money became his; his money became mine.

Occasionally I miss the responsibilities and independence. No, if I'm being honest with myself, I miss it a lot, particularly the financial independence. My identity and sense of self-worth were tied up with my job. I felt that I had achieved something in life, that I was recognised and admired even. A successful pharmacist. But something had to give, and Hudson and I decided that I should be the one to relinquish my career. At the time, I chose that willingly, but times change. At least my daily yoga practice is bringing me calm and acceptance, and perhaps that elusive self-confidence might start to seep back.

I'm wiping yoga mats with disinfectant wipes when Vanessa strides into the studio. This is her business and her premises; I'm just one of several teachers who run classes here, and we're all beholden to her. She's strident and controlling and expects gratitude from all her staff. I'd love to be out of her clutches. That's the plan but there's a long way to go first.

'Are you done?' Vanessa asks. She's about to lead a rebounder class and is wheeling out loads of little trampolines.

'Yes,' I say, gathering up my belongings. She throws me what can only be described as a filthy look and I wonder what I've done wrong this time. I'm not going to hang around to find out. With my big canvas bag over my shoulder, I hurry out of the studio edging past Vanessa's students, who are pouring in.

'Amelia!'

I glance up and see Katya.

'Got time for a coffee? Romy, Paige and I are nipping across the road.'

I glance at my watch, but I'm not sure why I check the time because I have no other commitments today. 'Sure.' I grin, happy to be part of 'a gang'. We four are all teachers at Vanessa's establishment. Katya teaches Pilates, Romy specialises in aerial yoga and barre work, Paige runs the

Vinyasa classes whereas I focus on Ashtanga and restorative yoga. I'm pretty sure my classes are the most popular. Only last week Vanessa asked if I could run an extra four classes each week.

Vanessa's studio, called Vitality with Vanessa, used to be a small department store on the high street. When the department store closed down, the place was empty for a couple of years, until Vanessa, an investment banker in her previous life, took it over and turned the premises into three large rooms with sprung floors, perfect for fitness classes. It's directly opposite an independent coffee shop called Eat Cake that serves the best homemade cakes in Sussex. Vanessa was furious when it opened up, because unsurprisingly, her students, feeling virtuous after a fitness class, hop over the road and indulge in a triple-layered chocolate cake or donuts filled with fresh cream.

The coffee shop is always buzzing and today is no different. As Katya and I walk in, Romy stands up and waves at us. She and Paige are seated at a small round table near the back of the shop, both nursing coffees.

We all air-kiss each other.

Romy turns to Katya. 'How's the wedding planning going?' Romy is a willowy woman with cornrow hair and flawless ebony skin.

'I'm exhausted,' Katya says as she sinks onto a chair. 'It's such hard work organising a wedding, and it's not even a big one.'

Somehow I doubt that, because, along with our partners, we've all been invited. I can't say that my husband Hudson is too thrilled about the prospect of attending the wedding of someone he's never met but we're going whether he likes it or not. Katya is the youngest of us four by over a decade and she's chosen to have a boho wedding in a field, where she and her husband-to-be will arrive bare-back on horses. I'm sure she'll look stunning with her bright blue eyes and flowing blonde hair.

'What can I get you, ladies?' the server asks Katya and me.

'A fresh mint tea, please,' Katya says.

'I'll have the same, please,' I add.

'I can't wait for your wedding,' Paige tells Katya. Paige is around the same age as me, in her early forties, with choppy shoulder-length hair the colour of wheat, and deep-set green eyes. She wears heavy makeup, even for her yoga classes, and I wonder if she's covering up acne-scarred skin. Paige's daughter Taryn is in the same school and year group as our daughter, Marnie. Not that they're friends. Paige has been a yoga teacher at Vitality with Vanessa for about six months, but I've only got close to her in the past couple of months, largely because Romy has included me in their friendship group. She reminds me both physically and personality-wise of a girl on my pharmacology course who always tried a little too hard, who I reckoned felt inferior because of her difficult start in life.

'Still loads to do, although I've chosen the flowers,' Katya explains. 'I'm going to have garlands of daisies in my hair and in my posy and we'll have wildflowers in jam jars on the tables. I'm getting really excited. Not long to go now. Have you all chosen what you're wearing?'

'I've ordered a stunning cornflower-blue dress from an online shop,' I say.

'That colour will look fabulous on you,' Romy gushes.

The truth is, I'm getting nervous about my order. I spotted the most beautiful silk dress on a website and I placed the order nearly four weeks ago. It still hasn't arrived. I emailed the shop, a website called Luxall-London, and eventually received a tracking number. I'm concerned because the tracking number is from China, yet the shop's website states they're based in London. I've got a suspicion I might have been scammed and zone out as the others talk about the dresses they'll be wearing. I wonder if I'm going to have to raid the back of my wardrobe.

'How are your grand plans going?' Romy asks me.

'What grand plans?' Paige quips.

'Amelia is hoping to turn her barn into a wellness retreat, aren't you?'

'Oh wow! That sounds amazing. Tell me more.' Paige leans towards me, her face open and eager.

'I've got planning permission to convert our barn and I hope to one day run yoga classes and wellness retreats from there.'

'Will you need teachers?' Paige asks. 'If so, count me in!'

I laugh. 'Of course.'

'Anything to get away from vile Vanessa,' Katya adds. We all snigger.

'So when will you be up and running?' Paige asks.

I sigh. 'I haven't got the money to do the building works at the moment. Costs have rocketed and I'm not sure when I'll be able to do it.' The money that I saved from my job as a pharmacist went towards our house. All that's left is a nest egg squirrelled away in a savings account allocated by Hudson and me to fund Marnie's university education.

'That's a shame,' Paige adds.

'Can't Hudson help?' Romy suggests. Romy and I have known each other the longest, coming up for five years now, and her husband is good mates with Hudson. No doubt

Hudson has been bragging about his business and his varied investments, implying that we're loaded. And in comparison to many, we are, except there's a hefty mortgage on the house. For now, my yoga teaching brings in a pittance. The problem with my 'grand plan' is that my husband doesn't think converting the barn into a wellness retreat is a sensible idea. He doesn't want strangers coming onto our property and nosing around. As he travels so much, I'm not sure why he's bothered. He doesn't think we'll get a return on our investment and has dismissed my detailed business plan and carefully worked-out financial projections. I disagree and it's a big bone of contention between us.

'Hudson isn't sold on the idea,' I admit.

A couple of hours later and I'm back at home. We live in the Sussex countryside, three miles' drive from Beacham, where Vanessa has her studio. Not far from the sea, our tiny hamlet is located at the foot of the South Downs. Our house, once a brick farmhouse, is set far apart from the others, at the end of a long drive that winds between trees and hedgerows. We also have a ramshackle barn and a one-acre garden. I love the house and the setting with its beautiful views, but occasionally wish I didn't have to get in the car to go everywhere. But it's a perfect place to raise a child, and our black Labrador, Clover, gets gorgeous walks.

The post has arrived, along with a small plastic-wrapped parcel from China. At long last. I just hope that the dress is as beautiful as it looked in the photo. There's so much tape, I have to use scissors to cut it, and the garment has been compressed to such a degree, there's a whoosh of air when I open the package. I take out a thin sliver of fabric that crackles and sparks as it slides through my fingers. It's blue, it's a dress of sorts, but it is absolutely nothing like the photograph of the dress I thought I was buying. This garment is made from cheap nylon, the stitching is visible on all the seams, and I know without putting it on that it will look dreadful. I let out a groan. As I feared, I've been scammed. I just pray that I can return it and get my money back, money I can ill afford to lose.

I let the fabric slip back into the plastic packing and mentally kick myself. I should have known better. I grab my old laptop and navigate to the online shop. It's still there: Luxall-London, with a photograph of two older women standing in front of the window of a smart-looking clothes shop. The strap line says:

> Sadly, the day has come to shut down our boutique and spend more time with our grandchildren. Thank you to all our loyal customers from the past twenty years. But before we close our doors, we have something special for you: our beautiful collection is now available with discounts of up to 80%! Once the stock has gone, it's gone forever.
> With love and gratitude, Margaret and Vera.

With a sinking heart, I realise that Margaret and Vera most likely don't exist and probably never have done. I scroll through the website to find the help email and fire off a message, requesting a refund due to the dress looking nothing like the one that was advertised.

I feel like such an idiot. That sensation that I'm just not good enough; that time has passed me by; that I let everyone around me and myself down. When Marnie was young, I didn't miss my pharmacy job, but these days I do. Of course, it wasn't compatible with having a child; I had to travel too much. Except now, I barely recognise the woman that I once was. It's as if every year that's passed since I quit work, my education and career success have been further peeled away, leaving behind the insecure child from a hard-up, working-class family. It doesn't help that Hudson has confidence in bucket-loads, as if he's making up for my deficiencies.

My husband has a successful travel agency business which has grown rapidly in the last decade, and against all odds, weathered the pandemic. We live in a beautiful house but money has definitely been tighter the past few years. Even so, Hudson wasn't keen on me resurrecting my career. And he was right. I was able to be there for Marnie when she needed me the most. Except at some point, being a mother and homemaker became not enough. Gut-churning panic ate away at my days along with the sense that I had no legacy and no independence. With hindsight, I needed to be needed. I still do. And then I was introduced to yoga and it became my salvation. It saved my sanity, improved my physical health, and now it's a source of income, albeit modest. At long last I feel like I'm doing something worthwhile. Except perhaps I'm more fragile than I realised. I've been scammed, and those feelings of being small and worthless hit me all over again. And it's accompanied by a strange fear that my comfortable little world might come tumbling down at any moment.

CHAPTER TWO

PAIGE

I stand in the mirror and do a twirl. Yes, I look good. The dress and bag might be borrowed – well, actually, stolen, except I'll be taking them back, so that makes it borrowed, right? I've tucked the tag carefully inside the fabric and I bought one of those magnet devices from Amazon that removes the security tags from garments. When I take the dress and bag back to the shop, I'll explain that my husband bought the garments for me and didn't give me the receipt. I'm believable, and if necessary, I'll turn on the tears. It works every time. No one knows about my 'borrowing' skill; not Dean, my partner, nor Taryn, my daughter. The dress is a pale blush pink that looks great with my blonde hair and skims over my curves.

There are heavy footsteps behind me and a whistle. 'You look a million dollars, love,' Dean says.

'Thanks,' I say, turning to pick up the matching handbag off the bed. I glance at Dean. I wish I could say the same about him, but despite the rented suit and silver tie, he still looks rumpled and dishevelled. What is it with him? Most men look a million times better in smart clothes, but not our Dean. I sigh. 'Come on, we'd better get a move on.'

I have to say I was surprised to be invited to Katya's wedding. It's not like we know each other well, but I guess if she was inviting Amelia and Romy she could hardly leave me out. To be fair, we haven't been invited to the wedding ceremony, which, according to Katya, is for family only, but we have been invited to the big celebration afterwards. And so here we are, parked up in a field, watching the other guests trot along a freshly mown path, stiletto heels digging into the earth, making it hard for the women to walk elegantly. To hell with that. I take off the rented shoes that I can't afford to sully (rented, because even I would struggle to shoplift shoes), and walk barefoot towards the marquee. As I glance back, I note a few other women following my lead, carrying their shoes in one hand, glittery clutches in the other. That's the thing with me: I'm a leader.

'Hold on,' Dean says breathlessly, trying to keep up. I'd rather he didn't. The other male guests look so suave and sophisticated in sharply tailored suits, and some men are even wearing morning dress, long-line jackets. I can't decide whether they make them look like penguins or really dapper. I spot Katya and her new husband frolicking in a field, a photographer directing them as they pout and contort in various Instagram-worthy poses. A huddle of people stop to stare. There's no doubting that Katya looks a million dollars. She's wearing a white silk slip of a dress and has a garland of wild flowers woven into her hair which she's wearing down in big, flowing curls. Her skin is bronzed and her muscles well defined. She's staring up lovingly into the eyes of her husband. What the heck is his name? I can't remember. We get swept up with the fast-flowing stream of people and walk into a huge white marquee, its ceiling filled with balloons in pale pinks and beige. I tut. I thought Katya was eco-friendly. There's nothing ecological about several hundred latex balloons. I can make out about twenty tables dressed with white tablecloths decorated with numerous jam jars in differing sizes filled with grasses and what look like wildflowers but have probably been cultivated in a greenhouse. The look is countryside bohemian but I'm not sure it quite hits the mark. I'm walking towards a huge stand with a table plan on it when I come face-to-face with Amelia.

'I'm so glad to see you!' she gushes. 'I don't know anyone here. Do you?'

'We've only just arrived, so I'm not sure.' The chances of me knowing anyone other than Amelia, Romy and Katya are almost zero.

'I've checked out the table plan and fortunately, we're all sitting together.' She may think that's fortunate; I'm not so sure.

Dean appears at my side and grasps my arm. He's always awkward in social occasions and I sense his tension. He's annoying me today and I shrug him off. He could at least have gotten a haircut. Amelia is looking at him expectantly.

'Oh, sorry. This is Dean, my partner,' I say, introducing them.

'And Hudson is just over there, getting me a glass of champers,' she adds. On cue, a man appears holding two champagne flutes. Unlike Dean, who is in an ordinary blue suit, Hudson is wearing black tie, a sharply cut black suit with satin collars and a pale-yellow silk bow tie. But it's not just his expensive clothes that strike me; this man is incredibly good-looking with dark hair, greying at the temples, pale blue eyes and a strong jaw. Amelia has done really, really well for herself.

'Hello,' he says in a husky voice, his eyes running all over me. He hands Amelia a glass of champagne but his eyes don't leave me.

'Hudson, this is Paige and her partner Dean. Paige and I work together at Vanessa's studio.'

I take the lead and put out my hand. 'It's a pleasure to meet you,' I say. I can tell immediately that Dean won't like Hudson. He's one of those suave, poshly spoken types, no doubt privately educated, the sort of man who makes Dean feel instantly inferior. Even though I've told Dean numerous times that he's worth a thousand of the Hudson types, he doesn't believe it. Just because he's a plumber and a bit rough around the edges doesn't mean he's less of a man than someone like Hudson, who probably has a degree or two from some fancy university. At least that's what I used to tell myself. We make casual chitchat, accepting glasses of fizz and canapés from servers who all look younger than Taryn, my sixteen-year-old daughter. I stand just a little too close to Hudson, brushing his arm as I bring my glass of champagne up to my lips. He explains that he has a chain of boutique travel agencies specialising in tailor-made trips for people with more money than sense. His words, not mine. I ooh and aah and watch Amelia out of the corner of my eye, but she doesn't seem fazed by my flirting with her husband. Perhaps she's used to other women coming onto him, or perhaps she doesn't care.

Before long, we're being ushered to our tables and the bride and groom enter the marquee to huge applause. Katya is glowing, lapping up all the attention, waving and twirling and blowing kisses like a true diva. God, I wish I could be her right now.

We take our seats at our table, the one furthest away from the bride and groom's top table. I suppose we've been labelled as the least important guests. I shouldn't care, but I do. I sit down between Amelia and Hudson.

'Your dress is beautiful,' I say to Amelia, even though it isn't. Frankly, it looks like it's a couple of sizes too large for her, and the shade of purple does nothing to enhance her complexion. It's hardly surprising that Hudson can't keep his eyes off me. 'Is that the one you ordered online?'

'I thought you said it was cornflower blue,' Romy adds.

'I had to send that one back.' Amelia lowers her eyes.

'Oh dear. Didn't it fit?' I ask.

For the first time, Amelia seems to clock her husband, who is deep in conversation with Paul, Romy's partner. As if she doesn't want him to hear, she leans forward and says in a conspiratorial whisper, 'I think I was scammed. I feel like such an idiot.'

'Oh no,' Romy says. 'What happened?'

'It was nothing like the photo or description, and now I've got to send it back to China.' She speaks so quietly I can barely hear her. I lean close to her and can't help but inhale the scent of her sickly floral perfume.

'What's the name of the website?' I ask, a little nugget of an idea forming at the back of my head.

'Luxall-London,' Amelia whispers.

'Gosh, I hope it wasn't too expensive,' I add. Amelia grimaces. And that's all the answer I need.

The first course arrives; a salmon mousse with a minuscule portion of salad. I monopolise Hudson for a while, asking about his business, letting my arm gently nudge his.

And then I turn back to his wife. Amelia seems awkward and I can't work out why; it's as if her mind is on something else.

'Your bracelet is gorgeous,' I say. Indeed it is: a platinum band inlaid with big sparkling diamonds, Cartier perhaps.

'Thanks,' Amelia responds. 'We had a bit of a tough time a couple of years ago when Marnie was really ill. She almost died but, thank God, managed to pull through. Hudson gave me the bracelet as a commemoration of Marnie's life, I guess.'

I would like to ask her more, except someone hits the side of a glass and as the ringing sound permeates the marquee, everyone falls silent. We listen to some deadly boring speeches given by the best man and the father of the bride, and then, at long last, the main course arrives. Partridge for the carnivores, some vegetarian tagliatelle for everyone else. The partridge is largely bone and frankly, a bit ridiculous.

'Tell me more about your ideas for your yoga retreat,' I ask Amelia, knowing that this question will get her talking. She witters on about the classes she'd like to give and the holistic remedies she wants to offer, and her ideas for marketing it far and wide. I zone out, just adding in supportive platitudes, telling her that I think it's a brilliant idea and that she absolutely must do it, even if she has to remortgage their house.

When she gets up to go to the toilet, I turn towards her hunky husband. We're deep into a chat again, largely about his extensive travels, with me pretending I've visited countries that I haven't even heard of. He spends a lot of the time staring at my cleavage and letting his leg graze against mine.

'So what do you think of Amelia's new project?' I ask, my eyes wide and head tilted to one side.

He frowns.

'The yoga retreat in your barn,' I add.

'Oh that,' Hudson says, a hint of dismissal in his voice. 'A pipe dream. I can't see it taking off and besides, the thought of a bunch of braying women on our property fills me with horror.'

'But Amelia is such an amazing yoga teacher. Her classes are always full.' I pause for a moment, gently biting my lower lip. 'Except I have to agree with you. I don't see how it could be a commercial success. The market is over-saturated and as lovely as your wife is, I think she's a little commercially naive. Please don't tell her I've said that because I adore Amelia.'

He laughs. 'You're speaking my language now.'

'I mean, I looked at some of the ROIs in her projections and it would take about twenty years to pay back the capital investment she wants to spend.'

'You're right. You need to talk some sense into my wife. Let her carry on teaching her little yoga classes but that's that.'

For a moment I actually feel a tiny bit of pity towards Amelia. Hudson might be a looker but he's hardly the supportive husband. And then she's back from the toilets and the conversation switches and we're talking about the new headmistress of Stanford Grammar School, the school that Taryn and Marnie go to in Beacham.

Once the meal is over, Dean and I don't stay long at the wedding. I'm a nobody here and the last thing I want to do is dance with Dean. Amelia, Hudson, Romy and Paul take to the dance floor, which enables us to slip away without anyone noticing.

Back at home, I check out Luxall-London's website. Amelia is such an idiot to have fallen for it because it's absolutely obvious it's a scam. All you need to do is check out the IP address, the length of time the website has been running, and the reviews on Reddit. But then again, I'm a techno genius; it's how my brain works, and it was my line of work until a few years ago. My comfort zone. I set up a new email account and send Amelia an email to the address I've lifted from the website she has promoting herself as a yoga teacher. It's a one-pager site, far from impressive, and attracting zero traffic, so I'm not sure why she bothers. I type out the following:

Dear Ms Myers,

Please accept my sincere apologies for sending you the wrong item. Your dress should have been sent from our boutique in London but unfortunately was sent from our wholesaler in China, who dispatched the wrong item. I've been away from work for a few weeks, nursing my husband who has now passed away, and take full responsibility for the mix-up. Please rest assured I will investigate and sort this.

Yours Sincerely,
Margaret

After sending the email, I carefully remove the dress I wore to the wedding and inspect it, checking that there aren't any little marks or stains that a shop assistant might notice. Happy that it's spotless, I fold the dress neatly, slipping it into a carrier bag.

Dean is already asleep by the time I'm out of the shower and ready for bed. As I close my eyes, I think of Hudson, with his thick dark hair and chiselled jaw. I wonder what it would feel like to have his fingers exploring my body, his wide lips on mine. And then I think of Amelia and how she has all the luck. A handsome, rich husband, living in a gorgeous house. I console myself with the thought that Amelia's luck is shortly going to change.

THE NEXT DAY there is an email from Amelia thanking Margaret for her kind note and requesting her money back. Oh, Amelia! You really are self-obsessed and weak, and really rather stupid. In fact, she's proven herself to be exactly as I had labelled her. The entitled type for whom everything always turns out so perfectly. But not for any longer, Amelia. No. I'm going to enjoy playing with you and your handsome husband, Hudson.

I'm rarely home when Taryn gets in from school, but today I need to talk to her. Our house is small. Nothing like Amelia's mansion. It's a two-bedroom, one-bathroom semi on a long row of terraces. There wasn't much choice when we moved here but despite my initial reservations, it's beginning to feel like home. My daughter is sixteen and about as different to me as is possible. Sometimes that makes it hard to bond with her, especially now she's going through her goth stage with spiky black hair that, against her pale complexion, makes her look like a ghost. Taryn wears chunky black boots, black clothes and black makeup. Honestly, she looks hideous but Dean bites a chunk off me whenever I criticise Taryn's looks. You'd never know that he wasn't her real dad.

'Hi, darling!' I shout out as she stomps into the kitchen with the footsteps of an elephant. 'Good day at school?'

'What's it to you?'

'Look,' I say, swallowing my annoyance at her rudeness. 'Do you know a girl called Marnie in your year?'

'Yeah, vaguely. Why?'

'I'm friends with her mum and I thought it would be fun for the four of us to get together.'

'No way.' Taryn's shoulders tense up.

'Why? Her mum is lovely.'

'Well, Marnie's not.'

'Could you perhaps make an effort, for me? We could go out for supper, watch a film perhaps.'

'She's a bitch.'

'Oh, come on, Taryn. You just said you hardly knew her.'

'She and her friends are a bunch of bullies.'

I stand up, suddenly, tipping the wooden chair over. 'Have they bullied you?' I ask. Taryn knows that I don't stand for any nonsense; that if anyone bullies her, they have me to deal with. I might not be the most maternal person in the universe but all guns come out blazing if anyone hurts my daughter.

'It's fine, Mum. Just chill. Look, I don't want anything to do with Marnie and I don't want to meet up with her. It's bad enough having her around at school.'

'What does that mean?' I ask, bristling at the thought of Amelia's daughter behaving badly towards Taryn.

'Let it go, Mum. It's nothing. She's just an idiot. I'm going to do my homework.' She takes a glass from the cupboard and pours herself some water from the kitchen tap.

'What would you like for supper?' I ask to her retreating footsteps, thinking about what I will do to Marnie if I find out that she's been bothering Taryn.

'Whatever.'

The trouble with my daughter is she's exceptionally

intelligent. There's talk that she might be Oxford or Cambridge material. It's not like she's had much support from Dean and me, at least not on the academic side. Schoolwork just seems to come naturally to her. Because she does so well at school, I let her get away with more than I should – the answering back, the rudeness and the ridiculous dress sense – because when your child comes home with glowing school reports and prizes, there's not much to get annoyed about. After I hear her bedroom door slam, I pick up the phone and call Amelia.

'Recovered from the wedding?' I ask.

'Just about. You disappeared early,' she replies.

'Dean had an early start. Look, I was just talking to my daughter Taryn, and she mentioned how lovely Marnie has been to her at school. I was thinking it would be fun for the four of us to get together, go out for a pizza or something and perhaps take in a film. What do you think?'

'That would be wonderful!' Amelia exclaims with such enthusiasm it makes me wonder if she actually has any other friends. 'When were you thinking?' We agree on Saturday late afternoon.

Half an hour later, over our pasta supper, I turn to Taryn. 'We're meeting up with Amelia and Marnie on Saturday afternoon.'

'You have to be fucking joking! Why don't you ever listen to me?'

'Language, Taryn,' I say.

'You might be meeting up with them but I'm not.'

'Yes, you are, and it'll be lovely. It's important to make new friends.'

'You can go without me.'

'Ah, come on, love,' Dean says, patting Taryn's hand. He's always had an easy way with her and she listens to him.

'We stand up to bullies in this household, Taryn,' I say. 'If she's being a bitch to you, then let's charm her with kindness.'

Dean laughs, knowing that isn't my normal way. Taryn stares at me as if I've lost my marbles, and perhaps I have. 'You wait and see,' I say. 'We'll have a lovely time.'

CHAPTER THREE

MARNIE

'We're meeting Paige and her daughter Taryn in Beacham this afternoon,' Mum says. When she first mentioned the 'get-together' I'd gone apoplectic. What mother foists their friends' children on them when they're our age? I mean, I'm nearly sixteen, not some little kid whose mum can boss me around. Besides, Taryn is a weirdo, all goth and sulky and a complete swot.

'It's not convenient,' I say, instantly losing my appetite for the piece of toast in front of me. 'I've got revision to do.'

'You've been working really hard recently and I think it would do us all good to go out for an early supper.'

'No, thanks.' I get up from the table, but Mum is not going to let this one go.

'It's non-negotiable, Marnie. If you don't come, you don't get your pocket money this month.'

I throw my hands up into the air. 'But that's blackmail.'

'I'm sure we'll have a lovely time and if in the unlikely event we don't, there's no need to see Taryn again.'

'Hardly. We're at the same school, and what if she starts

hanging onto me? She's so cheugy,' I mutter under my breath. And she is. She only started at our school at the beginning of the year and I'm not sure she has a single friend. Taryn never makes eye contact with anyone, she wears skinny black jeans with slashes at the knees and has spiky black hair. And most of the time, she comes top of the class in every subject. I don't know why Mum is so desperate for Taryn and me to be friends but I have zero intention to hang with her at school. It's not like my friendship group is great at the moment but I'm not that desperate.

Except when Saturday afternoon arrives and Mum promises to give me double pocket money for joining her at supper with *our* new friends, reluctantly I accept. I just hope that none of my actual friends see us. That would be so unfunny.

Paige and Taryn are seated at a table for four and Paige jumps up and greets Mum as if they're long-lost friends. It's so lame. They've only known each other a few months and it's not like they're besties. They work together. Taryn raises her blackened eyes at me and nods. Olivia and I haven't exactly been nice to Taryn these past months. I might have said some mean things which she overheard, and now I'm sitting opposite her, I hope she doesn't mention anything because that would be awks. She's wearing over-ear headphones, a brand that I've been craving for ages but are really expensive.

'Take those bloody things off,' Paige says, trying to make a grab for the headphones. Taryn ducks and rolls her eyes at me. That's the second time she's looked at me in less than a minute and I wonder if the keeping-eyes-to-the-ground thing is something she affects at school to avoid everyone.

'Marnie is addicted to music too,' Mum says as she settles into the chair next to me.

'Hardly addicted,' I mutter. Taryn throws me a brief grin.

'So what sort of music do you like listening to?' Mum asks Taryn.

'You won't have heard of it so why do you bother asking?' I interject.

And then we're interrupted by a server who takes our drinks order. White wine for Mum and Paige, Coke for me and a green tea for Taryn. A green tea?! When the server's gone Mum and Paige are deep in conversation and Taryn and I are just sitting there, not saying a word, avoiding eye contact with each other. I've got literally no idea what to say to her so I repeat Mum's question. 'What sort of music do you listen to, then?'

'Bands such as Groan the Growl and Pretensa Beats. You've probably never heard of them.'

'You have to be joking!' I exclaim, leaning across the table and almost toppling over my empty glass. 'I love them. I'm saving up to see Pretensa Beats when they come to London in July but no one wants to go with me.'

'I will,' Taryn says.

'I've literally never met anyone who likes that kind of music. All my friends think I'm weird.' And that's true. They all listen to Billie Eilish or Kendrick Lamar; so boringly mainstream.

Taryn laughs. 'I'd say we're just ahead of the curve. I bet you anything that Groan heads Reading Festival in the next couple of years.'

'God, I hope you're right.'

And then we're off. Talking about our favourite bands

for the rest of the meal, all my preconceived ideas about Taryn banished. We agree to share our Spotify lists on Monday at school and exchange socials so we can stay in touch. I want to hate Mum for being right but actually, it's a relief. Taryn may be a bit weird but we've got a lot in common.

The next day, as I'm walking into school, I see Olivia and Lola up ahead of me. I sprint to catch up with them and nearly run into Ryan.

'Oi, watch out!' he says. I slow down to walk alongside him, but he turns away from me, talking in a low whisper to a couple of his mates. My heart sinks. Ryan is hot. He's got floppy dirty-blond hair that he keeps gelled back from his forehead, and dazzling blue eyes. He's one of the most popular boys in school, with loads of friends, and he swaggers rather than walks. I've fancied him for ages, and two weeks ago he actually talked to me. It was a proper conversation and when the bell rang, he placed his hand on my arm and said, 'We need to hang sometime.' Except ever since then, Ryan has been ignoring me, like he is now.

I pretend not to be bothered and catch up with Olivia and Lola.

'Ryan just spoke to me,' I say breathlessly.

'We're talking,' Olivia says in a sarcastic voice. 'Don't interrupt us.'

It's been like this with Olivia and Lola for a few days now. They've been snubbing me and I don't know why.

'Why are you being like this?' I ask.

'Why are you being like this?' Olivia repeats in a singsong voice, and Lola just laughs.

I slink away, my shoulders rounded, dreading another whole day at school, and not knowing why my friends have turned on me. At the lockers, I catch sight of Taryn. Before, I might have been embarrassed to have Taryn as a friend, but now I reckon it's not such a bad thing. But she disappears before I can catch up with her. Taryn and I aren't in the same classes because she's cleverer than I am and in the top grades for every subject, but when the bell rings at the end of the school day, she materialises in front of me, and I don't mind.

'Do you want to hang after school?' she asks.

'What, today?'

'Why not?'

'Okay,' I reply, and then think that Mum will go ape-shit if I don't come home on time. But she was the one pushing for Taryn and me to be friends, so I ask if Taryn wants to come back to my house. Her face lights up as she says yes.

I wish I could get the bus home except I can't. We live in the middle of nowhere and there's no public transport, so Mum has to pick me up every day. It's embarrassing. As soon as I turn seventeen I'm getting my own car. At least Mum's agreed to park a couple of streets away so no one sees me get into her Volvo. How very dull and middle-class.

'Hello, Mrs Myers,' Taryn says as I open the rear passenger door for her.

'Is it okay if Taryn comes over for supper?' I ask.

'Of course it is.' Mum looks really pleased but then she ruins it by saying, 'I hope you're going to do your homework and not just listen to music.'

'Taryn is top of the class in every subject,' I say. 'She's going to be helping me out.'

We haven't discussed that and I turn in my seat and mouth, 'Sorry' to Taryn. She just shrugs.

An hour later and we're in my bedroom, Pretensa Beats

playing at full volume, making the house shudder. Mum appears and asks me to turn the music down. I do a bit.

Taryn is lying on the floor and I'm on my stomach on the bed. 'Where did you go to school before you came to Stanford Grammar?' I ask.

'Different schools,' Taryn says. 'We've moved a lot, mainly for my dad's job. What about you? Have you always lived here? Your house is so big and beautiful.'

'Thanks,' I say, wondering where Taryn lives if she thinks this place is so lovely. 'I'm glad our mums work together, otherwise we'd have never become friends.'

Taryn glows with the compliment.

'Has your mum always been a yoga teacher?' I ask.

'No, she retrained quite recently.'

'Mine too. And thank goodness she's got something else to focus on.'

'What do you mean?'

I sigh. 'I got meningitis a couple of years ago and nearly died. I was in hospital for three weeks and off school for three months. After that, it was like Mum wrapped me up in cotton wool. She was breathing down my neck literally all the time. Talk about a helicopter mother. She was in my face twenty-four seven. She didn't even want me to go to school. She's got a little bit better recently but she still treats me like I'm a baby.'

'Hospitals freak me out,' Taryn says, before edging forward, opening her rucksack and pulling out a couple of books. 'My brother was in hospital. Do you want me to help you with your maths homework?' she asks.

After supper, Taryn still hasn't made a move to return home and I wonder if she wants to stay the night, but then Mum appears and says that Paige will be collecting her in an hour's time. We go onto Spotify and talk music. There's a song I really love called 'Into the Ether,' and I start singing it.

'You've got a really good voice!' Taryn says. She switches the music off. 'Sing it again.'

And so I do. I stand in the middle of my bedroom, grab my hairbrush and pretend that I'm some cool pop star, bellowing out a hit. And then I collapse on the floor laughing.

'Seriously, Marnie. You've got a brilliant voice. You're every bit as good as most of the artists making it big.'

I'm not sure I believe her. I think Taryn is just being nice. It's true that I used to be in the school choir until I dropped it because there were better things to do.

'Sing it again.' She switches on the track, quite quietly so my voice booms over the top, and then Taryn takes out her phone and records me. I prance around the room, flicking my hair backwards and pretending that I'm in an arena performing to thousands of adoring fans. And then I'm laughing all over again.

'That was so good! You should upload it to Insta and tag Pretensa Beats.'

I sink onto the end of the bed. 'You're not just saying that?' I ask.

'Trust me. I'm dead serious. What's the worst that could happen?'

'Everyone taking the piss out of me at school,' I say.

'If you get crap comments, then just remove the video, but I really don't think you will. Or if you want, I can post it on my account.' She's fiddling with her phone. 'You've got way more followers than me so hardly anyone will see it if I post it.'

I don't like that idea so I agree to post it myself, and I do as she suggests and tag Pretensa Beats. Ten minutes after I've posted it, Mum shouts up the stairs that Paige is here and Taryn has to leave. And ten minutes after she's gone, I've got more likes on my new post than I've ever had before, and even Ryan has liked it and posted two flame emojis. I do a jig around my bedroom.

The next day, I'm checking the 'Gram before school and OMG! I've got two hundred and twenty-seven likes and forty-two comments. I have never had that before. Perhaps that silly little dream I had of becoming a pop star might turn into reality. Perhaps Taryn is right and I really do have talent. And then I see I've got a DM. I click on it and it's from someone called Jax James. I click on his profile and double OMG! He's an A&R working for a talent agency. The message reads:

> *Great rendition, Marnie. You should enter our online competition. Here's the link.*

I click on the link and it takes me to a website where you have to pay twenty quid to enter a singing competition but the prize is the possibility of being signed. It's worth every single penny.

At school, I make a beeline for Taryn and throw my arms around her. She looks quite shocked.

'What's that for?' she asks.

'There's an A&R that's suggested I enter a singing competition. You were right! I think I might be quite good.'

'I'm always right.' Taryn laughs. 'Of course you should enter, but if you win, remember me!'

'I need to record myself singing the song and then upload it to the website.'

'Why don't you do that at lunch? You can use one of the practice rooms in the music department.'

'Will you come with me?' I ask.

'Of course I'll help.'

I slide my arm into Taryn's and we walk together to the geography department. Olivia and her posse throw me quizzical looks and one of her friends mock-sticks her finger down her throat. I know they don't understand why I've become friends with weird Taryn, but that's because they don't know her. Well, I suppose I don't really know her yet either, but so far she's nothing like I thought she was going to be, and I think we could become close.

The morning passes by so slowly but eventually, Taryn and I meet up at the cafeteria, wolf down our lunches and head to the music department. The small practice room is perfect because it's soundproofed. Taryn records me singing on my phone and when we listen back, she's really supportive, telling me I sound great. I hope she's right because I upload it to the competition website, pay the twenty quid and press send. Mum gave me double pocket money this week, so at least I still have twenty pounds left over.

Later that night, back at home, I'm in bed, double-checking my social media, and decide to send Jax a message. With a pounding heart, I type:

I uploaded my entry this afternoon!!! Thanks so much for the opportunity.

He replies almost immediately.

Cool. I'll make sure I listen to it.

I find it hard to sleep as I imagine Jax being blown away by my voice and Mum telling the school that I've landed a record deal and that I'll have to be home-schooled because I'm going to be on the road, travelling the world, singing in sold-out arenas. And then I snort aloud because I'm getting carried away and I know deep down that that will never actually happen. But it's nice to dream.

The next day there's nothing from Jax and my hopes are dashed. I'm so stupid for believing I could make it big. It isn't until I'm in bed that evening scrolling mindlessly on my phone when I notice a message request. It's from Jax James Personal. My heart nearly thuds out of my chest as I click on it.

> Hiya, Marnie. Your submission is great. I've passed it on to my manager. I'm messaging you from my personal account because the other account is for business only. Hope you don't mind. I just wanted to say that you're hot and hope we can meet up someday. Jax P.S. – I don't use this account much but if you want to contact me, do it here!

I let out a yelp. Jax James fancies me! I accept his request and flip back to his account. He's only got five posts on his account and fifteen followers. A bit weird but he did say that he doesn't use his personal account much. He's really hot too, with short black hair and dark eyes.

I can't believe someone so much older and gorgeous likes me! I study his photos on both his personal and business accounts and reckon he must be late twenties. Most of his pictures and reels are of musicians and there are only two or three photos of him, his arm around people I don't recognise, a bottle of beer in his hand. He's wearing a cool bomber jacket and slouchy jeans, and he's got the best smile, wide, with sparkling white teeth. There's a gold stud earring in one ear, a chunky gold chain around his neck and a tattoo on his right arm which I think spells out something, but despite trying to enlarge the photo, I can't make out what it says. I wonder what he'd think if he knew I was only fifteen.

It takes me ages to decide what to say to him. In the end, I text:

Ur really good-looking too! Thanks for the message.

A moment later, he messages again.

Tell me about urself.

Nothing much to say. Uv got the coolest job!

Yup, I think so 2. Thought ur audition was rizz.

Wow thanx! Really?

Really. Ur so gorge. Not delulu at all. Have u got a boyfriend?

My heart hammers when I read that message. I reply.

No.

Or a girlfriend?

Not into girls.

What, not at all? Thought everyone was bi these days.

Not me. Really don't fancy girls and the dyke-like ones with short hair and butch clothes give me the jeebies.

The dots start and then stop and there's no reply. Immediately I wish I could delete that comment without it looking weird. Because I'm not that sort of person and I wish I hadn't said that. It's just that I like boys and Jax in particular. Oh God, I'm an idiot. I wait for ages but he doesn't message. But just as I'm dropping off to sleep my phone pings.

Sorry, got waylaid with work. I'm stoked we've connected. Sleep tight gorgeous and let's chat again in the morning. Will be dreaming of u.

He signs off with a winking emoji and a red chili pepper and I think I'm going to explode.

CHAPTER FOUR
AMELIA

I'm thrilled that Marnie and Taryn have become such close friends. When I first met Taryn I was rather wary. She dresses in an odd way but she's clearly a very bright girl and I'm hoping that will rub off on Marnie, who doesn't find academic work easy. Before she got sick, I made Marnie take all kinds of extra-curricular activities, as well as getting her extra coaching in maths and English, but when you think your child is going to die, that changes your perspective. Now, I just want her to be happy and healthy. I'm confident she'll find her way in life.

As Taryn is around our house most days after school, I'm seeing a lot more of Paige too, who has to drive over to collect her daughter. I like Paige. She's a bit different than my other friends with her down-to-earth, blunt manner which sometimes verges on rudeness. The other day, Katya turned up to Vanessa's studio in a new athletic outfit. She asked us if it suited her. I would have lied and said it was lovely, but Paige just blurted out that the colour drained her complexion.

Katya looked hurt, but in some ways, it's better to be told the truth, isn't it?

This afternoon, I'm having a bit of a clear-out, hoping to list some old clothes to sell online. I'm trying to save every penny I can and if I can earn a little extra, I will put it towards my retreat building fund. I'm in the kitchen writing descriptions on my laptop for all the items of clothing while the girls are upstairs doing their homework – at least I hope they are. Marnie's last school report wasn't great and if she doesn't buckle down, she might not even pass her GCSEs. Hudson will go apoplectic if that happens. He has Marnie's life all planned out. A Levels, a degree in a good university preferably studying something like law or accountancy, and then a climb up the corporate ladder, followed by taking over his business. I just can't see that happening.

I hear the crunch of tyres outside and see Paige pull up in her little white Polo. She hops out of her car and strides up to the back door.

'You're so kind to have Taryn yet again,' she enthuses as we air-kiss.

'It's no problem, and if she can help Marnie increase her grades, then so much the better.'

Paige seems comfortable in our house these days, but when she first came here, there was an uneasy awkwardness. I noticed how her eyes grew large as she took in my big, square designer kitchen with its pale sage units and sparkling white marble work surfaces. She walked over to the large Aga and ran her fingers over the pale cream doors. Then she stared at my Quooker tap as I poured her a glass of sparkling water. I wondered if she'd never been in a kitchen such as mine, with all the mod cons. But then she swivelled towards me and grinned, and in her typical blunt manner said, 'What a beautiful kitchen. You must be loaded!' Taryn and Marnie had been sitting at the kitchen table and I noticed how Taryn flinched when her mother spoke.

Today, Paige is dressed in leggings and a padded jacket and her trainers squeak on the limestone tiles. 'What have you got here?' Paige asks, pointing at the two black bin liners filled with old clothes.

'Just stuff I'm trying to sell. Coffee or tea?' For a moment, I wonder if she's going to ask to take a look, but then she pirouettes to face me.

'Tea, please.'

As I'm placing a tea bag in a mug, Paige sits down at the kitchen table and asks, 'By the way, did you ever get your money back from that online dress shop?'

My shoulders sag. 'No. I got well and truly scammed.'

'You're not going to let them get away with it, are you?'

'I'm not sure what else I can do beyond reporting them to my bank or hopping on a flight to China.' Frustratingly, I've heard nothing from Margaret since I responded to her lovely email.

'I've got a bit of experience in this. I got well and truly scammed too, a couple of years back, but I was damned if I was going to let them get away with it. Do you want me to help you write another email?'

I'm surprised. Paige seems to be a good enough yoga teacher, with lots of energy, but I don't get the opinion she's particularly educated. Her texts are littered with emojis and she uses abbreviations that the kids use. Last week, when she posted a note on the door to her class, her handwriting was large and spiky and almost illegible.

I accept her offer and place my laptop on the kitchen table. She dictates an email which I type, and it's punchy and to the point, threatening legal action and promising to mar the reputation of the shop. I'm impressed and wonder if I've misjudged her. I don't hit send straight away because I'm a little nervous of the repercussions of the strong words. And then I tell myself, '*Grow a backbone, woman!*' I've never liked confrontation, or managing people for that matter. My pharmacy job suited me because I was dealing with processes and paperwork more than personnel. These days Hudson takes over contentious bills or unexpected parking fines. He likes dealing with disputes and does a fine job of it. Does that make me seem pathetic? A bit, I suppose, but it makes for an easier life.

'So how's the plans for your new yoga studio and retreat coming along?' Paige asks as she leans back in her chair, both hands clasped around the mug of tea.

I let out a puff of air. 'It's all stalled. I just don't have enough money. Building costs have gone crazily high.'

'I was thinking. Why don't you rent a room at a local hotel and run a weekend retreat as a proof of concept? Sure, you're not going to make as much money as if you were running them from your premises, but it'll be a start. Show that there's a need for what you're doing and then you can go to Hudson or the bank and they might loan you the money.'

'It's a great idea,' I say. 'In fact, I've already mapped out how I would run a weekend retreat, it's just I haven't actioned it yet.' To be truthful, I've been worried it might not work, and sometimes it's easier not to try something than to face failure. My relationship with Hudson is so rocky at the moment, I'm just keeping my head down and praying that the good times return.

'I hope I'm not talking out of turn, but I'm a little shocked Hudson isn't supporting you,' Paige says. I glance up at her in surprise. 'It's just that when we were talking at Katya's wedding, he seemed so proud of you and appeared to love the idea.'

'Really?' I question. That's the complete opposite to what my husband has said to my face. Not that he isn't proud of me; honestly, I wouldn't know. But he's been adamant that we don't have the funds to invest in developing the barn, and he also isn't keen on 'opening our house up to the public.' Perhaps he's saying one thing to me and another to other people. Or perhaps Paige got the wrong end of the stick.

'If you want any help running a weekend retreat, I'd love to lend a hand. Free of charge, of course, because we're mates. Besides, I've got a vested interest in you being successful so that I can come and work here and get away from vile Vanessa.'

'Thanks, Paige. That's really kind. I may well take you up on that.'

THIS EVENING, Hudson has returned from a business trip. I've lost track if he's been in Prague or Panama, but he's dumped his overnight case in the hall and is slumped in front of the television.

'How was the trip?' I ask, passing him a glass of wine for which he doesn't thank me.

'Fine. Did you pay the bill for the dentist?'

This is what we are reduced to. Perfunctory conversations discussing bills that need to be paid, appointments that need to be booked, whether we can afford to buy a new washing machine, as ours is on its last legs. I try to remember when either of us said, 'I love you.' I recall the days when we were so close we would share our most mundane of thoughts.

In the early years of our marriage, our love was all-consuming, we frequently finished each other's sentences, and dreamed about a future full of laughter and children and wealth. Somehow, it's all gone wrong.

I sink onto the sofa with a heavy sensation of sadness, wondering where the affection has gone.

'Oh, I almost forgot to tell you,' he says, turning the sound of the television down just a little. 'I've been head-hunted for a job.'

'A job?' I frown. 'But you run your own business.'

'Yes, but the job's got lots of potential.'

I'm confused.

'Don't worry, Amelia. I'm not going to take it,' he says without looking at me. 'Thought you might be pleased.'

'Pleased?'

'Oh, never mind.'

'Talk to me, Hudson,' I say. Except he scowls, shrugs his shoulders and turns the sound up again. I debate questioning him further except I know that look. His lips are firmly closed, his eyebrows knotted together, eyes focusing on the television screen. And I'm not in the mood for another argument. Of late, I've been wondering whether Hudson chooses to travel so much because he wants to be away from home. It's not like he couldn't send members of his staff to check out new hotels. I recall the early days when I used to accompany him everywhere, even bringing Marnie along when she was a baby, much to the abhorrence of the hotel owners who assumed their offer of a free stay in return for promoting their business to his customers extended to him and him alone. But as Marnie got older and went to school, Hudson started to go alone. Occasionally I wondered if he cheated on me with some glamorous guest or rep, but when he'd return from the airport and throw his arms around me, then head straight for a shower before tugging me to bed, I was reassured that it was me he wanted, and only me. Except he doesn't do that anymore.

A couple of months ago I signed up for therapy, but when in that first session, my therapist asked me to talk about my relationship with Hudson, I found I couldn't. I didn't want a stranger to know that our sex life has petered out, that we lie on our king-size bed without touching, that he's resentful of me for being at home and I'm resentful of him for all the travelling. I didn't return to the therapist and instead promised myself that I would sit Hudson down and have a proper talk with him.

And I did. Three weeks ago. I made a lovely supper, chose a good bottle of wine and when we finished, I asked, 'Can we talk?' My heart was hammering.

'Of course,' he said with a frown. 'What about?'

'About us. Our relationship. I don't think you're happy and I'm not sure that I'm happy.'

He stared at me with an expression of disbelief. We sat in silence for what seemed like forever. Tears began welling in his eyes and I wondered if I'd got it all wrong.

'I know the last few years have been tough but... do you want a divorce?' He stared into his almost empty glass of wine.

'No, of course not,' I said. 'I just want to talk about us. How do you feel?'

He shrugged. 'I don't know.'

'Are you happy with the way things are?'

'I think so. I don't know what you want me to say.'

And then his phone had rung and, to my disappointment, he had answered it. The conversation was over and we haven't returned to it.

While Hudson is watching the television, I think about Paige's suggestion for a yoga retreat. I go into the kitchen and put my laptop on the table. Clover comes to lie at my feet. Marnie's dreadful music is permeating through the ceiling, but I try to ignore it. I make a list of local hotels, and then study their websites to find out if they have suitable rooms to rent where I might be able to house ten women for a weekend of yoga classes. And then there's the ping of an incoming email.

Dear Ms Myers,

Please accept my sincere apology for taking so long to respond to you. Things have been difficult this end with closing the business. Please supply me with your bank details and a copy of the invoice and I will refund you in full immediately.

Yours Sincerely, Margaret

I respond with my bank details and literally ten minutes later, the full amount I spent on the dress lands in my account.

I send Paige a text message thanking her for her help. She responds with a thumbs-up emoji.

Later, in bed, Hudson and I are lying in the dark, as normal, not touching.

'Tell me more about the job offer,' I say.

'I'm tired,' Hudson replies, and then he turns over, his

back towards me, and tugs the duvet tightly around his shoulders.

CHAPTER FIVE

PAIGE

'What's this for?' Dean is holding out our credit card statement, shaking the piece of paper in front of my face. 'And this?' he says, stabbing his finger at various lines of text. 'And this?'

'Calm down!' I exclaim. 'It's stuff I needed, new shoes for Taryn and the wedding gift for Katya. Hardly an extravagance.' I'm tempted to tell him that I stole the bloody dress I wore so he didn't have to pay for it, but I know how furious he'd be, how disappointed, so I hold my tongue.

'We can't afford it!' Dean is raising his voice, his face turning increasingly puce.

'What do you mean, we can't afford it? You're out working all hours and I'm bringing in some money from my yoga classes.'

'Pocket money. Not even enough to pay a single bill. I told you you need to be careful and now we're maxed out.'

'Stop shouting at me!' I hate that Dean is in control of all our finances, that I need to justify what I'm spending. And he's so bloody sanctimonious about it, stressing when we go into the red. I stomp over to the fridge and take out a bottle of white wine, pouring myself a very large glass. I don't offer him any.

'I am not prepared to be in the situation we were in before, Paige!' I can feel my blood beginning to boil. It's never good when my blood begins to boil.

'I thought plumbers earn six figures,' I spit, knowing full well that Dean has never achieved anything near that. He might be a good plumber but we're relatively new to the area and it's hard to get traction in a place where plumbing and heating family businesses have been around for decades. 'Perhaps you should try harder.'

He takes a step towards me. He knows how I hate it when someone invades my personal space, how it makes me react like a terrified animal, how I can't help myself but go on the attack. And yet he takes another step forward and for a moment I wonder if he's going to kiss me, but no, his eyes are narrowed and he's spitting out his words. 'You need to rein in the spending, Paige.' With his nose practically touching mine and his stale breath on my face, I can't stop the anger from rushing through my veins. I've been here so many times before, times when I've been unable to control myself, times when the consequences of my actions have been so much worse than the initial trigger. I know I need to stop myself. I know I'll regret it if I hurt Dean. But the fury is immense, making it hard for me to breathe, causing me to grit my teeth, to want to scream, to lash out.

'Enough!' I shout.

Dean steps away just in time, just as I grab my glass of wine and hurl the remaining liquid at him. I don't wait for his reaction and storm out of the kitchen, through the back door, into the garden, clutching the now-empty glass.

'Breathe!' I hear the therapist's voice in my ears. 'Take several deep breaths.' Except the fury is too strong and instead I squeeze the wine glass so hard it splinters in my hand, shards of glass clattering to the paving stones, other pieces digging into the soft palm of my right hand. The pain calms me instantly. It's so much more effective than any stupid deep breathing. I watch my blood seep to the surface of my skin and drip down my wrist. It's been a long while since I hurt myself in a visible place and I wonder if this will hamper my ability to teach yoga. But I had no choice. If I hadn't stepped out in that moment, I would have hurt Dean. And I couldn't do that because Taryn is upstairs.

I leave the shards of glass on the ground and walk back to the kitchen. Dean has gone and I can hear the low pitch of his voice as he talks to Taryn in her bedroom. I hold my hand under the cold tap in the kitchen sink and watch the blood disappear down the plug hole. There are footsteps behind me. Quickly, I switch off the tap and wrap a tea towel around my hand.

'What have you done, Mum?' Taryn asks, that disapproving sanctimonious look on her face. Thank goodness my anger is more tempered towards my daughter. To be honest, I was worried when she was born. Knowing myself, knowing my quick temper, I was terrified that the incessant mewling of a baby might send me over the edge. That I might hurt her. Except I never did. Somehow maternal love mellowed my fury, towards her at least.

'Cut myself on the wine glass. The damned thing shattered in my hand.'

She throws me a look as if she doesn't believe me. Taryn is too damned clever. I've got brains but not at Taryn's level. How I managed to produce a daughter like her, I've no idea.

'Do you want me to bandage it up?' she asks.

I accept her help. Wordlessly, she finds the first aid box and takes out some steri-strips, removes a small shard of glass stuck in my palm with some tweezers and then wipes it down with disinfectant before pulling my flesh together to stem the bleeding. Five minutes later, my palm is throbbing but clean and the bleeding has stopped.

'Thanks, love,' I say. Still Taryn says nothing. I hate that I'm a disappointment to her, yet what can I do?

The next day, Amelia has invited me, Romy and Katya – who is recently back from her honeymoon – over to her house for coffee and the chance to look through Katya's wedding and honeymoon photos. I'm the last to arrive. I really didn't want to come, except I'm on a mission and I need to remember the bigger picture. So here I am in the home of a woman I detest, forcing myself to fawn over the photos of someone I'm completely indifferent towards.

'Amelia!' I say warmly, giving her the compulsory air-kisses. 'So kind of you to have us over, yet again.'

She places one of her perfectly manicured hands on my arm and I want nothing more but to shrug it off. Instead, I grit my teeth and give her a little shoulder bump. Oh, we're such buddies!

'What have you done to your hand?' she asks, noticing the padded plaster on my palm.

'Stupid accident washing up. A wine glass broke in the sink.'

'Ouch,' she says. 'Will it affect your teaching?'

'No, it should be fine.' Whether it will or not remains to be seen but I have an extremely high threshold for pain and as Dean so unnecessarily pointed out, I need the money from teaching. He's still being off towards me but I have a plan, a plan that should put a great big smile on his face.

'So, girls,' Amelia says as we approach the kitchen table. 'Paige came up with the brilliant idea that I test my retreat concept and run a weekend away in a hotel somewhere.'

'Excellent,' Romy adds.

Yada, yada, yada. I zone out and gaze around Amelia's huge kitchen. You could probably fit the whole of our house in this space. She has all these grandiose plans and is feeling so sorry for herself because her filthy-rich husband won't indulge her little whims and pay for their barn to be converted. Why doesn't she go out and earn some proper money herself? Stand on her own two feet rather than be reliant on her partner. And no, I'm not being hypocritical here. I'm only earning pennies from teaching yoga because I couldn't return to my previous work. The fact that I'm reliant on Dean is out of my hands. It's not what I wanted. Up until a few years ago, I was the main breadwinner, but sometimes life throws you a curveball and I've had way too many of those.

Their barn is visible through the kitchen window. I have to agree with Hudson. If I had a home like this, I wouldn't want to have a bunch of over-privileged women turning up on my land, waving their flabby butts in the air and indulging in me-time. As if they even need it. Most of them haven't got a clue what real life is like.

'And Paige...'

I zoom back into the conversation at the sound of my name.

'Good on you, girl!' Romy says.

I haven't got a clue what she's talking about until Amelia mentions how chuffed she is that she's been reimbursed by

Luxall-London. It's beyond me why Amelia is so upset about a dress when she's got a whole wardrobe of them. If she's living in a place like this, she's hardly going to miss a couple of hundred quid. Nevertheless, I have the bigger picture in mind and it serves my purpose that she's been refunded the money for the rubbish gown. In fact, the more I think about it, the more the plan evolves in my mind.

I butt into the conversation. 'There's a new wine bar in town that's just opened, called Chica's. I thought I'd try it out. Anyone free to join me tonight?' I ask.

'Tonight?' Amelia says, the tone of her voice suggesting that this is the most outrageous of suggestions. I backtrack because I am aware that I can be a bit over-enthusiastic from time to time.

'Well, maybe tonight is too soon, but another night this week?'

The others look at their phones and the only night we're all free is tomorrow, although Amelia makes a big fuss about trying to find a babysitter. Pathetic, considering Marnie is fifteen. Do they really not let her stay at home by herself? I suggest that Marnie spends the evening at our house with Taryn and, with some reluctance, Amelia agrees. A flicker of excitement rushes through me.

Chica's is a small bistro-come-wine bar, all fancy, with glass tables and little wooden platters filled with crudities and nibbles. Large copper pendants hang from the ceilings and the shelves behind the bar are made out of wood attached to the trunk of a tree to make it look like the tree has sprouted shelves. Spirits are served in copper mugs and the wine glasses are tall and thin, looking more like champagne flutes. This afternoon, straight after school, Marnie and Taryn came over to our house and I saw how over-privileged

Marnie looked around our small home, her eyes widening, her lips curled ever so slightly in disgust. Yes, it's small, an ex-council house and nothing like the fancy place she's grown up in, but it's clean. It'll be good for Marnie to see how the other half live. Who knows, before long, she might be grateful to be living in a home such as ours.

As planned, I'm the first to arrive at Chica's. I order a bottle of wine plus a triple gin for Amelia, the cheapest wine and the cheapest gin on the extensive drinks menu. Amelia makes a big thing about how she can't digest wine and that she has to stick to champagne or spirits. It makes me want to vomit that she doesn't realise how pretentious that sounds. Anyway, I hope she appreciates my kind gesture. Making sure no one is looking, I drop the pill into the gin and tonic and give it a quick stir with a glass stirrer just as Romy arrives, annoyingly early as always. Katya and Amelia aren't far behind. We greet each other as if we're best friends, which is ridiculous since we've only met through our yoga teaching, and if you really think about it, we're all competitors. All the same, it suits me to play along.

'This is a cute place,' Romy says. 'Cheers!' she holds up her glass of wine. We all raise our glasses.

'Goodness, I need this!' Amelia says, taking a large sip of her gin. 'Thanks, Paige.'

I nod. The talk is the usual mundane chatter, mostly bitching about Vanessa. She's not the most pleasant of characters but it might be worth us remembering that she is our boss. If it wasn't for her, none of us would be teaching.

Amelia gets drunk very quickly, and fortunately, I don't think the others really notice. She's particularly loose-lipped, complaining about Hudson, going on about her yoga studio dream yet again. Boring. Boring. The next round is on her, and she orders herself another gin and a further bottle of white wine for the rest of us; no doubt better quality this time.

I make my excuses and disappear to the toilets. I wait for another woman to wash her hands, and then when I'm alone, I lean against the door so that no one else can enter. I take the new burner phone with the new SIM from my handbag, block the number and dial. It takes a while for her to answer.

'Good evening. Is this Amelia Myers?' I put on a strong Liverpudlian accent, an accent that I've perfected over the years.

'Yes.'

'I'm sorry to be disturbing you, Mrs Myers, but I'm calling from Redcore Bank and I can see that there has been fraudulent activity on your account. Please, can you give me your account holder number for verification purposes?'

There's a long pause and I can hear the clatter of glasses and the hum of voices in the background. 'How do I know you're really the bank?' she asks. She's definitely slurring the words now.

'Please feel free to call me back on the number on the reverse of your card. However, I would urge you to change your password. May I read out the last transactions you've made?'

'Sure,' she says.

'Chica's wine bar five minutes ago. Prior to that, the purchase of an Apple MacBook for three thousand and fifty-five pounds at 5.55 p.m. today, and prior to that an online purchase from John Lewis to the value of nine hundred and forty-three pounds. You have exceeded your credit card balance by three thousand pounds.'

'No!' Amelia exclaims. 'I haven't bought anything today except a round of drinks!'

'These purchases did flag up as being unusual, hence the reason for this call. I can block your card with immediate effect and look into getting these charges reversed; however, I need you to change your password. Can you do that, Mrs Myers?'

'Yeah, of course,' she mumbles.

'I do need to ask you a few further questions for verification purposes. Who do you have direct debits with?'

'Um, not sure,' Amelia says. 'I'm–'

I cut in. 'I won't keep you long as it sounds like this is not a good time. Please confirm the balance on your account.'

'Which account?' The words are drawn out.

'Your current and savings accounts?' I say.

'Dunno but at least twenty thousand in my savings account.'

'Yes, I can confirm that that is correct. I will need you to change the password to your whole online banking account, otherwise we cannot guarantee that the thief won't access your other accounts.'

'It's not just my credit card?' she asks, every word slurring more than the last.

'No, it's affecting all your accounts. Have you clicked on any links that perhaps you shouldn't have done or made any purchases that seem dubious with hindsight?'

'The dress I bought that came from China, from Luxall-London. Might be them.'

'That's very helpful, Mrs Myers. I will put a block on your account, and once you've changed your password everything should be back to normal. In the meantime, I wish you a very pleasant evening.' I hang up and burst out laughing, only having to control myself when I hear footsteps. I move away from the door and let warm water pour over my hands as the door to the ladies' toilets swings open and a stranger walks in.

A minute later, I'm back with my friends. 'You look like you've seen a ghost,' I say, placing a hand on Amelia's shoulder as I return. To my delight, Romy and Katya are deep in conversation and don't even glance up as I slip back into my seat.

'Just had a call from the bank saying there's fraudulent activity on my account.' If I didn't know what she was saying, I'd be hard-pushed to make out the words. She's looking very pale and I hope that she doesn't throw up. I'm going to have to get her home soon.

'You'll need to change your password,' I say, picking up her phone. I hold it out to her but she doesn't take it.

'Would you like me to help you?' I ask. She nods. I hold the phone up to her face and it opens up. 'Do you remember your customer number and password?' I ask. I glance towards Romy and Katya, but they're looking at something on Katya's phone and paying us no attention. This is risky but it will be so very worth it if I can pull it off. A flicker of excitement plays in my stomach.

'My customer number?' she murmurs. It's obvious that there's something not right with her now and I need to chivvy her along.

'Concentrate, Amelia,' I say in a low voice. 'Where can I find your customer number?'

'Notes. Redcore.'

I navigate to her notes and search for Redcore, and what an idiot! She's actually written down her customer number. I surreptitiously take a photograph of it and then input it into the banking app.

'And your pin number?'

She recites it very slowly.

'Right, we're in,' I say. 'You need to change your pin number. What number can you remember?'

She looks at me, her eyes watery and her gaze unfocused. I'm going to need to get her out of here quickly.

'How about Marnie's birthday?' I suggest.

She nods. '14th of January.'

'Are you feeling alright?' I ask, talking a little louder this time.

'No, not really,' she slurs.

'I think we'd better get you home.'

I turn to the others. 'Amelia is feeling sick. I'm going to take her home.'

'Oh goodness!' Katya exclaims. 'Poor you. You don't look so good, Amelia. Do you need any help, Paige?'

'No, you two stay here and enjoy yourselves. Our daughters are together so I'll collect Marnie and take her and Amelia home. We'll see you soon.'

I help Amelia to her feet, pick up her bag and place her phone inside it. Then I link my arm through hers and support her as we walk out of the wine bar.

'Think I'm going to be sick,' Amelia mutters. And a moment later she vomits onto the pavement. How disgusting.

I'm livid. I was sold the drug by a mate I met in prison and she promised me that there wouldn't be any side effects. Clearly, I was fed a lie. But no worries, I'll tell Amelia she must have got food poisoning, so perhaps this will work out for the best. I've got the information I need and that's all that matters.

CHAPTER SIX

MARNIE

I've been messaging Jax practically non-stop. It feels like he's the first person in the whole world who truly understands me. I'm pretending that I'm twenty and in my final year at uni studying psychology because it must be fun knowing how the human brain works. I'd thought about saying I was studying music management but reckoned that was too risky. He and I share the same taste in music and he seemed really impressed that I know so many upcoming bands and spend hours on Spotify checking out new music. He said I should think about getting a job in music if my singing career doesn't take off. I wonder if he'll be able to help me. There's no way I'll really be studying psychology because I'm crap at science but I'd love, love a job in music. I've been researching music colleges and my first choice is Berklee College of Music in Boston, USA, where I can study music management. It would be so cool if I could go there but the fees are ginormous. Hopefully, Dad will be prepared to pay.

I'm in a maths lesson and I don't understand a word of what Miss Eisner is telling us. Everyone says she's the best maths teacher in the world, which just confirms that I must be really thick. She's super-patient, so I'll go and talk to her after class. But then my phone buzzes on my lap and the screen lights up. It's Jax, again.

> Are u free next Saturday night to meet up at KOKO in Camden? There's a band playing I want to check out. Would be gr8 if u could join.

I squeal and Miss Eisner locks her eyes on mine.

'Is there something you'd like to share with the class, Marnie?' she asks.

'No, I'm sorry,' I say, my face reddening.

She walks along the centre aisle, passing everyone else's desks until she's standing next to mine. I try to shove my phone into my pocket but she sees me. She holds out her hand and I've got no choice but to give it to her. The rest of the class snigger. What if she sees the messages? That would be a complete disaster. She takes the phone and walks back to her desk, slipping it into a drawer. 'Come and see me after class, Marnie,' she says.

I wish Taryn and I were in the same lessons but she's in the top set and I'm in the bottom one. I can't wait to show her the messages later. She's going to be completely stoked for me.

When the class finishes, I pack up my rucksack and walk to the front of the class, ready to be scolded and given an order mark. Except Miss Eisner surprises me.

'Are you finding these concepts tricky?' she asks.

I nod and annoyingly find tears starting to well in my eyes.

'First of all, you know that it's forbidden to be using your phone during class.'

'I'm sorry,' I murmur. 'I won't do it again.'

'I'd like you to stay behind after school on Thursday and I'll talk you through what we're studying this week to make sure you understand it. But I'm only prepared to give my time to students who are committed to working. If you don't put in the hours and concentrate in class, next time I won't be so lenient and you'll be in line for a detention. And keep your phone switched off during the school day. Do you understand, Marnie?'

I nod my head and mutter, 'Thank you so much, Miss.'

She reaches into her drawer and removes my mobile phone, handing it to me without so much as glancing at it. Such a relief. I scurry out of the classroom and head towards Taryn's locker. As expected, she's there waiting for me so we can go to lunch together. My other friends seem to have melted away, but I don't care, because Taryn and I are really tight.

'You are not going to believe it!' I say, opening up my phone. 'Jax has invited me to meet IRL the weekend after next!'

Taryn's eyes widen. 'But what are you going to do? He'll know you're not 20 when he sees you, and how will you get into a club when you're so underage?'

'I don't know. I'll worry about that nearer the time, but first I'm going to accept.'

'You're going to London all by yourself at night?' she asks. Taryn looks super-impressed.

'I'll find a way.'

I send Jax a message.

I'd love to. Can't wait to meet you!!!

It's really tough getting through the day because all I can think about is how I'm going to get to London at the weekend. Dad's due home tomorrow night and he's a softer touch than Mum. I'll see if I can persuade him to take me, pretending to be meeting up with some friends. I haven't seen much of Dad recently, and he and Mum have been arguing even more than normal. They think I don't notice, but I do. It's pretty bloody obvious.

By the end of school, I'm disappointed that I haven't had a reply from Jax, but when I'm in the car with Mum, my phone starts pinging. Making sure that Mum has her eyes firmly on the road in front of us, I open a message from Jax and I have to stop myself from screeching out aloud. He's sent me some pics of himself. The first pic is him standing barechested in the mirror, just his chest and stomach on display, muscles well-defined and the buttons of his jeans open so I can see the top of his boxer shorts. Oh my God, he's so sexy, like some model. When the next one arrives, I slam my hand over my face. I've just received my very first dick picture.

'What's up, love?' Mum asks, glancing at me. She wasn't well last night after going out with her yoga teacher friends. She says it was food poisoning, but she seems fine today.

I turn the phone over and shove it into my bag. I've never seen an actual willy before. Not having a brother, I suppose I've been a bit sheltered. Of course, us girls have giggled over porn videos, but mostly they're just embarrassing. And now I'm shaking because this is real. What am I going to do? Jax is so hot and he obviously thinks I am too.

Mum is wittering away about goodness knows what, and

as soon as we're home, I run upstairs and lock myself in the bathroom. Another message has arrived.

U seen me now I wanna c u. Can't wait!

Oh God. I know this is the sort of thing we're not meant to do. They've told us this at school and Mum gave me a lecture a year or so ago. But he's sent me his pics first. And he's a real person with the coolest job ever. I scroll back up to his photos and have a good look at his dick pic. It's a bit gross actually, and I can't look at it for too long. What am I going to do? Jax is my first proper boyfriend, someone who likes me for me. I mean, he hasn't even seen me properly, only the video that I uploaded of me singing and then some pictures on my Insta feed.

I take off my school shirt and stand in front of the mirror in my bra. Taryn's got much bigger tits than me and I don't even have any decent underwear. I hike my breasts upwards and make my bra straps tighter. That looks a bit better. The lighting is quite good too with the down-lighters throwing shadows so it looks like my cleavage is bigger than it is. I take a photo of myself in the mirror, cutting off my head like Jax did in his photos. I take several more and choose the best. I hesitate for a moment and then press send. I groan. I hope he likes what he sees.

The response is immediate. My heart is pounding as I wait for the little dots to turn into words.

Ur gorgeous!!!!

I let out a breath of relief.

Take off ur bra. I wanna c everything.

I'm not sure what to do because there's one thing sending a photo of me in my bra, quite another sending a nude.

Plse!

I hesitate and another photo comes through with a message.

I'm hard just thinking about you. I bet you're bussin.

OMG – it's a great big bulge in a pair of boxer shorts!
Have I done that to him? It makes me feel so powerful and, for the first time, really excited. Without thinking any more, I unstrap my bra and take another series of photos in the mirror, angling my body so my boobs look bigger. I press send.

Wow! How many peeps have u slept with?

How am I going to answer that? What will he think if I tell him I'm a virgin, that not only have I never slept with anyone, I haven't even kissed a guy? My cheeks flush with shame.

'Marnie!' Mum is shouting for me and I can hear her footsteps on the stairs. Shit. Hurriedly, I clip my bra back on and pull on my shirt, tucking it into my skirt.

'What are you doing in there?' she asks. 'Are you alright?'

'Yeah, fine,' I say, emerging from the bathroom with my phone hidden in my skirt waistband.

'Dad's not going to be home for supper tonight so I was wondering if you'd like a pizza?'

She treats me like I'm some little kid getting all excited about choosing the topping on my pizza.

'Don't care,' I say and trot into my bedroom. My phone pings again and I can sense Mum right behind me. 'Olivia's mum is taking her to London on Saturday and then to see a show afterwards and she's invited me to go with her. Can I go?' I ask. It's easier for me to lie to her when she's not looking at my face. I lean down and take out some school books from my rucksack.

I can sense the hesitation and I really want her to say yes first time around. 'It's not just any show,' I say, still with my back to her. 'It's a play we're studying for our English GCSE.'

'Oh how lovely,' Mum replies. She's in the doorway to my bedroom now. 'Which one is that?'

'Hamlet,' I say. We are studying Hamlet but I've no idea if it's being performed anywhere in London. What I do know is that Mum wouldn't recognise Olivia's mum if she was standing right in front of us. Olivia's mum is some high-flying lawyer and she never does drop-off or collection; in fact, I've never met her, even when I've been around to her house. Olivia and her younger brother are being looked after by a nanny called Hazel.

'Let me think about it and have a word with Dad,' Mum replies.

'What's there to think about?' I turn now to look at her. 'You can't carry on wrapping me up in cotton wool forever.'

Mum flinches. We've had this conversation so many times. The thing is, after I nearly died from meningitis, Mum became increasingly protective of me. It was okay for the first year, but now it's stifling. It's not my fault that I'm an only child. Mum needs to start chilling.

'What time will you be back?' she asks.

'Dunno. Late, I guess, because the show doesn't finish until about 11 p.m.'

'Perhaps I can have a chat with Olivia's mother,' Mum suggests.

'You're being ridiculous, Mum. I'd be going with her parents. It's safe. There's nothing to worry about. All I need is some cash to pay her back for the tickets.'

'How much is a ticket?'

'Don't know yet, but I'll find out.' I pause. 'Does that mean I can go?'

She sighs. 'I'll think about it.'

CHAPTER SEVEN

AMELIA

It's Friday morning and I think I'm going to throw up. I'm on my banking app and it makes no sense whatsoever. I have £453 in my joint current account with Hudson and zero balance in my savings account. I refresh the app wondering if there's some glitch. I get the same balances every time I refresh. What the hell has happened? There should be nearly twenty-two thousand pounds in my savings account. It's money that I've been saving since Dad died, wondering if I should invest it to get a better rate of interest, but hopeful I can use at least some of it on the barn conversion. The rest, Hudson and I have allocated for Marnie's university studies. It doesn't make any sense that the balance is zero. With trembling fingers, I navigate to my transactions and see that two days ago the whole sum was sent to Pay4u2u. That name sounds familiar. I gasp when it hits me. I made the payment to the Chinese clothing company through Pay4u2u, a PayPal-like website. Except I didn't transfer any funds from our savings account. I never touch that account. Never.

I try contacting Pay4u2u but of course, there's no telephone number, just an online chat function. I click on it and pace the kitchen as I wait for someone to respond. Eventually, I see the name Priti light up and a message that says:

How can I help you today?

I explain that the balance of my savings account was withdrawn and sent to Pay4u2u and that it must have been fraud. I demand to know where the money has gone. Except Priti is clearly reading off a script and my increasing frustration gets me nowhere.

I'm sorry, ma'am, but we can't tell you where the money has gone. The payment looks as if it was made legitimately so I suggest you contact your bank. I wish you a good day.

And then she's gone.

I swallow bile and call my bank. At least I get to speak to a real person this time. I explain the situation to the operator.

'I can see that you made a payment for £21,798 but it was made to your account at Pay4u2u using your banking app. I don't see any fraudulent activity, Mrs Myers. I will forward this to our senior fraud team who will investigate further.'

'Will you refund me the money?' I ask.

There's a pause. 'I'm afraid you'll only be reimbursed if we believe that fraud has taken place.'

'But it has!' I exclaim.

'We'll be back in touch within 28 working days,' she says.

'28 days!'

'That's our expedited process,' she explains. 'Normally it's six to eight weeks.'

I slump on the chair.

'Is there anything else I can do for you today, Mrs Myers?'

'No, thanks,' I say and then hang up. I tug my hair into a tight bun as I pace the kitchen, and then I glance at the clock. I'm late.

Grabbing my handbag and yoga bag, I apologise to Clover, our black Labrador, for only giving her a short walk this morning, and hurry to the car. I can't think of anything other than the lost money. What if I never get it back? It's not only my dreams that will be out of the window but Marnie's too. It was meant to be our nest egg for her university education. And how am I going to tell Hudson? He'll be home tonight.

My yoga class is full, as it normally is. Yet I just can't muster the energy that I usually bring to the class and have to force myself to stay present. No one complains but my ladies leave faster than normal. There's a knock on the door and Romy pops her head around.

'Are you recovered?'

I tilt my head to the side.

'When we went out to Chica's. Paige said you were feeling ill and you left early.'

'Oh that,' I say, my cheeks reddening. I can't remember the last time I was actually drunk and I don't think I drank that much, so I must have had some sort of food poisoning. The whole evening is a blurry haze. And yet, apparently, I transferred the full amount in my savings account to Pay4u2u. Even if I'd been completely drunk, I wouldn't have done anything as stupid as that. It must have been fraud.

'I felt terrible at the time but was fine in the morning. No, it's not that. I've got other stuff going on.'

'Oh,' she says, padding into the studio. 'Are you alright?'

'It's not the best of days,' I say.

'What's up?'

'I've been scammed. I've lost every penny in our savings account.'

'Oh my God!' Romy exclaims. 'What happened?'

'I don't know.' I sigh. 'They're investigating but all the money has gone and I've no idea how I'm going to tell Hudson.'

'That's terrible. Is it anything to do with the bank calling you the other night?'

'What?' I ask.

'You got a call from your bank telling you there was some fraudulent activity on your account and you changed your pin code.'

I stare at Romy. I have literally no recollection of that. Why can't I remember it? I fumble in my bag for my mobile phone and search back through my calls received list. Romy is right. I received a call from a withheld number at 8:15 p.m. on the night we were out. I look at my banking app and I see I supposedly made the transfer at 10:23 p.m. Was I so drunk that I did something stupid? I try to recall the evening and all I remember is Paige leaving me at my front door and waving goodbye, and me clambering up the staircase apologising to Marnie, telling her I must have food poisoning. I threw up in the toilet, went to bed and slept the whole night through. But now, all I can think about is how disappointed Hudson will be and whether I did something really stupid.

Hudson doesn't make it home for supper. I should be annoyed because I made his favourite coq au vin, and when he eventually walks through the door, three hours later than he'd said he'd be home, it is overcooked and dry. I remember how not so long ago I'd be all knotted up with worry if he was late home, catastrophising about a terrible accident, a plane falling out of the sky or a dreadful car crash on the way home from the airport. I wonder when I began to accept his tardiness, when it stopped to matter so much.

He opens the front door and shouts a generic hello. Then he strides into the living room where I'm pretending to watch television and leans down to give me a perfunctory kiss on the cheek. He catches his shoe on the edge of the coffee table and grumbles an expletive before disappearing upstairs. It strikes me that he's permanently angry these days, muttering obscenities over the smallest of things, such as a bin bag splitting or him losing his keys. Sometimes I think he's angry with me, that perhaps he wants a new life, the one that we dreamed of but that never materialised. Yet he seemed genuinely shocked when we had our futile conversation, and I don't want to open that can of worms again. Despite everything, I still love him.

Marnie comes bouncing into the kitchen. 'Dad says I can go to London with Olivia.' She grins. A small and quick victory that under normal circumstances would infuriate me. Except today I'm not that bothered because all I can think about is the money. The money that was allocated to her tertiary education. The money that has vanished.

Hudson has changed into casual clothes, his hair damp from the shower. 'How are my favourite three girls?' he asks. Clover pushes her nose into his legs and he strokes her soft, black back. Even though he's asking the question, Hudson isn't smiling. We never laugh together anymore.

Marnie says, 'I'm going to bed. See you in the morning.'

And she's gone before either of us can attempt to hug her or wish her a good night. It's like we're all little planets, floating around each other, making sure we don't knock each other off our lonesome trajectories.

Hudson slumps into his armchair. 'I'm exhausted too.' He yawns.

'So you said yes to Marnie going to London,' I say. 'I wanted to discuss it with you.'

'She's nearly sixteen, Amelia. She needs to spread her wings.' I've heard this refrain a lot recently.

'Except she's playing us off against each other.'

'Stop worrying about her. Stop smothering her.' He grabs the television remote off the coffee table and changes the channel to the news, then turns the sound off.

I may worry about our daughter, but it's not surprising that I do. Not considering what we went through, how we so nearly lost her. And it's easy for Hudson to be critical when he's never home. I feel a knot tighten in my chest, and I stand up.

'I'm going to take a bath,' I say.

He nods without looking at me.

If it wasn't for my guilt over the missing money, I'd switch the television off and pull Hudson to his feet. Then I'd either slap him or pull his face down to mine, kissing him deeply. But of course, I do neither. Instead, I promise myself that I will tell him about the missing funds. Soon.

CHAPTER EIGHT

PAIGE

I've got an appointment with a surgeon called Dr Harrison on London's Harley Street. I did my research and he's the best of the best, a cosmetic surgeon with literally thousands of five-star reviews praising him on creating perfect faces for his clients. I don't want to look completely different and certainly don't want pouty lips and overly chiselled cheekbones. But I do want a straighter nose and ears that don't protrude like ridiculous flaps at the side of my face. I promised myself that as soon as I came into money, I'd get my face fixed. When I was a kid, Mum took every opportunity to tell me I was fat and ugly and I'd never find myself a man. Well, she was wrong about that. I may not have the most beautiful face but my body is good, lean, with medium-to-big tits and a shapely bum and legs. After falling in love with Frank and then hooking up with Dean, I wasn't too bothered about my ears and nose, until I landed in prison. Those bitches were brutal. They called me Jumbo because of my long snout and sticky-out ears, and a name like that sticks in your head. It doesn't help that my new profession as a yoga teacher means I'm surrounded by other women, many of whom have definitely had work done, even if they proclaim they haven't. I'm pretty sure that Amelia has regular Botox, and those boobs are definitely too perky to be her own. Not that she'd admit it, of course.

So here am I, sitting in a waiting room that looks more like the lobby of an exclusive five-star boutique hotel. There's a book on the table with photos showing the before and after pictures of Dr Harrison's clients. If I didn't know better, I'd think they'd been photoshopped. Some of the women looked like dogs before treatment, and afterwards, whilst they might not grace the pages of a magazine, they're attractive enough. I've already got good bones, so it shouldn't be too hard for the doctor to make me look stunning.

A woman enters the waiting room, dressed in a designer suit, her hair scraped back off her symmetrical, overly smooth face.

'Ms Miller?'

'Yes, that's me,' I say, standing up.

'Dr Harrison is ready to see you now. If you'd like to follow me.'

We walk along a plush, carpeted corridor with paintings of mountains lining the walls, and then she pushes open a door. Dr Harrison stands up from behind his desk. The room is large and bright, with an examination bed along one wall and a bowed window looking onto the street beyond.

'Please take a seat,' he says, indicating to the chair opposite him. 'It's a pleasure to meet you, Ms Miller.' He glances down at a form on his desk, no doubt the form that I had to fill in online, giving my credit card details and a brief explanation as to what I want to have done. 'So you're looking to adjust your nose and pin back your ears. Is that correct?'

I nod.

'Before I examine you, I'd like to understand why you feel you need to have the work done.'

'Sorry?' I say.

'Regrettably, there are too many unscrupulous doctors out there who will give their clients whatever they request, rather like picking something off an extensive menu. I don't work like that. I want to make sure that my clients have fully understood the emotional and physical implications of any work we do, and to ensure that the raison d'être for cosmetic surgery is sound.'

'I've given this a lot of thought,' I say hurriedly.

'I'm sure you have, Ms Miller. May I call you Paige?'

'Of course.'

'So, Paige. If I may, I'd like to do a little probe into your state of mind. Why is it that you are seeking this surgery?'

'Because my nose is too big for my face and my ears stick out.' I shift uncomfortably in the armchair.

'Have you had any psychiatric or psychological treatment at any time in your life?'

'I'm not sure what that has to do with me being here.'

'My dear, there are no trick questions. I just want to ensure that you understand the emotional implications of cosmetic surgery.'

I bristle. This man is patronising me.

'Tell me a little about your background, starting with your childhood.'

I open and close my mouth. My background is none of this man's business, and I most certainly will not be sharing my secrets with him.

'I don't see how that's relevant.'

'We need to ensure that we're a good fit, you and me,' he says. 'Humour me by answering a few of my questions, and then we'll do a physical examination.'

I pick up my handbag and stand up.

'I don't think so, Dr Harrison.' I can feel the anger beginning to boil. How dare this man probe into my past, or into my psyche? I just want a bit of a chisel and a few stitches. 'I don't need to justify myself to you or anyone else.'

Before he can respond, I turn around and stride to the door, pulling it open and slamming it behind me. What a complete jerk. To hell with Dr Harrison; he won't be getting my business. I stride quickly but I hear footsteps behind me.

'Ms Miller,' a female voice says. 'We will be taking payment for your initial consultation from your credit card.' I look over my shoulder at the woman who collected me from the reception room and stick my finger up in the air. 'Fuck off to that,' I say and literally run out of the front door. I'll cancel the card and then they can stick it.

I'm raging as I stride down Harley Street. What a hideous experience. I'm going to have to find someone else who doesn't ask such probing questions. My breathing is fast and shallow and I pick at the scab on the palm of my hand, welcoming the pain as little droplets of blood rise to the surface. I find myself on Marylebone High Street, walking by a jewellery shop. In the past, I might have stolen a few items from such an establishment but today I have money in my pocket. Besides, I can't take the risk. I open the door and step towards a wall of jewels. My eyes fall on a pair of diamond earrings that glitter. Yes, they have my name all over them. I get a buzz of excitement as I imagine wearing them to our next yoga teachers' get-together. They're the sort of thing that Amelia might wear. A little blingy but largely classy.

'I'd like to try those,' I say, pointing them out to the shop assistant. Five minutes later, they're in my ears and I'm heading back towards the station. There's nothing like a little shopping to make a woman feel better about herself.

On the train home, I take out my phone and type out an anonymous review about Dr Harrison. It takes me a while to perfect it but when I do, I'm pleased with myself.

> *Avoid Dr Harrison, cosmetic surgeon, like the plague! He touched me inappropriately, refused my request to have a female nurse in attendance, and made hurtful comments about my appearance. He wanted to do way more work than I'd requested. When I complained, he sent me a bill even though I didn't have any work carried out! I'm told that lots of women have complained about him but he employs a PR agent to squash all the negative reviews. You've been warned!*

Using a fake name, I post the review everywhere online, on search engines, across social media, and anywhere I can find that mentions cosmetic surgery or Dr Harrison. By the time the train pulls into the station, I've got a huge smile on my face.

That evening, Dean is home for 6 p.m. as he always is. He looks tired and heads straight to the fridge to remove a beer. The thing with Dean is he's really observant. It never fails to surprise me because largely, I've found men to be utterly unobservant.

'What's those sparkles in your ears?' he asks, peering at me.

'New earrings. Do you like them?'

'What the hell, Paige. We can't afford–'

I cut him off. 'They're fake, you idiot. But they look good, don't they?'

He nods, then takes his beer can and walks upstairs. A couple of minutes later, I hear the sound of the shower. I never wanted to take on the traditional roles in a relationship but as Dean works longer hours than I do, I accept that most nights I prepare our supper. I don't mind cooking so long as Dean or Taryn clears up. I like the precision of following recipes, juggling lots of things at once.

Twenty minutes or so later, Dean stomps down the stairs into the kitchen, no doubt in search of another beer.

'Why have you got a thousand pounds in your purse?' He stands there with his hands on his hips.

'What were you doing rifling in my handbag?' I snap back, slamming a lid onto a saucepan.

'It was perched on the edge of the bed and I knocked if off onto the floor by mistake. Why have you got so much money in cash? You're not up to your old tricks again, are you, Paige?'

'No!' I exclaim. 'I got it from Vanessa for working overtime.'

He gives me that look, the one that suggests he doesn't believe what I'm saying, but I stare back at him, and as normal, Dean backs down. He knows that if we get into an argument, it always ends badly. And he probably remembers our last fight, when I chucked the wine at him. He knew perfectly well that the wound on my palm was a result of my temper and not an accident from washing up, but he didn't say a word. And he definitely knows that a repeat performance is more likely to result in him being hurt than me.

Dean turns away from me, and as predicted gets another beer out of the fridge, but this time he sits down at the kitchen table.

He pulls the tab off the can and drops it onto the table. 'Paige, love. I don't believe you. Let's not fight, but the thing is, no one is going to give you a grand in cash for teaching a few yoga lessons.'

He's right, of course.

'You shouldn't be complaining about me having cash. It helps pay the bills.'

'I'm not complaining; I'm worried. We've been here before, haven't we, love, and last time it didn't work out so well.'

'I haven't done anything illegal!' I exclaim, mentally crossing my fingers because of course that's a blatant lie. 'Do you really think I'd take the risk of being sent back to prison?'

He shakes his head unconvincingly and clearly doesn't believe me.

The anger starts bubbling up just like the water for the pasta on the hob. I can feel my face flushing, my fingers starting to twitch.

'Take a breath,' Dean says.

But it's no good. I've had enough of phoney psychological treatment for one day and I can't stop myself from exploding.

'Don't fucking tell me what I should or shouldn't do!'

'I'm just worried, that's all.'

'Don't you trust me, Dean? Because you should. If we

don't have trust, what the hell do we have?' I'm shouting now.

'I trust you and I love you,' Dean says, trying to placate things. 'Let's not fight, Paige. But I do want you to tell me the truth.'

'I am!' I exclaim, lifting the lid off the saucepan and chucking a spoon into the boiling pan of water. A splash of water rises up and strikes my wrist and I let out a squeal of pain. 'You did this!' I say, realising I sound like a petulant child. 'I'm burned because of you!'

'I'm just worried. That's all,' Dean says with a sigh. He looks up at the ceiling and takes a swig of beer from the can.

I wonder for a moment what would happen if Dean walked out. I've pushed him really far so many times, yet he always seems to forgive me. Perhaps he stays because I'm good at sex, or because he knows he's punching above his weight with me. Or perhaps it's because he genuinely loves Taryn. Occasionally, I wonder if he stays due to pity and worry that I'll go completely off the rails without him. Of course, I don't ask. I'm sure I'd be absolutely fine without Dean but for now, it suits both Taryn and me to have him around.

The burn on my wrist stings like crazy and I find myself lifting up the pan. I can see the boiling water flying through the air, cascading over Dean's face, and I hear his scream piercing my eardrums.

'What's for supper?' Taryn asks as she saunters into the kitchen. I put the pan back down on the hob and let out a loud breath. Thank goodness for Taryn. It's what always happens when she's around; the fury of the moment is diffused.

'Mum's making some delicious-smelling pasta sauce,'

Dean says. There's such warmth in his eyes as he looks at Taryn.

I turn away from both of them and bite down hard on the skin on the inside of my mouth. *Saved for now, Dean,* I think. But in my gut, I know time is running out. Next time, he might not be so lucky.

CHAPTER NINE

AMELIA

'We need to talk,' I say to Hudson as he dumps his briefcase and coat and slumps into the kitchen. My heart is hammering. I'm dreading his fury, or worse, his disappointment. Paige is bringing Marnie home from school and I suppose now is as good a time as any. He walks to the fridge and removes a beer, popping open the tab and pouring it into a glass.

'What about?' Hudson sits down in his normal chair.

I decide to tell him without any preamble. 'I've been scammed. I've lost the money in my savings account.'

'You what?' He turns to stare at me, his nose wrinkled with confusion.

'I'm sorry, but it's all gone, and I don't know if I'll get it back. The bank is disputing it.'

'You are bloody joking, right?'

'It's not a joke.' I can't bring myself to look at him.

'Well, then you need to sort it, Amelia. Fucking sort it.' He stands up then, kicking his chair back, picking up his glass of beer and storming out of the room. I don't know what I was expecting, but not this. His perpetual avoidance. I slump into the chair he's just vacated and lower my head into my hands. I know I need to sort it, but I was hoping Hudson might show an iota of sympathy, or have some ideas to help me sort it. Instead, he's walked out.

After ten minutes of not knowing what to do, I haul myself up and walk out of the kitchen into the hall. I can hear Hudson on the phone in his study. I decide to leave him to it and I make supper.

Half an hour later, Hudson is back in the kitchen, and I brace myself for his anger, except his expression is strangely unreadable. He sits again.

'I'm taking the job offer from Globus Planet. They'll be purchasing the travel agency.'

I stare at him, feeling confused and dismayed. How come he hasn't discussed this with me? Besides, he only told me the other day that he wasn't accepting the job offer.

'They want me to stay working for the company and to move to the head office in Manchester.'

'Manchester?' Manchester is 250 miles away. The shock makes me grab the seat of my chair.

'Yes. I'll have to be there full-time. I can start next week. It might be good for you and me to have a bit of distance for a while.'

'Distance?' There's a stab in my chest. I thought Hudson and I were meant to be trying to improve our marriage, not distance ourselves further.

'You, Marnie and Clover can join me in a few weeks, once we've found a new school for Marnie. We can rent the house out or put it on the market. I've already spoken to a couple of estate agents and they reckon we can get good money for this place.'

'What!' I exclaim. 'You're moving next week and you expect us to up sticks and go too, just like that?'

'That's pretty normal when the main breadwinner has to relocate, isn't it?'

'No, Hudson!' I stand up and start pacing the kitchen. 'A marriage doesn't work like that. You're meant to discuss major life decisions with me, not just sell your business and take a job on the other side of the country and present it as a fait accompli. And what about our life here? Marnie is sitting her GCSEs this year and I've got a business.'

He scoffs. 'Hardly a business.'

'We cannot take Marnie out of school. Are you out of your mind?' I pick up a teatowel, scrunch it up and let it drop onto the countertop.

'Well, what do you propose?' His voice has an edge of sarcasm.

'I can't believe you've just dumped this on me. Why haven't you told me about this before? Surely it's been months in the planning.'

'Well, I did mention it. Besides, I've had offers before that have come to nothing, and what's the point in getting your hopes up unnecessarily?'

'I don't think you should take the offer. It's too much of a disruption.'

'What!' Hudson throws his hands up into the air. 'You don't understand, Amelia. It's a done deal and I have no choice. I have to do this for the continuation of the business. Besides, it will be good for all of us. Eventually, I'll have more time to spend with you, and Manchester is an edgy town, a great place for a teenager to grow up. I've looked into schools and colleges and there are several that are really highly rated.'

I'm literally speechless. A few days ago, Hudson said in passing that he'd been offered a job, but the truth is, he must have been planning this behind my back for months, just assuming that we can up sticks and relocate several hundred miles away with little interruption to our lives. I don't want to go. I have no desire to live in a big city far away from my friends and family, and the last thing Marnie needs is the disruption of moving schools right before her exams. And what about Mum? She's coming over tomorrow; she's arthritic and she needs me. My yoga students need me. I stare at Hudson and once again wonder when it was that we grew so far apart. It's one thing not talking about our feelings; it's quite another planning a relocation to the other side of the country without discussing it with your spouse.

'Well, just think about it,' he says, getting up and walking towards the door. 'I'm going to take a shower.'

I listen, stunned, as he stomps upstairs. This is not acceptable! He can't just walk away when we haven't finished the conversation. I race upstairs after him.

'Hudson, wait.'

He's standing in our bedroom, his shirt removed. I notice that he's put on weight around his midriff, the beginnings of a middle-aged paunch. A few hairs on his chest are turning grey. He's getting old and I hadn't even noticed.

'I can't go, and Marnie can't either. At least not until the next academic year.'

'In which case I'll go alone. I'll come home at the weekends as often as I can.'

'So that's it?' I ask. 'Decision made unilaterally?'

'As I've already told you, Amelia, there is no choice.'

'And you expect me to have to do everything, do you? The childcare, the dog care, managing the house, paying all the bills and working. Essentially being a single mum.'

'You're hardly paying the bills, aren't you? Sure, you might write out the cheques, but the money that's in our account is thanks to me. I'm working my guts out so you can live this life of luxury. And then you announce that you've lost our money. You've actually lost it! It's the height of irresponsibility, Amelia.' He waves his hands around.

I'm stunned. Is that what he thinks? That I enjoy being financially reliant on him? Doesn't he realise that's why I trained as a yoga teacher, why I have ambitions to open my own studio, so I can contribute too?

'And how do you think our marriage is going to work with you being away all week every week? It's been bad enough as it is.'

He shrugs his shoulders, almost as if he doesn't care, and that makes me furious. 'Do you want our marriage to break down? Is that what all this is about? An easy way out of being married to me?'

'Don't be melodramatic, Amelia. This is a great job offer and one we can't afford to turn down. If you won't move, then what's the alternative? We'll just have to try a bit harder, won't we?'

'But I am trying!' I exclaim, feeling exasperation. And that's when we both hear a creak from outside our bedroom. I walk to the door, fling it open and glance down the stairs, just in time to see Marnie's back disappearing out of the open front door.

'Wait, Marnie!' I shout, worried how much of this conversation she's heard, upset that I'd forgotten that Paige was bringing her home. I run down the stairs and out of the front door. Paige's white Polo is pulling away, but Marnie runs after it, waving her arms, and the car comes to a halt. Marnie's feet are pounding the gravel and she races up to the car, pulls open the rear door and flings herself inside. I watch with dismay as I realise Marnie has fled with Paige.

CHAPTER TEN

PAIGE

Poor Marnie is in quite the state. Apparently, she overheard her parents having a massive argument, something about Hudson moving to Manchester, and now she thinks her parents are getting divorced. I wonder if there's any truth in that and find it hard to hide my smirk at the thought of Amelia's distress. There I was thinking she was living in paradise.

My phone rings as I turn onto the main road. Amelia, no doubt, so I let the call go to voicemail. I'll ring her back in due course and let her sweat for a bit.

'Mum and Dean argue all the time,' Taryn says from the back seat, as if that's going to console Marnie.

'It's just banter,' I add. 'Keeps the relationship on its toes.'

'Gross, Mum,' Taryn says. 'Anyway, if your parents move to Manchester, you can stay with us.'

Right, I think to myself. And how's that going to work? Will Taryn really want to share her bedroom with Marnie and will the Myers pay me to feed and clothe their daughter? Nope. That is not going to happen, but I won't burst the girls' bubble quite yet.

When we're back home, I glance at myself in the hall mirror, pleased with my new look. I haven't had any surgery but I did treat myself to a new hairstyle thanks to a very expensive colourist and, of course, the sparkling new diamond earrings. I can't wait to see Amelia's face when she sees me.

I stick a ready-made lasagne into the oven and tell the girls to get on with their homework. I wait another thirty minutes and then call Amelia. I've had three missed calls from her.

'Sorry,' I say, pretending to be breathless. 'I hope you weren't worried, but Marnie was really distressed, so we calmed her down, did a quick shop and now I'm making them a lovely homemade supper. I'll drop her back to your house later on.'

'Oh,' Amelia says. 'That's really kind of you but I can't ask you to come over here twice in one evening. I'll happily collect her from yours.'

To date, I've succeeded in keeping Amelia away from our house. I don't want her condescending pity when she sees how small our place is in comparison to hers, how run down our street is. As our lives increasingly intertwine, I'm not sure how much longer I'll be able to keep her away, but I'm going to try.

'I absolutely insist on bringing Marnie back,' I say. 'You've got enough on your plate and besides, I need to do a quick shop at Tesco's for stuff I couldn't get earlier, so it's barely out of my way. And I don't want you to worry about

Marnie. You know what it's like; when we adults have a little tiff, the kids get all uptight about it. I've reassured Marnie that you and Hudson are as tight as ever. I am right, aren't I?'

'Yes, yes. It was just unfortunate that Marnie overheard us. Hudson is having to take a job in Manchester, which is far from ideal.'

'Oh, really? Well, I shouldn't worry. Distance makes the heart grow fonder and all of that,' I say. 'Think of the fun you could have without him being around. You could even get that yoga studio off the ground and he wouldn't be any the wiser. Anyway, I'll drop Marnie back a bit later and, in the meantime, you put your feet up and make up with that lovely husband of yours.'

'Thanks, Paige. You're really kind.'

Yes, I think to myself. *I am really kind. Yes, Amelia dear. You really can trust me.*

I drive Marnie home at 10.30 p.m., which I'm sure is much too late for a school night. I can imagine how twitchy Amelia will be, but indebted to me as she is, there's not much she can do about it. Marnie is silent around me, which is rather frustrating, but I remind myself – one step at a time. The lights are all on in the Myers' residence. Such a waste of electricity; so typical of the rich. Marnie hops out of the car and I follow her. Amelia is at the front door before we reach it.

'Thank you so much for bringing Marnie back,' Amelia gushes.

I step up to the front door so I'm bathed in artificial light. My earrings should be glistening and my hair all shiny except, frustratingly, Amelia doesn't seem to notice.

'Are you teaching tomorrow?' I ask.

'I am.'

'Great, me too. Let's catch up for a coffee. I hope you've mended things with Hudson.' With another quick shake of my new locks, I head back to the car. Amelia shuts the front door before I'm even inside. She's such a self-centred, selfish woman, it makes my blood boil.

The idea hits me as I'm driving back home. Why am *I* never the centre of attention? Why does no one truly notice me? That might sound a little childish and all me, me, me, but when you've been through as much hardship as I have, I think it's a fair enough thought. Why don't nice things ever happen to me? Am I less deserving than Amelia or Katya? In many ways, I should be more deserving because I wasn't born with a silver spoon in my mouth. My mother hated me and never failed to remind me how much of a pain in the butt I was to her, but at the same time expected me to wait on her hand and foot. I've had to work for every little thing myself; I've suffered terribly. I think of how beautiful Katya looked on her wedding day, how she was the centre of attention, and it gets me thinking. Dean has asked me to marry him loads of times and I've always said no. I mean, what's the point? It's not like I'm going to inherit a fortune from him when he dies, and he's a good dad to Taryn whether we're married or not. Except perhaps now is the time to say yes. I've got money and we can afford a lovely wedding. And it's about time that I'm the centre of attention, isn't it? I let the thought drip-feed overnight and the more I think about it, the better an idea it becomes.

The next day, I've finished my one and only yoga class. Why is it that I've only been asked to lead one class whereas Amelia gets to run several every day? I really need to talk to Vanessa, except this morning, I'm leaning into positivity and self-love, whatever the hell that is. I see Katya and Amelia chatting next to the water machine and I hurry towards them.

'Hi, Paige,' Amelia says before returning to her conversation with Katya. Neither of them notices my new hairstyle. In fact, they barely glance at me. The bitches.

'I've got some exciting news,' I say. They both stop talking and turn towards me. Katya's thin eyebrows rise up. 'I'm getting married!' I exclaim.

'Oh my goodness, that's fantastic news!' Amelia says. 'When did Dean ask you?'

'He's asked me numerous times over the years but this time I actually said yes. It's so exciting!'

'Congratulations,' Katya says, although there isn't much enthusiasm in her voice. Perhaps she thinks it's too soon for her to be usurped as the blushing bride. Stupid cow.

'Anyway, it's a bit hush-hush at the moment as we haven't even had the chance to tell Taryn. So if you wouldn't mind keeping it to yourself for a few days...'

Amelia does that silly zipping up of her lips motion, and with a spring in my step, I hurry away.

For once, Taryn comes straight home after school.

'Darling,' I say, putting my arm across the kitchen doorway to stop her from leaving the room. 'I've got a huge favour to ask of you and if you say yes, I'll give you a hundred pounds.'

She eyes me suspiciously.

'Could you go to Marnie's house this evening or otherwise stay up in your room?'

'Why?' She crosses her arms over her chest.

'Because Dean and I are going to have a romantic dinner. I'm doing it as a surprise for him.'

'Why?' She scrunches up her nose.

'Just because. We need to do these things to keep our relationship alive.'

'Gross, Mum. I can't go to Marnie's. Her grandmother is over.'

'Well, you can stay upstairs then. I'll make you some food and bring it up on a tray, and if you keep out of our hair for the evening I'll give you a hundred quid as a thank you.'

'Since when have you got a hundred pounds to spare? Normally you're so tight I can't even get a pound out of you.'

'I've come into a bit of money recently, not that it's any concern of yours.'

I see a flash of worry on her face.

'All above board,' I say. 'Now chop-chop, and I'll bring you some food later.'

I spend the next hour preparing steak, chips and mushy peas for Dean – his favourite meal. It's not exactly gourmet but Dean has simple tastes. I've got a bottle of champagne cooling in the fridge and a ready-made chocolate gateaux, which I'll pretend I made. I lay the table with the only tablecloth we own and light a few candles, then I hurry upstairs and change into a slinky dress. I survey myself in the mirror and am pleased with what I see. Sure, the nose and the ears aren't fixed yet, but my body is both curvy and toned and I look a million dollars. And then I hear the slamming of his van's door. There's loud, thumping music coming from Taryn's bedroom but at least her door is closed. I hurry downstairs just as Dean walks into the hallway.

'Wow! You look good!' he exclaims. I throw my arms around his neck even though he's wearing his overalls and stinks of sweat and the faint hint of drains. Dean appreciates me and that feels good.

'I'm cooking you your favourite meal so hurry up and get showered,' I say, ushering him upstairs.

'What is it? My birthday or something?' He grins. I pat him on the backside and he climbs the stairs.

Half an hour later and he's sitting at his normal place at the kitchen table. I wish he'd made an effort with his clothes and had bothered to shave but he's not to know how special this evening is going to be.

'What's all this?' he asks, gesturing at the lit candles and neatly laid table.

I don't answer, but walk to the fridge, take out the champagne, pop the cork and pour us each a large glass. 'There's something I want to ask you, Dean Smith,' I say. I wonder if I should get down on one knee, but the dress is really tight and I think I'll pop the zipper. Dean's eyes widen.

'Stand up,' I say, as I hand him the glass of champagne. He's frowning now.

'Will you marry me?' I ask, fluttering my eyelashes and pouting my red lips ever so slightly.

'Seriously?' he asks.

'I'm dead serious.'

'Of course I will, you silly cow!' he says, placing his glass on the table and wrapping his thick arms around me so that the champagne slops out of my glass.

The silly cow bit wasn't quite the reaction I was hoping for, but Dean looks truly chuffed. He smashes his lips down on mine and shoves his tongue into my mouth. I pull back.

'Steady on, tiger,' I say, putting the palm of my right hand on his chest. 'We've got a yummy meal to get through first.'

'I haven't got you a ring, though,' Dean says.

'Don't worry, there's time for that.'

'I can't afford much, love, and I know you like your diamonds.'

'I've got a bit of cash. I can lend you the money and then you can pay me back,' I suggest. Dean looks a bit suspicious but doesn't say anything.

'I can't believe you actually want to do it,' he says. 'After all these years.'

'You've been good to me, and good to Taryn. I think we should formally become a family, don't you?' It strikes me that neither of us has said that we love each other. In fact, I'm not sure we've ever said it. But then Dean is a means to an end and he's not the sort of bloke to rock the boat. He's steady, is my Dean, and that's what Taryn has needed. Steadfastness.

I finish off the steaks and pile his plate up high.

'Smells delicious, Paigey,' he says. He only calls me Paigey during sex. Of course, we'll have to have sex tonight, which is annoying as Dean is a wham, bam, thank you kind of man, despite me trying to teach him otherwise. He takes a big mouthful of steak and chews it loudly.

'I've been thinking this for a while, love. But now you've suggested we get married, why don't we take this opportunity to start again? We can move somewhere up north and have a smallholding. Be self-sufficient, live off the land. I've always dreamed of having my own pigs and chickens, and if you want to still do a bit of yoga, you can do that by Zoom. The north of Scotland is so beautiful and rugged, and we wouldn't need much money to live a good, healthy existence. What do you think?'

What do I think! Is he off his bloody rocker? How well does Dean actually know me? I'm a city girl. I need the bright lights and the buzz of people and nice, material things.

There is not a hope in hell that I'm going to be living in some shack in the middle of nowhere in the remote, freezing cold of north Scotland.

'Let's think about it,' I say, throwing him a wide and very fake smile. 'We've got a wedding to plan first.'

'Nothing too extravagant, Paige,' Dean says, bringing the tone of the evening right down. 'Just a registry office wedding and a nice meal down the pub for you, me and Taryn.'

'No, Dean. I haven't waited my whole life to get married to have a meal down the pub. I want the full shebang. A church wedding, flowers, a meal in a marquee like Katya did.'

Dean pales and I laugh.

'You don't need to worry about the money. I've told you, I've come into some money and I've been squirrelling it away especially for this. We can afford it, I promise you.'

He looks really dubious and is about to say something when I lean across the table and put my finger over his lips. 'You don't need to worry. I'm not the sort of person who makes the same mistakes twice.'

'Promise me?'

I nod. 'Anyway, we need to tell Taryn the happy news. She's going to be chuffed to bits.' I push my chair back and walk over to the shelf where we keep our crockery and glasses. I remove another wine glass and half-fill it with champagne. Then I walk to the kitchen door, open it and shout up the stairs. The music is still thumping and knowing Taryn, she won't hear me. I shout her name and when I get no response, I hurry upstairs, knock on the door and fling it open. She's hunched over her desk and starts when I tap her on the shoulder.

'Dean and I have got something to tell you. Can you come downstairs?'

'Thought you wanted me to stay in my room,' she says, without looking up from her school-issued laptop.

'We did but now you can come down. I've got some food for you.'

She huffs but eventually gets up and follows me downstairs. That's the thing about Taryn; she's a good girl really and barely takes after me.

'Well, this is all very romantic,' she says, in a snarky voice.

I hand her the half-filled glass of champagne.

'I don't drink alcohol,' she says.

'Oh come on. It's a special occasion. At least take a sip.'

'What's up?' she asks.

'Dean and I are getting married and we'd like you to be our chief and only bridesmaid.'

'What?' A grin emerges on her face. She plonks the glass down and throws her arms around Dean's neck. She's been asking for him to adopt her for years, but we've never got around to it. Taryn has never met her birth father. The bastard left me when I told him I was pregnant.

'You happy, love?' Dean asks Taryn as he strokes her back.

'Eh, yes. You're crazy for wanting to marry her but I'm stoked you're going to be my proper dad.'

'I've always been your proper dad,' Dean says.

I have to break up the love-in between my husband-to-be and my daughter. 'Right, take your supper and leave Dean and me to our romantic evening, okay?'

'And the hundred quid?' Taryn asks.

'You'll get it in the morning.'

Later, when Dean is pumping himself into me and I'm pretending to enjoy it, I find myself imagining it is Hudson lying on top of me. I wonder what it would feel like to have a classy man make love to me, someone who actually knows how to make a woman feel good rather than taking their lead from cheap porn. And then I wonder: what have I done? Am I saying yes to marrying Dean just because I want a wedding? The truth is, I am. Then again, I've always known I'll be getting rid of Dean at some point, whether we're married or not. And if we are married, then there must be plenty of legal and financial benefits. So what the hell. I will go through with it and enjoy myself in the meantime.

There are two wedding dress shops in Beacham, neither of which I've visited before. I called the smartest one in advance, and using my poshest of fake accents, made an appointment for Taryn and me. It's called Grace's Wedding Boutique and has beautiful satin gowns hanging in the window and swirling letters painted on the shop sign. Just inside the entrance is a little side table with a bottle of champagne cooling in a silver bucket and several champagne flutes. Classical music is playing softly through hidden speakers.

For a teenager who pretends to be a goth and views herself as a bit different, Taryn is ridiculously excited. She's brought Marnie along too, which actually I'm quite glad about, because I'm hopeful she'll talk Taryn out of choosing a black bridesmaid dress. Obviously, I'm not going for the full white meringue look, rather something simple and elegant, more suited to an older bride. But this is my first marriage, so I'm going to stick with white or cream.

As we enter, a shop assistant steps forward. She's

wearing a boxy suit and her hair is pinned back over her broad forehead with a thick Alice band.

'Hello. I'm Grace. Welcome to my boutique. Can I help you?' She peers down her nose at me. I bristle.

'I'm getting married and am looking for a dress for me and my daughter.'

Grace turns towards Marnie and says, 'I'm sure we can find you something pretty.'

'I'm the daughter,' Taryn says while Marnie reddens.

'Oh,' the woman replies, looking Taryn up and down as if she's something the cat dragged in. I feel that anger surge through me, but I dig my fingernails deep into my palm, reminding myself that I'm the customer here and she's just a stupid shop owner.

'And what is your budget?' Again, Grace looks down her nose at me and I can tell that she's thinking I can't afford shit, and that I should be dress-shopping at M&S and not at her fancy boutique.

'How much are your dresses?'

'They start at two thousand pounds and go up to ten thousand.'

I can feel the smile slipping off my face.

'Is that within your budget?' she asks, giving me such a snooty look, I want to slap her face.

'It's less than my budget,' I say quickly.

'What the hell, Mum!' Taryn mutters.

Ghastly Grace wrinkles her forehead, looks me up and down and scowls as if she doesn't believe me. She's staring at my Tesco shoes when she should be hurrying out the back to select my dresses. I can't stand this condescending cow.

'Do you want our fucking business or not?' I exclaim. I stride over to the little table with the champagne bottle, pour myself a glass and drink the whole thing in one go. Marnie and Taryn are staring at me with round eyes.

'Come on, girls,' I say. 'This witch doesn't deserve our business.' I storm out of the shop with the girls galloping behind me.

'God, what a cow,' I say, as we stride along the high street. 'Let's go to the other shop.'

THIS SHOP ISN'T as fancy, but it does have rails stuffed full of wedding dresses and a shop assistant who talks with a Brighton accent and doesn't ask me how much money I've got. When I describe the kind of dress I'm looking for, she disappears around the back to make a selection. Meanwhile, the girls are rifling through a rail of bridesmaids' dresses, all of which Taryn is rejecting. Normally Taryn spends every minute of her waking day typing into her phone, her fingers flying over the screen, but today she hasn't even looked at it.

'What's your colour theme?' Marnie asks me.

'I'm thinking blues. Do you think you can get Taryn into a blue dress?'

Taryn groans, but she doesn't outright reject the idea. 'They're all so fancy,' she says, as she pulls out a long sky-blue satin dress. 'Just not me.'

'It could be,' Marnie suggests, and for a moment I'm rooting for the daughter of my enemy.

A few minutes later and I'm in a large changing room trying on five dresses. Each time I walk out into the shop the girls ooh and aah and I feel truly great about myself. But it's the fifth dress that is the one. It's a pale cream colour, silky satin with a cowl neck and simple spaghetti straps, and it makes me feel like a model.

'This is it,' I say, as I twirl in front of the girls. 'Do you agree?' They both nod, and very sweetly I notice tears in Taryn's eyes. 'Right, your turn now. I'm going to select some dresses for you to try on.'

'Must I?' Taryn groans.

'Yes,' Marnie and I reply in unison.

Clutching a handful of dresses, Marnie accompanies Taryn into the changing room while I sit in the boutique on a luxuriously padded chair. I'm thinking about the price tag of my chosen dress. Just over three thousand pounds. It's a crazy amount of money for a dress that I'll wear once, but I remind myself of that cliche: I'm worth it and I have all that money thanks to lovely Amelia. As I'm sipping from a glass of champagne (not as nice as in the other shop but served to me willingly) I notice that Marnie has left her handbag and coat on the chair. It's a Michael Kors bag open at the top. It's rather disgusting that a fifteen-year-old girl has a designer handbag, and it looks new, not even like one of Amelia's castoffs. I can hear the girls chatting and giggling, so I pull the bag towards me and look inside. She has the normal rubbish; a purse with twenty quid in it, some cheap makeup and a plastic hairbrush. And then I notice a set of keys. Her house keys, I assume. Without too much thought, I grab the bunch of keys, drop them into the zippered section of my handbag, a designer knock-off that I bought at a market stall for a tenner, and then push her bag back to where I found it. Who knows, those keys might just come in handy.

Dress choices made, I suggest to the girls that we go for a drink before returning home. We're not far from Eat Cake, the coffee shop opposite the yoga studio. They each choose a cake and a drink and I send them off to find us a table. Having paid for it all, I'm just about to sit down with the girls, when I see someone I recognise striding along the pavement. It takes me a second to place her but then I realise it's snooty Grace. I jump up.

'Just popping out to get some money from the cashpoint,' I say. 'Don't eat my cake!'

Taryn throws me a confused look, but I ignore her, scoot through the coffee shop and hurry out of the door. The bitch is ahead of me, walking purposefully. But just as I catch up with her, she stops at the traffic lights, obviously intending to cross the road. There's quite a little crowd gathered, and she, of course, is at the front, her pointy shoes sticking out over the edge of the pavement. There's a rubbish truck approaching, driving a little slower than I would have liked, but just as it approaches us, I step right up behind Grace and shove her really hard in the back. She stumbles and falls into the road. There's a scream and then more screams, but I've edged away from the little crowd and I'm striding back towards Eat Cake. I don't look back once. I don't hesitate, I don't glance over my shoulder, I just walk purposefully, pushing the door open and marching to the girls and sitting down at their table. I dig my fork into a piece of chocolate cake.

'Yum,' I say. 'This is really delicious.'

When I drop Marnie back at her house, Amelia invites me in for a cup of tea.

'Did you choose a dress? What's it like?' she asks eagerly.

I show her the photograph on my phone that Taryn took of me modelling my wedding dress.

'Oh my goodness, you look absolutely stunning!' Amelia gushes. 'That's the most beautiful dress; so very elegant. I can't wait to see you walk down the aisle in it.'

I pause for a moment. Amelia has made a massive assumption that she's going to be invited to my wedding. I control a snort. What if I didn't invite her? What if I invite Romy and Katya and even Vanessa but not Amelia? How would she react then? The thought is tempting. Amelia would feel so left out, humiliated even. Except, no. I don't want to show my hand this early and let Amelia know that we're only pretend friends. I need to do something way worse, something that will truly hurt her. I've been wanting Amelia to pay for too long. So no, I'm going to do something that really makes her suffer.

CHAPTER ELEVEN

MARNIE

Mum is completely overreacting. I've lost my house keys, probably when I was out with Paige and Taryn wedding dress-shopping, and I've had to tell her.

'You need to be responsible, Marnie!'

'It was a mistake,' I say. 'We all make mistakes.'

'But what if someone finds it and realises whose keys they are? We're going to have to change the locks.'

'That's ridiculous! The keys have got no identification on them. How is anyone going to know who they belong to?'

'Have you asked all your friends? Did you leave them at Taryn's house?'

She's the first person I asked, and no, she hasn't seen them. They've probably been dumped in a rubbish bin somewhere. I don't know why Mum is making such a fuss about it, but she makes a fuss about everything these days. It's like she's strung out, and goodness knows why. She's pissed that Dad is moving to Manchester but really, she's got nothing to be so tense about. He's not around much anyway.

Meanwhile, things are going pretty well for me. I mean,

really well. I was super-worried about telling Mum about the lost keys because she's actually agreed for me to go to London on Saturday! Well, more like Dad said I could go and she had to agree. She thinks I'm going with Olivia and her mum but actually, I'm going alone. It's a risk, I know, but so worth it. The thing is, I need my keys to let myself back into the house when I come home late at night, so that's why I had to fess up. I've got it all planned out. Mum will drop me off at the station in the afternoon. I'll take a bag and get changed in the train toilet, then I'll get the tube to the nightclub and hang around somewhere near there until it's time to meet Jax. I'll have to make sure I don't miss the last train home, which is a pain, because it means I've got to catch the 11.05 p.m. train from Victoria, which is way too early, but I've got no choice in that. Then I'll take a taxi from the station back home. At least I'll get a few hours with my boyfriend.

I'm trying to focus on my French homework but the words are all a jumble. Jax has messaged me a bit less the last few days but we're still sending each other loads of messages and cheeky photos. He's got the most beautiful body and although I still like Ryan, Jax is a real man whereas Ryan is still a boy. Not that Ryan has even glanced in my direction at school. Before, I might have been upset, but now I'm with someone so much better. I wish I could show Jax off to everyone at school. Except I can't. Not even Taryn. Despite her edgy looks, she's a bit of a prude and I don't think she'd approve of the pics. And now he's messaging me again.

Can't wait to meet u!

You too! X

I add an x and wonder if that's too much.

8 p.m. outside Covent Garden tube. Italian for supper and then onto a club. U'll luv it.

Can't wait.

An hour later another message pings through.

I need 2 c all of u.

??

Nkd.

So far I've only sent him photos of my boobs and I'm not sure about this. And then he sends me a photo of himself. The whole of his body from his neck down to his feet, and he's completely naked, with a massive hard-on. My cheeks flame red as heat spreads through my body. Oh my God! He is so hot. I slap my hand over my face. He's a real man and he wants me!

This is what u do 2 m, Marnie. Just thinking about u. Ur turn now.

It takes me over an hour. I shower and shave, nicking my skin and making myself bleed and then wondering how much hair I should or shouldn't have. Will it be obvious that I'm a virgin just by looking at my photo? I try different poses in the mirror, crossing one leg over the other, leaning over the sink trying to push my boobs together, and I take a gazillion different shots.

He sends me another message.

Still waiting.

And in the end, I just choose one at random and hit send.

He replies immediately with a thumbs-up emoji. Somehow that seems like a bit of an anti-climax, but what would I know? I'm new to all of this.

The hours drag by but eventually it's Saturday and then it's Saturday lunchtime and then it's time for Mum to take me to the station. I've packed a short black bandeau dress, and makeup. Stuff that I bought when I was out shopping with Taryn; stuff Mum doesn't know I have. She'd go apoplectic if she saw me in that outfit.

'Have a lovely time,' she says as she waves me off. 'And say thank you to Olivia's mum.' I run into the station, holding my phone over the ticket barrier and racing down the stairs to the platform. The train is surprisingly busy but I manage to get into the toilet and with some difficulty get changed. When I emerge, I walk back to my seat, passing a mother with two girls, probably eleven or twelve years old. They stare at me and their mother frowns and then throws me the filthiest of looks. I sit down and a couple of boys, probably not much older than me, let out a whistle. One of them makes an obscene gesture and the other bursts out laughing. I feel really uncomfortable now, so I tug on my coat and cross my bare legs. I try to ignore the boys for the rest of the journey, but I can feel their eyes on me. At Victoria Station, I keep my coat firmly tied around me and walk towards the tube. There are crowds of people and I suddenly feel a bit scared. Literally no one knows I'm here. I could be abducted and Mum and Dad would never find me. I keep my eyes on the ground and walk quickly heading towards the tube. The crowd sweeps me downwards and it takes me a little while to work out which tube line I need to take. The Victoria Line to Green Park and then I need to change onto the Piccadilly Line. I've got three hours to kill so I suppose it doesn't matter if I get a bit lost, although I need to keep an eye on what I spend. I've only got fifty quid on my phone.

Eventually, I get out at Covent Garden and it's drizzling with rain. I shiver. I'm not wearing enough clothes and my legs are freezing. And there are so many people. Too many people. I wander around for a bit but I don't want to go too far in case I get lost or freeze to death. Eventually, I find a Starbucks, buy myself a coffee and find a seat. Time goes by so slowly. I message Taryn, pretending that I'm in London with Dad doing boring stuff. She's so excited about her mum and Dean getting married in a couple of weeks' time. I asked if her mum was pregnant, because what's the rush? They've been together forever. She sent a laughing emoji and said being pregnant was not a reason for getting married, and then I felt a bit foolish. All the same, I don't understand why there's this big hurry. But I'm happy for Taryn because she's happy. On the whole, she doesn't smile much. I play games on my phone and then notice that my phone battery is down to 12% and I haven't brought a charger with me. It starts to get dark outside and eventually, it's 7.45 p.m., so I hurry back to the tube station. I send Jax a message.

Here early. Waiting at the entrance. C u soon!

I can see that he hasn't been active on Instagram since early this morning. I guess he's had a busy day and now he's probably hurrying to meet me. My heart is hammering in my chest. What if he doesn't like me in the flesh? What if we miss each other? That's silly; he'll call me if he can't find me. He's got my mobile number. I hop from foot to foot, constantly glancing at my watch. It's exactly 8 p.m. now and there are so many people milling around. I'm looking everywhere, trying to make out his face. At 8.05 p.m. I wonder if I've got the correct exit. I find the road sign and send him another message.

Waiting at the exit on James Street.

When it gets to 8.15 p.m. I'm literally shivering with cold and there's a gnawing feeling in my stomach, and it's not just hunger. I go back onto Instagram and it looks like he hasn't seen my message. Has something bad happened to him? Perhaps he's sick, in hospital. Perhaps something happened to someone in his family. Just before 8.30 p.m. I decide to call him. I realise that we've never actually spoken; I mean, people of our age don't, do they? It's all done via messaging. But there is a call button on Instagram and I've come all of this way and we have such a good connection. At 8.33 p.m. I press the call button. A female voice says, 'This number is no longer in service.' I pull the phone away from my ear and stare at it. What the hell? I press the call button again and get the same message. Tears spring into my eyes as it dawns on me what's happened. I've just been ghosted. Jax has done a disappearing act. I look back through my messages and realise the last one I got was that thumbs-up emoji when I sent him the nude photo. I swallow as I realise what's happened. He didn't like what he saw. He didn't like what I look like and now he's ghosted me. I can't help but burst into tears. It feels like he's stabbed my heart and stolen all of my dreams. I'm sobbing now, running my hand over my nose to wipe away the snot, not caring that people are staring at me.

'Are you alright, dear?' An old woman is peering at me. Her face is completely wrinkled and she's holding two plastic bags full of bottles that jangle as she moves. Her breath stinks.

'Yeah,' I mutter. 'Thanks.' I turn and run down the steps into Covent Garden tube station. My phone is ringing and, for a moment, happiness floods through me. But then I see that the caller is Taryn. I want to speak to her, to tell her what a fool I've been, to ask if I can come over to her house. Except I don't. I send her call to voicemail.

I go into the toilets at Victoria Station and change into the clothes that I wore when I left home. I feel more like me now, and not so self-conscious. It crosses my mind that Jax might have turned up, but when he caught sight of me, he didn't like what he saw. Perhaps it wasn't just the nude photos. Or perhaps he didn't come at all. Whatever. I just want to sob. I take the next train home and a taxi from the station. I get the taxi to drop me off at the bottom of the drive because if she's still awake, I don't want Mum to see that I've come in a taxi. She's expecting me to be dropped off by Olivia's mum in some fancy car, no doubt.

The lights are on upstairs when I let myself in through the back door with the new key that Mum gave me. Clover wags her tail so much when she sees me, it's as if her backside is going to fly off. I sink onto the floor and bury my face in her soft fur, crying softly.

'Hey, Marnie. You're home early.' I jump. Mum is standing in the doorway in her dressing gown. 'What's up?' She crouches down and peers at me. 'Why are you crying?'

'I had a massive argument with Olivia. Just stupid stuff.'

'Oh darling.' She tries to put her arms around me but I push away. I know she means well but I wish she'd stop treating me like a little kid. 'How was the play?'

'Going to bed,' I say, and edge out of the room before running upstairs.

I get the first text message two days later. I've started leaving my phone in my locker as Ms Eisner insisted, and it's probably just as well because if this had arrived during a lesson, it would have been a disaster.

> Send me £200, otherwise I'll share the photos. Send the money via Monzo. Details here. By the end of today.

I drop the phone onto the floor and have to scramble to pick it up. I stare at the phone. The message has come from a number I don't recognise. My fingers are trembling as I message back.

> Who's this?

A laughing emoji.

> Have you been sending nude photos to other people too???

I let out a strangled sob. This is Jax. Jax, who I thought liked me.

> Why are you doing this?

There's no answer. I try calling the number but it goes straight to voicemail and I don't leave a message. I feel sick, really sick. I shove my locker closed and rush towards the toilets, brushing past Ryan.

'Hey, Marnie! What's the hurry?' He grins at me, this boy whom I used to really, really like, but I don't hang around. I make it to the toilets and dry-heave. I don't have £200. I don't even have £20 after my trip to London, where I wasted all my pocket money. And who will Jax send the photos to if I don't pay up? What if he puts them on the internet and attaches my name? My whole life will be ruined. Everyone will laugh at me, I'll have to leave school, I'll never get a job, and I can just see the disappointment on Mum and Dad's faces. What will Ryan think? He and his mates will never stop laughing at me. And worst of all, I can't tell anyone because I've been such an idiot.

I send another message.

> I don't have the money.

The school bell rings and I've got to get to a science lesson. I return to my locker and shove my phone inside as if it's toxic.

I can't concentrate for the rest of the day. I avoid Taryn at lunchtime, worried that if I see her, I'll blurt out the truth. And then, when I pick up my belongings at the end of the day, I see I've got another message.

> Steal it from your parents. Or sell something.

That evening, Dad is home and I can hear my parents in the living room, bickering, which is all they seem to do these days. I tiptoe upstairs and into their bedroom. Mum leaves her handbag on a chair in the corner of the room. I open it, search inside for her wallet. She's only got £30 in cash, but then it hits me – cash is no good. Jax wants me to wire him the money, but how am I going to do that if I haven't got it? I could ask Mum for an advance on my pocket money but I only get £20 a week, so that's not going to work. I leave the £30 and wander despondently into my bedroom.

I message.

> I can't get you the money today.

Surprisingly, an answer comes back quite quickly.

> Feeling very generous. You've got till 10pm Friday. Then I'll put the photos online. But it's gone up to £250.

I bury my face in my pillow. How the hell am I going to get so much money? I debate telling Mum the truth, but the look of disgust I know I'm going to see on her face is too much to bear. Besides, she'll probably drag me off to the police and then things would get really bad.

> I don't know how to get £250.

> Steal stuff. Sell it in town. Or send it to my PO box. Let me know. Time is running out.

CHAPTER TWELVE

AMELIA

It's Paige's wedding in a week's time. I'm so happy for her; it's as if she's floating on air, going around with a permanent smile on her face, with her new, gorgeous hairdo. I have to say that I was surprised she and Dean have organised the wedding so quickly, but I suppose at this point in our lives, if you've made a decision, you might as well get on with it. I'm rifling through my wardrobe trying to work out what to wear tonight, trying not to think about the dress from China and all the missing money in our savings account. Hudson has gone to Manchester this week and we didn't part on good terms. He doesn't seem to get it that he can't just spring a relocation on me with no notice and expect it to be all right. Marnie was absolutely horrified when I told her we might move north, and frankly, after overhearing our fight, I didn't blame her for running off to Taryn's house. I then had to backtrack and say that it wouldn't be until she'd finished her exams and if she really didn't want to go, then we wouldn't.

The missing money is permanently on my mind. I contacted the police and they were completely disinterested, as was the bank. Because I supposedly made the transfer myself, they're saying they're not liable. But of course, they are still 'investigating' and I'm just praying that I will be reimbursed.

I took Paige's advice and have started planning a yoga retreat weekend. I've booked a lovely reception room at Northgate Lodge, our local hotel, for a weekend, and have secured a reduced room rate for my retreat clients. I created a little leaflet and handed copies to all of my clients at the end of my classes. I'm a little nervous Vanessa might find out as, strictly speaking, I'm soliciting her customers, but then again, she doesn't do weekend retreats. And to my delight, I've got ten women signed up. Ten women who are prepared to take the time out of their lives and trust me enough to believe that my retreat will make them feel better about themselves. I'm excited but also nervous, not least because Northgate Lodge expect me to put down a deposit for the rooms and meals and I haven't got the money to do it. I only asked my customers to pay a 10% deposit, and that isn't enough to secure the hotel booking. I know, I know, I was stupid. Naive. But I haven't done this sort of thing before and I never expected to lose all my money and be maxed out on my credit card. I'm thinking of asking Hudson tonight if he'll lend me the money. I haven't even shared with him that I'm planning the weekend.

This evening, I'm hoping our little family will come together and we can put aside our arguments and disappointments. It's my birthday. We've had a tradition for the past few years of going to dinner at Northgate Lodge for my and Hudson's birthdays. They have two restaurants: the Spa restaurant where my clients will eat, and the main hotel restaurant which has a culinary rosette and serves exquisite food along with eye-watering prices too. I had debated messaging Hudson and telling him that perhaps we should not go this year, but then decided I didn't want to bring the money woes to his attention. He has enough to contend with starting a new job. He left for Manchester on Sunday evening and we've had cursory conversations every evening since. I'm a little surprised that he didn't ring me this morning to wish me happy birthday, but I assume he'll be doing it in person. Marnie also forgot it was my birthday, and when I reminded her that we'd be going out for supper tonight as normal, she seemed quite dismissive. I'm worried about her. She's been acting strangely the past few days, even less communicative than normal. I hope the thought of moving isn't going to affect her studies.

I pull out my go-to black dress to wear for supper tonight and lay it on the bed. Then I open my jewellery box but, weirdly, my precious bracelet that Hudson gave me after Marnie was ill isn't in the slot I normally keep it in. I search through the rest of the box and then pull out the contents of my top drawer as well as my bedside cabinet. I'm sure I last wore it to Katya's wedding and I would have definitely put it away. There's a slight panic in my chest because not only is this the most valuable piece of jewellery I own, but also it's particularly sentimental. I take a deep breath and start looking all over again. But then my phone rings.

'Is this Mrs Amelia Myers?' It's a male voice and I'm expecting this to be a cold call, especially as the number comes up as withheld.

'Yes,' I confirm.

'I'm calling from Shoreham police station. We have your daughter, Marnie.' My stomach roils.

'Marnie? Oh my goodness, what's happened to her? Is

she alright?' I feel myself go into a panic as I glance at my watch, my pulse pounding and my knees trembling. It's 3 p.m. and Marnie should still be at school.

'She's fine, but you'll need to come to the station to collect her.'

'But what's happened? Is she hurt? Does she need to go to the hospital?'

'There's nothing physically wrong with her but you do need to come and collect her. Ideally as soon as possible.'

'Yes, of course. Is she a victim of a crime?'

'We will explain everything when you arrive.' And then he hangs up on me. Immediately I try calling Marnie but her phone is switched off and it goes straight to voicemail. I grab my bag, apologise to Clover for leaving her alone, and hurry to my car. It's a fifteen-minute drive to Shoreham and I speed as fast as I can to get there, trying but failing to think of a reasonable reason why Marnie might be at the police station. I find a space on a residential street opposite, not bothering to look if I'm allowed to park here or not. Only as I'm switching the engine off do I think about calling Hudson. I glance at my watch. He'll probably be on the train on his way south and as there's nothing he can do to get here faster, I decide to ring him later, when I know what the situation is. Hurrying out of the car to the squat, red-brick building opposite, I realise with a jolt that I've never been inside a police station. What an uneventful, mundane life I've led.

I push through the doors and walk into a lobby with no one inside and then up to an unmanned front desk. I press an old-fashioned gold buzzer and a moment later a uniformed officer walks through a door behind the Perspex counter.

'My name is Amelia Myers. I'm here for my daughter, Marnie.'

He nods at me slowly, as if trying to evaluate me, and it does nothing to ease the knot in my stomach.

'Wait there,' he says.

A couple of seconds later, a door opens to the side of the desk and he beckons me to follow him. We walk down a short corridor and then he pushes open the door to a small room, more like a cubicle really. Marnie is sitting on a grey plastic chair. She looks up at the sound of us, her face red, blotchy and tear-stained.

I move as if to rush towards her, to sweep her up in a hug, but the police officer says in a firm voice, 'Please take a seat, Mrs Myers,' pointing at the chair next to Marnie.

He's a portly man whose uniform stretches over his barrel chest. His face is lined and weary, as if he's seen too much and is fed up with it all. 'Marnie was caught shoplifting in Samuel's jewellers this afternoon,' he says as he settles into the chair behind the desk opposite us. As he shifts, the chair creaks.

'No, that can't be right!' I exclaim.

'I'm sorry, Mrs Myers, but she was caught red-handed and has admitted it.'

'Marnie?' I turn to look at her, my voice sharp with shock. Marnie keeps her eyes on the floor and visibly shrinks away from me.

'We're letting her off with a caution this time because it's a first offence. But, if she is caught again, then she will be prosecuted. Do you both understand?'

I nod vigorously, trying to comprehend what Marnie was doing out of school and how she could have shoplifted when we've tried so hard to instil in her right and wrong.

The officer slaps his palms on the table. 'Alright. We don't ever want to see you again, Marnie. Understood?'

She nods and mutters, 'Sorry,' her eyes still down, her face shrouded by her hair.

The officer stands up and shows us out of the police station. Marnie and I walk in silence across the road to the car but when we're inside, I turn to her.

'What the hell? What on earth were you doing?'

'Don't shout at me,' she says, shifting towards the passenger window and away from me.

I take a deep breath because losing my temper isn't going to help, even though I'd like to. 'Start at the beginning and tell me exactly what happened.'

'I've said I'm sorry,' she murmurs.

'Not good enough. Why were you out of school?'

'Because everything is going to shit and I didn't want to be in school and you won't understand, Mum, so just let it go.' She's sobbing now and I'm at a loss as to what to say. I start the car engine.

'If you're having problems at school, you need to share them with me, and together we can try to work things out. We can talk to Mrs Chase.'

Marnie doesn't say anything, so I continue. 'Have some other kids set you up to this, love? Because I know it's not in your nature to commit a crime. What was it they wanted you to steal? Jewellery for a friend?'

Marnie hides her face in the crook of her arm and swivels so that her back is facing me. I sigh. If she's not going to talk to me, then we might as well go home. Perhaps Hudson can talk some sense into her later. We're both silent on the short journey home.

The second I open the front door, Marnie rushes past

me, up to her bedroom and slams the door shut. I know she's hurting but I deserve an explanation. So much for a fun birthday. I message Hudson.

> What time will you arrive at the station? I'll collect you.

The little dots start up and then stop. It takes him another three minutes to send the message and all it says is:

> Station?

> What time does your train get in?

> I'm in Manchester. I've got a late meeting so thought I'd take the train in the morning.

Disappointment and dismay sit heavily on me as I realise that Hudson has forgotten it's my birthday. I've had nothing from him. Not a card, no flowers, no present, and now he's not even coming home. I don't know whether to laugh or cry. I pick up the phone and call him.

'It's my birthday,' I say dully. 'I thought you'd booked us a table at Northgate Lodge.'

'Oh shit,' Hudson says. 'Sorry, Amelia. I completely forgot the date. There's so much going on here with the new job and everything.' There are voices in the background and I can't tell if he's in a busy office or a bar. 'Look, love. I've got to go now but I'll call you later. And sorry again.' He hangs up before I can respond, before I can tell him that Marnie was caught shoplifting and that this is one of my most miserable birthdays ever.

CHAPTER THIRTEEN

PAIGE

I'm putting away the yoga mats when Amelia pops her head around the door. 'Are you free for a coffee?' she asks. I'm about to say no, because I have zero desire to spend time with Amelia, but there's something in the tone of her voice that makes me look up. She looks awful. Her hair is greasy and pulled back into a ponytail and, very unusually for her, she doesn't appear to be wearing any makeup.

'Sure,' I say, experiencing a little dart of glee. 'Give me five minutes.'

'What's up?' I ask, as we cross the road together heading to the coffee shop. I haven't got the patience to listen to Amelia moan about how miserable her life is. I have so much to do for the wedding, needing to visit the florist, confirm my hair and makeup, sample the dishes we're going to eat for our buffet lunch. But as always, I have to remember that my focus is Amelia and the plans I have for her. I wish I was a more patient person, but it's just not in my nature.

We stand in the queue, with the scent of freshly brewed coffee and the clatter of china and voices swirling around us. 'Things aren't great with Marnie,' she admits, which does take me by surprise. Taryn hasn't said anything, but then again, Taryn doesn't say much. I'm about to ask what she means, but we're at the front of the queue.

'Can I get you a coffee?' Amelia asks. 'And a cake?'

'A coffee would be great. Thanks.'

We carry our mugs to the only free table and sit down. Immediately, she leans forward and I brace myself to listen to a juicy bit of gossip that I can use against her at a later date.

'I had the shittiest of birthdays,' she sighs.

Oh, for goodness' sake. She's a forty-something-year-old woman. Who bothers with birthdays anyway?

'Hudson forgot it and didn't come home, and Marnie, well, please don't tell anyone, but she got caught shoplifting.'

I try very hard not to smile, to show shock and compassion and all of the emotions I guess I should be displaying upon receiving such news.

'Of course, you can trust me,' I say. 'I'm sorry to hear that. Marnie, shoplifting? That's quite the shock.'

'She point-blank refuses to discuss it with me other than repeatedly saying sorry. I'm worried that she's got in the wrong crowd, that some kids have put her up to it. That she's being bullied. I was wondering if you could ask Taryn if she knows anything.'

I bristle slightly. Is she implying that Taryn might have been shoplifting too? No, my daughter is too much of a Goody Two-Shoes. After what I went through, she's turned the other way. Sanctimonious, ruthlessly honest, little Miss Perfect. Only a couple of days ago, she said that she intended to study law when she goes to university, and then will become a barrister. I've no idea where all these ridiculous grandiose ideas come from; certainly not me.

Fortunately, Amelia doesn't wait for me to respond and carries on. 'And Marnie skived off school. She was caught shoplifting in the middle of the afternoon when she should have been in lessons. I'm wondering if she's upset because Hudson has moved to Manchester.'

I suppress a grin. 'Could be, or perhaps she's just being a teenage rebel. It's normal behaviour at that age.'

'Has Taryn ever done anything like that?'

My initial reaction is to stiffen, to take offence that she's suggesting Taryn might be a bad influence. Just because we live in a smaller house than her and don't have her privileges doesn't mean I haven't taught my daughter morals. Except I manage to check myself and settle my features into a neutral look. I throw her a sympathetic smile.

'Me and Taryn are like Edwina and Saffy in *Ab Fab*. She's been a Goody Two-Shoes her whole life. Dean and I joke that Taryn was born aged fifty.' I take a sip of coffee and tilt my head to one side, conspiratorially. 'There is one thing I do, just in case. I've put a tracker on Taryn's phone. You know, just in case anything happens to her. Have you done the same?'

'Only Find My Phone, but she can switch that off.'

'There's a sneaky little app you can install so you can track the phone without her being able to switch it off. Do you want the details?'

She nods eagerly, so I share the app with her.

'And how are things with Hudson? I'm sorry he forgot your birthday.' I'm not in the slightest bit sorry; in fact, I think it's rather hilarious.

'He's working crazy hours. He's in the head office at

Globus Planet in Manchester while they're finalising the sale of his business. Of course, I was disappointed he forgot my birthday, but he did come home the next day with a massive bunch of flowers.'

'So you made up?' I ask.

Amelia shrugs her shoulders. 'Kind of.' She takes a sip of coffee and then plonks it down rather hard. 'Actually, not really. I've decided to go up to Manchester on Thursday. Katya's offered to take over a couple of my classes and I was wondering if you could do the others?'

'Sure,' I say, bristling slightly. She could have asked me first.

'I'm hoping that it'll be easier to have a proper chat away from home and try and sort out some of our differences. Actually, I was wondering if there was any possibility Marnie could stay the night with you?'

'Of course,' I say, perhaps a little too eagerly. 'And Clover? Who's looking after the dog?'

'My lovely cleaning lady, Julia, is having her.'

Of course Amelia would have a cleaner. Women like her are much too posh to lower themselves to clean up their own mess. We chat a little more, but my mind is on other things and before long, I excuse myself, saying I've got some important wedding planning business to attend to.

The next day, I'm dressed in my smartest, sexiest dress with a trench coat over the top and high heels, sitting on the train to Manchester. I've no idea if my little plan will work, but it's worth a try. Globus Planet's offices are easy to track down, located in a red, turreted building not far from Piccadilly Station. If Amelia is correct and Hudson really is working hard, then I've likely got a long wait ahead, but that's all right. It will be worth it. There's a Costa Coffee almost opposite the front door to the office block and I find a table in the window with a perfect view of the door across the road. Around 5 p.m., hordes of people pour out of the building and I'm concerned that I might miss him, but I can't hang around the office front door for too long in case the security officer gets suspicious. By 6 p.m., Hudson hasn't appeared and I'm tempted to go over the road and ask for him at reception. I give it another few minutes, and then I spot him.

I race out of Costa Coffee, pushing past a couple of dawdling women, and stride along the pavement until I'm walking just behind him. He's wearing a grey suit, a coat over his arm, and carrying a leather briefcase. His head hangs low, and he's strolling along quite slowly, so I'm able to keep up. And then I get lucky. He turns into an off-licence. I wait outside, my heart hammering, a huge smile on my face. A couple of minutes later, he emerges, a plastic bag in his hand weighed down by the outline of a bottle. I walk towards him.

'Hudson?' I ask, my voice hesitant. He glances up and stops walking abruptly. He frowns at me for a moment, a flicker of recognition in his eyes but as if he can't quite place me.

'It's Paige. Amelia's friend and colleague. We met at Katya's wedding and our girls are best friends.'

'Paige!' he exclaims, his tired face lighting up with a grin. 'What on earth are you doing here?'

'I could say the same to you!' I laugh. 'I'm from Manchester. My mother lives here and I'm up visiting her. What about you?'

'I'm working here now. Up here during the week and back to Sussex for the weekends.'

'Oh goodness! Amelia mentioned that you were working

away from home but I didn't realise you were in Manchester. What a coincidence!'

We smile inanely at each other for a few seconds and then both speak at once. 'After you!' I exclaim.

'Are you heading back to the station?' he asks.

'No, I'm staying with my mother tonight, although she hasn't got a clue who I am any longer so sometimes I wonder why I bother. It's sad and depressing. But anyway, I'm sure you've got plans,' I say, gesturing towards the plastic bag with the name of the off-licence on it. He blushes slightly.

'Actually, I haven't. If you're not in a hurry to get away, would you like to go out for a drink?'

Bingo!

I glance at my watch and take a long beat to reply. 'That would be lovely. Thank you.'

He takes me to a wine bar located on a quiet side street. I perch on a high stool at a tall, circular table and while he's gone to place the order, I edge my stool so it's a little closer to his. Hudson returns with a bottle of white wine and two glasses.

'So how are you finding Manchester?' I ask, as we clink our glasses together.

'I'm having to work harder than I've ever worked, so, to be honest, I haven't got to know the city. Days are long with work, and in the evenings I'm trying to find a decent flat to rent. The company have given me my current one, but it's only for the first month and then I'm on my own.'

'So Amelia and Marnie aren't joining you?'

He sighs. 'Not until Marnie's finished her GCSEs. The timing wasn't great.'

'It must be lonely being in a strange city all week long.'

'It's early days but I'm hopeful I'll make some friends in due course.'

'No one at your office befriending you, then?' I ask. He's a good-looking man. There must be a few people giving him the once-over. It makes me wonder how faithful he's been to Amelia over the years.

He coughs and I wonder what he's hiding. We make small talk for a while, he asks me about my yoga teaching but glazes over when I describe it, so I ask him lots of questions and he puffs his chest out as he talks about himself. When we've finished the bottle of wine, I say, 'Well, I really must be off now. I'm sure you've got supper plans and things to do. I'll just grab a sandwich somewhere and kill time in the dreadful spare room in Mum's care home. But it was lovely to see you again.'

He doesn't miss a beat. 'If you're not doing anything this evening, would you like to join me for supper? There's an Italian around the corner that has become my local.'

I pause and hesitate for a few beats, just long enough not to appear desperate. 'I don't want to intrude,' I say.

'Not at all. I will enjoy the company.'

Double bingo!

Disappointingly, Hudson turns out to be dull. I knew he would be entitled and pleased with himself, but I had had higher hopes for him. Despite his travels all over the world, he is small-minded and ever so conservative in his views. Not that that changes my plans for the two of us. I can do dull. As he's wittering on about the integration of his business into the Manchester firm, I wonder how he would react if I told him the truth about me. That my ordinary backstory of being a mum and loving partner with a passion for yoga is in fact a front. That I have been to prison and mingled with women who would literally eat Hudson for breakfast and spit him out for elevenses. I imagine how his handsome, symmetrical features would distort with shock and disgust. And that's why I say nothing. I have work to do and Hudson is one of my pawns.

We finish off another bottle of wine, or more like he drinks most of it because I'm pacing myself. And then he orders us both a digestif and the restaurant gives us a complimentary Limoncello. I'm slightly tipsy, but Hudson is definitely under the influence. He insists on paying for the meal, which is just as well, as I had no intention of contributing, and then we're out on the street, shivering in the cold night air. As I walk, I intentionally weave into him, giggling and apologising. He links his arm into mine to steady me.

'Where's your flat?' I ask, edging very close to him so that I accidentally on purpose bump my hip against his.

'Just around the corner.'

'A nightcap?' I ask. 'I don't fancy going back to the old people's home yet. It's so depressing there.'

He hesitates for a moment and then says, 'Sure.'

Hudson is living in a serviced apartment. One of those places with a twenty-four-hour concierge and the need to sign in and out. The apartment is nice but bland, a bit like him, really. There is a small sofa and an armchair in the bare-walled living room, and a grey, open-plan kitchen.

He opens the bottle of red wine that he'd bought earlier in the evening and pours us each a large glassful.

'When is Amelia coming to keep you company?' I ask, knowing full well what the answer is.

'She's due tomorrow but not for long, I think. She doesn't want to move to Manchester.'

'If you were my husband, I wouldn't let you out of my

sight,' I say, fluttering my eyelashes. 'You must be very lonely here.' I gaze around the small apartment. 'When do you have to be out of here, and have you found somewhere else to stay long-term?'

'Honestly, I haven't had the time to visit any places and have just looked online,' he says, as he sinks into the armchair opposite me.

'Shouldn't Amelia be helping you?' I ask, and then wave my hand in front of my face as if to dismiss that thought. 'No time like the present.' I take my phone out of my handbag. 'Let's see if we can find you somewhere. You need a place that's more homely than this and perhaps in a block that has communal facilities, such as a gym or cafe so you get to meet people.'

He nods. I pat the sofa next to me and say, 'Come over here and we can look together.'

Hudson hesitates for a second but then steps over to the sofa. To begin with, I edge away from him, keeping an inch or so of space between us, but as we start browsing through possible rentals on my phone I shift nearer to him so that the full length of my leg is pressing against his. I can feel the warmth of him, the woody scent of his aftershave, his alcohol-scented breath on my cheek, and despite everything, I feel a faint sense of arousal and I'm pretty sure he does too. This is going to be such fun.

'What do you think of this one?' I ask, leaning so close that my breast touches his arm.

'Mmm,' he says, clearly unable to concentrate on the listings. Slowly I lower the phone and put it on the sofa arm.

'Are you feeling it too?' I ask in a husky whisper, placing my hand on his knee.

Hudson sighs loudly. 'I'm a man,' he says, briefly leaning

his head back against the sofa. Not exactly a profound statement. But then, to my surprise, he stands up and turns to look at me.

'Aren't you getting married soon?' he asks.

Shit. Shit. I need to backtrack fast. I get up too and step away from him. 'I'm sorry, Hudson. My bad.' Theatrically, I bury my face in my hands. 'It's all the booze we've drunk tonight, and I'm being a complete idiot. You're a very handsome man, but you're right, I was completely out of order. Please forgive me.'

'Of course,' he says. I can tell that he's flattered.

'I just need to use the bathroom and then I'll be out of your hair.'

'No hurry to leave,' he says.

'I think it's the right thing to do for both of us, don't you?'

He nods, but I'm sure I see regret in his eyes.

I'm furious. I misjudged that, came on too quickly, in my normal impetuous fashion. I should have known better. Should have played the longer game. But it's not too late to do some damage. Amelia is coming here tomorrow and I need to leave some things behind...

CHAPTER FOURTEEN

AMELIA

It's raining in Manchester. The city is humid and oppressive, which just adds to my unsettled mood. Hudson has agreed to leave work early so that we can have a full evening together. I told him that we needed to talk and I wonder if he thinks I'm here to tell him Marnie and I are moving to Manchester. We're not. But we do need to talk, to discuss our marriage.

I walk from the station to Hudson's apartment block, umbrellas bumping each other, trying to avoid the puddles forming on the pavement. It's weird going to an address where your husband of twenty years has been staying but where you've never visited. It's an unattractive apartment block with a concierge, and apparently, he's expecting me.

'Good afternoon,' I say. 'I'm here to collect the key to my husband's apartment. Hudson Myers in number forty-one.'

'Ah yes,' he says, opening a key safe behind him and removing a key with a fob. 'If you wouldn't mind signing the visitors' book, Mrs Myers.' He pushes a folder towards me and hands me a pen.

Hudson's apartment is small, dull and functional. I dump

my bag and make myself a cup of tea. He has very little in the fridge – just a carton of milk, a pot of jam, some old bread and a couple of carrots. I wonder what he's been living off. Hudson is able to cook but he chooses not to, except if we're having people over for dinner. Then he will select a complicated Ottolenghi recipe designed to impress our guests. On a day-to-day basis, he never cooks. Cradling a mug, I sit on the sofa and glance around. It must be rather depressing living here. There's a view onto a brick wall out of the window, and literally no colour in this open-plan kitchen-living area. I hope we can find somewhere more homely for him to move to, and perhaps we should rent a van and bring up some furniture and paintings from home. When I've finished my tea, I carry the mug over to the dishwasher and open it up. As I'm placing the mug inside I notice that there are two wineglasses stacked on the upper section. It takes a moment for me to realise that one of the glasses has the remains of red lipstick on the edge of the glass. With dismay, I reach into the machine and take out the dirty glass. That has definitely been used by a woman. My heart quickens but I tell myself that he could have entertained a colleague, that I've got no reason to believe that Hudson has been unfaithful.

Just as I shove it back in, the front door opens and Hudson steps inside. He looks tired, grey rings under his eyes, a show of stubble on his face.

'Hello, darling,' he says. He walks towards me and places a quick kiss on my cheek. 'I've got you a belated birthday present.'

He dumps his coat and briefcase on a chair and walks out of the living room into the bedroom. I follow him. Reaching on top of the chest of drawers, he lifts up a pale turquoise bag and hands it to me. I follow him back into the living room and open the beautifully wrapped gift. It's a pair of diamond earrings, small, understated, pretty. But they're not special like the bracelet he gave me. Which reminds me, I still haven't found it. I must look harder when I'm back home.

'Thank you,' I say, placing a kiss on his lips. Hudson steps backwards, almost as if I've scorched him. That is weird.

'Who came over for drinks?' I ask.

'What?' He frowns.

'You had a woman here for drinks.'

A flash of anger passes over his face. 'Have you been checking up on me?'

'No. I saw the lipstick marks on the glass in the dishwasher.'

'For fuck's sake, Amelia. The first thing you do is check out my dishwasher?' He has gone from zero to one hundred in a millisecond and I know in that instant that he's hiding something.

'I didn't check it out, I just saw the glasses. So who is she?'

'Nobody,' he retorts too quickly.

'Well, obviously it's somebody,' I reply, my chest constricting. 'Unless you've taken to wearing lipstick.'

'If you must know, my boss and his wife came over.'

I know he's lying. It's the way he turns away from me when he talks, how the vein throbs in the side of his neck, how he touches his nose with his right hand. Besides, there were only two glasses in the dishwasher, not three.

'You haven't come all of this way just to have an argument, have you?' Hudson turns to face me, his hands on his hips.

I need to take a breath, to recalibrate.

'I'm going to the loo and then let's sit down,' I say.

In the bathroom, I can't stop the tears. Our relationship is at an all-time low and now I know for a fact that Hudson is lying to me. There's a box of tissues on the sink, so I take one and pat my eyes dry, then put my foot on the pedal bin to open it. That's when I see another flash of colour. Crouching down, I look into the bin. There are two cotton wool pads, one with a hint of beige foundation on it, the other coated with the same red lipstick that was on the glass in the dishwasher. I gasp. Hudson has had a woman staying here.

I slam the lid of the bin shut and am ready to storm out of the bathroom, but as I step into the corridor, I hear Hudson on the phone. I pause for a moment, wondering if he's talking to her. Except he's reeling off some numbers and says something about a balance sheet. Tiptoeing, I pad into the bedroom and stand at the foot of the bed, looking around. He's pulled the duvet up over the pillows and the room is scrupulously tidy. I walk to the head of the bed and pull the duvet off, looking for any tell-tale signs on the sheets and sniffing the pillows. I see and smell nothing. But he could have changed the sheets before I arrived; in fact, he probably did. Then I lower myself to the floor and under the bed, right near the edge of the mattress, is an earring. It's a gold hoop with a little red-coloured stone hanging off the loop. I scoop it up and stare at it. It looks cheap but perhaps I'm wrong.

And now I'm livid. Clasping it in my palm, I storm back into the living room.

'We need to talk!' I say.

Hudson holds up a finger to me and that makes me even more furious.

'Now!' I don't care whom he's talking to, whether that person hears me.

'Sorry, Sam,' Hudson says. 'Can I pick this up with you in the morning? Something urgent has just come up.'

'What's this?' I ask, holding the earring out towards Hudson.

He frowns. 'An earring?'

I roll my eyes at him. 'And who does it belong to?' I spit.

'I've no idea.' He bunches up his shoulders.

'Stop lying, Hudson! I found this in your bedroom.'

'But I don't know whose it is,' he says, throwing his arms into the air.

'It obviously belongs to whatever woman you slept with, the one who left makeup pads in the bathroom bin and lipstick marks on the wine glass. Is she the real reason why you have relocated to Manchester so quickly?'

'Look, Amelia. I don't know what you're talking about. I haven't had an affair with anyone.'

'Stop bloody lying to me!' I'm shouting at him now, which I know isn't helpful, but I'm a mixture of furious and hurt.

'Calm down,' he says, which of course has the opposite effect on me. 'I'm truly sorry I forgot your birthday and that this move has happened so quickly, but I haven't done anything wrong.'

'So it's just a bizarre turn of fate that I found all of these things?' I say.

'They were probably left by the last tenant. The cleaners aren't very good.'

'Oh really? You're saying that your bathroom bin hasn't

been emptied in over a fortnight and the bedroom floor hasn't been vacuumed? I thought this was a serviced apartment.' My voice is laced with sarcasm because of course he's lying.

'I don't know who those things belong to.'

Hudson is getting red in the face now but he's not as angry as I am. I am seething. My husband has moved away from home and within a fortnight he's already cheating on me. Or has this been going on for ages? After all, he's had plenty of opportunity.

'You're lying, Hudson!' I shout at him. 'Call me when you decide to tell the truth but until then, stay away from me and Marnie.' I storm out of the living room into the hall, grab my coat off the peg on the wall, fling my handbag and overnight bags over my shoulder and tug the front door open.

'Wait!' Hudson says.

I swivel around and stare at him.

'I'm telling you the truth!' he says. 'And you can't keep me from my daughter.'

Well, it's perfectly obvious that he isn't telling the truth and frankly, he can go to hell. I walk out of the door, slamming it shut behind me. Furiously blinking back tears, I run down the stairs to the lobby area where the concierge is standing behind his desk. He looks up at me with an expression of surprise. I suppose I look rather more rumpled than I did when I arrived, no doubt with a blotchy face and reddened eyes.

'Have you seen my husband with another woman?' I ask.

He frowns, then he opens and closes his mouth.

I tilt my head and stare at him. I don't care if I make him feel uncomfortable.

'I'm sorry, but we don't get involved in marital disputes.'

And there it is. All the confirmation I need. If Hudson hadn't been cavorting with another woman, this stranger would have just said no, wouldn't he? I glance down at the desk in front of him and a thought crosses my mind.

'Shall I sign out of the visitors' book?' I ask.

'No need. If you'd just like to hand me back the keys, I can do it for you.'

'I'd like to sign out myself,' I say. 'Let's do it by the book.'

He knots his eyebrows together and pushes the open folder towards me. And then, fortuitously, his phone rings and he looks away. Quickly, I scour back through the signatures and flat numbers recorded in the adjacent column. There's nothing for Flat 41 today, so I quickly flick the page back to yesterday. And that's where I see it.

Flat 41 and a scribble. It's completely illegible, but someone visited Hudson's flat yesterday evening. I am trying to decipher the times, when the concierge turns to face me, puts down his phone and pulls the open book back towards him.

'What did she look like?' I ask, my voice bitter. 'Blonde, brunette, red-haired?'

'I'm sorry, but I can't tell you anything.'

'Can't or won't?' I stare at him for a moment, but his eyes are hard and his expression unrelenting and I know I'm not going to get any more information out of him. With my shoulders artificially pulled back, I stride out of the lobby, down the steps and onto the damp street below. I let out an involuntary sob as I head back towards the station.

CHAPTER FIFTEEN

PAIGE

To begin with I was absolutely furious that Hudson rejected me. Am I not good enough for him, not pretty enough, not clever enough? I've never been short of male attention and I know that I've settled low by choosing Dean. But I can't be with someone who is going to question me or dig into my background. It's not that I want to be with Hudson. He's a boring man, much too self-centred and full of himself. No, he's a means to an end. Having said that, his money wouldn't hurt. For a fleeting moment, I imagine us together. There's no way I'd live in Amelia's house out in the sticks, but I could see myself in a lovely Georgian townhouse, going to the theatre on Hudson's arm, having dull sex with him in return for unlimited spending. I suppress that dream and remember that however furious I might be that he pushed me away, my real focus is on Amelia. I'm hopeful she will have found the little gifts I left behind in Hudson's flat. I wonder how she got on with telling him about the 'lost' money. I can't imagine someone like Hudson taking that well.

As I don't have any classes today, I telephone Amelia.

'Just to say that all was fine with having Marnie to stay. I dropped the girls off at school this morning and they couldn't stop chattering.' That at least is true. 'How was your trip to Manchester?'

'I came home early.' Her voice sounds glum, as if all the energy has been extracted out of her.

'Oh no.'

There's a long pause during which I realise she's crying. I do an arm pump. Yes!

'I'm sorry, Paige, but I really don't want to talk about it.'

Well, that's a shame, but inside I'm dancing because it's extremely likely that my ploys have worked. 'I'm here if you ever want to talk,' I say. *Oh yes, Amelia dear. You can really trust me!*

That evening, Dean, Taryn and I are having a TV supper, as we regularly do. We're watching *The One Show* which is featuring some footballer I've never heard of. Taryn seems lost in her own little world as normal, writing on her phone in between eating. I can't be bothered to tell her off. And then, suddenly, she puts her phone down, grabs the remote and turns down the sound.

'Ow, what are you doing that for?' Dean asks.

'I've got something I want to tell you both.'

This doesn't sound very Taryn-like, so we both put down our cutlery. Her face is white but she's got two little pink blotches on her cheeks.

'What is it, then?' I ask because she seems to be struggling to spit out her words.

'I'm gay,' she says.

I snort. 'That's hardly a surprise. You only need to look at how you dress like a dyke to work that one out.'

'That's really bigoted, Mum,' Taryn says. 'You can't tell someone's gender or sexuality by their clothes.'

Dean is staring at Taryn, his lower jaw hanging open. I don't know why he looks so shocked, because it's no big deal in today's day and age. Besides, deep down I already knew.

'Say something, Dean,' Taryn says. Her eyes look watery.

'It's just a bit of a shock, that's all. So you like girls, then? You don't want to be with a boy?'

'That's generally what it means.' I let out a short laugh.

'Are you upset?' Taryn asks, with a quiver in her voice.

'It's just a surprise.'

Taryn grabs the television remote and turns the volume back on. A moment later, she leaves the table and I listen to her heavy footsteps running up the stairs. She slams her bedroom door shut.

'You didn't handle that well,' I say to Dean.

'How was I meant to handle it?' he asks, a look of genuine surprise on his face.

'She wanted you to approve.'

He nods slowly and then gets up from the table. He also disappears upstairs, and I can hear Taryn and Dean talking in her bedroom. I leave them to it.

The days whizz past and before I know it, there's just twenty-four hours until my wedding to Dean. I've got serious doubts. Although I would love to be the centre of attention, and I've planned a glorious day, it is only one day. The more I think about being married to Dean, the less appealing the idea is. Dean and I are in the kitchen while Taryn is still clopping around upstairs.

'Are you going to come off the pill?' Dean asks as he slurps his morning tea.

'What?'

'Let's have another baby. I mean, I love Taryn, don't get me wrong, but we need to have another child that's ours. And what better place to raise them than Scotland? What do you think, Paige? A new family, a new life?'

What I think is, you've got to be bloody joking. Firstly, at forty-one, it'll be touch-and-go if I can get pregnant, but secondly, I'm done with all of that. Why on earth would I want another child? And it's a complete joke, his idea about moving to Scotland. I have such great ambitions, whereas Dean wants a small life.

It's on the tip of my tongue to tell him that he's being completely ridiculous, but strangely the words don't come. Perhaps it's the look of longing in his eyes and the realisation that he and I want such different things. And then he goes off to work and I spend the rest of the morning pacing our small house.

I can't go through with it. I can't marry Dean. I'm going to lose a lot of money if I cancel but I'd rather that than making what is clearly a wrong decision. By midday, I'm in a bit of a state, so I call Dean and ask if I can come to where he's working.

'Everything alright, love?' he asks.

'Thought I'd bring you some hot soup. I've just made some.'

'That's kind of you.'

He gives me the address of an old factory on the edge of town that is due to be demolished to make way for a housing development. He's having to disconnect all the pipes, make sure that everything is sealed off. Hardly a glamorous job.

I've driven past the site a number of times but never paid it much attention. There's a tall metal fence surrounding it and as I pull into the entrance, I pass broken signs and one that is graffitied. The gate isn't secured, so I get out of the car and push it open, driving around the side of the building and parking next to Dean's van. The place is like a mausoleum and it gives me the creeps. Dean had mentioned that it's a horrible place to work, but it pays well. I get out of the car and look up at the three-storey red-brick building. There are rows of tall windows with black iron frames, and the glass is broken in many of them. Tall weeds grow up the side of the brickwork and a large, blue, iron door has also been graffitied. I should have asked Dean to come home for lunch rather than me driving out here. I walk up to the door and it opens with a deafening creak, as if the hinges haven't been oiled in decades. In front of me is a concrete staircase.

'Hello!' I shout. 'Where are you, Dean?'

'Come up the stairs and turn to the left.' His voice echoes as if he's in a cave.

The stairs are filthy and I'm pretty sure that they're lined with mouse shit. The place smells gross too. Nimbly, I climb the stairs and push open a swing door at the top. I'm in a huge room that I assume was once filled with machinery, but goodness knows what sort. I can hear hammering, so I turn to the left and follow the sound. And then I see Dean, dressed in his grey overalls, crouching down on the ground, surrounded by pipes in different stages of decay.

'This is a shithole,' I say as I approach him.

'I get the most glamorous of jobs,' he says, standing up and wiping his dirty hands on his trouser legs. 'Brought me some lunch, have you?'

I haven't.

'I want to talk about the wedding,' I say, feeling suddenly uncomfortable. 'I think it's a mistake and we should call it off.'

Dean snorts. 'You are joking, right?'

'I'm not.'

'We've just spent a bloody fortune on it,' he says. I don't point out that he hasn't spent a penny on our wedding; it's all been my money.

'That's not a reason for going ahead.'

'Why the change of tune, Paige?' He scratches the top of his head. 'It's normal to get cold feet, even when we've been together as long as we have.'

I stare at this man and I shudder. What did I actually see in him? I deserve to be with someone debonair like Hudson, rich and good-looking, and Dean is none of those things. The only thing he's good at is being a stable stepdad to Taryn, and now she's nearly grown up, she barely needs him. I've got money now too, and I'm sure I can get some more from where my windfall came from, so it's not like I even need Dean's paltry earnings. It's as if I'm seeing him for the first time; a slightly slobbish-looking man standing in an environment that I shouldn't be seen dead in. I don't belong with Dean.

'I've made up my mind and I'm calling the wedding off,' I say.

Dean's face crumples. 'Don't be silly, love,' he says, stepping forward and putting a dirty hand on my arm. I shrug him off.

'I'm not being silly. I'm being deadly serious. It was a mistake, and a mistake I'm willing to admit to.'

'But I want to marry you!' he says, rubbing his jaw as if I've just shared a conundrum.

'You need two people to marry.' There's sarcasm in my voice.

'Are you splitting up with me?'

'No, I just don't think we should get married. If something isn't broken, why change it?'

Dean takes a step towards me. 'But you were the one who wanted to get married. You asked me, in case you don't remember.'

'Of course I remember. But I've changed my mind.'

And then something snaps in Dean. He's generally a mellow man, but occasionally if he's pushed really far, he'll throw a hissy fit. 'You can't do this, Paige! You'll make us look like bloody idiots, and think of all the money we've wasted. You won't get it back, not at this late stage. And what about Taryn? Think about your daughter for once. She is so looking forward to it, happy to have a stable family at long last. You never think about Taryn, do you?'

'How dare you!' I shout, pushing my face up towards his. 'She's my daughter.'

'Which you never fail to remind me about, except you want me to bring her up. Who was it that looked after her when you were in prison? Who does she come to when she's got a problem? It's not you. You're so bloody selfish, Paige. Everything is all about you.'

'And yet you still want to marry me?' I retort.

'Because for better or worse, I love you and I love Taryn. I want to do what's best for her.'

'And you're saying I don't?'

'Mostly, no. You're fundamentally selfish.'

'You're the one who wants to take us away to some godforsaken place in the north of Scotland, to rip us away from our lives.'

'And you're the one who ruined our lives, Paige, in case you've forgotten.'

'Stop bringing that up!' I'm yelling now. A red mist rises

up inside of me, one that I recognise, one that I'm unable to stop. 'It wasn't my fault.'

'Nothing is ever your fault, is it? Except it was.'

The anger is choking me now, gripping my chest, making me desperate to lash out. There's a piece of copper pipe lying at Dean's feet and before I know what I'm doing, I've bent down and grabbed it.

'Oh yeah, as if violence is the way to go!' Dean says. This mild-mannered man whom I thought I loved, or at least cared for, is goading me. Doesn't he know what I'm capable of? How fury grips me like a long-lost lover's embrace. I lift up the copper pipe, which is lighter than I anticipated, and before I can stop myself I'm swinging it like a golf club, the momentum taking me by surprise, and with one long, sweeping blow the pipe smashes into the side of Dean's head. His eyes open and he wobbles for a moment, a look of shock gripping his features, making him look like a gargoyle. But then he stumbles over his tool box and he's flying, as if in slow motion, cartwheeling his arms uselessly, and he smashes into the filthy concrete ground, the side of his head bouncing, his eyes wide with shock.

A wave of power rushes through me, the sense that I'm in control, that I always get what I want. Dean isn't going to bother me again and I let a smile linger on my lips. Suddenly I'm startled, my heart missing a beat as something flies straight over my head. A pigeon settles on a window ledge before flying out of an open, broken pane of glass. I let out a little gasp and turn my eyes back to Dean, and that feeling of power vanishes. Shit. What have I done?

But no. I didn't do this. Dean goaded me, he asked for it, and it's not my fault that he stumbled over his equipment. He's sprawled on the ground, eyes closed, blood seeping from the side of his head. I swallow hard, bile taking me by surprise. Have I killed him?

'Dean?' I say, crouching down to look at him. I can't tell if he's dead or alive. My head is spinning and I feel dizzy. 'Dean, wake up!' I don't touch him, just in case. The bloody idiot. Why did he provoke me? I stand up and step backwards.

Oh God, I've killed him. I wanted to stop him, of course I did, but I've actually killed him. We're meant to be getting married tomorrow but that won't be happening. As I stare at his motionless body, I realise that this might be my salvation. No one knows where Dean is. No one knows what I've done, and I didn't really want to marry Dean. I'm going to be stood up at the altar. I'll go through with the wedding and will be waiting there for Dean, who won't turn up. It's not ideal being the jilted bride, but it'll still mean I'm the centre of attention. I'll get to wear the dress, get to have my day, just without my husband-to-be. And it's the perfect cover for Dean's unexpected disappearance. He'll have gotten cold feet and done a runner, and no one will be out looking for him, because they'll think he's a coward and a mean piece of shit for dumping me in such a heartless manner.

I run my fingers through my hair and let out a puff of air. Yes, this has worked out rather beautifully. Before I fully know what I'm doing, I've grabbed his van keys from his pocket, turned around and I'm walking back the way I came, down the filthy concrete stairs, a sense of relief putting a little spring into my steps.

CHAPTER SIXTEEN

MARNIE

I haven't been to a wedding since I was a kid and was bridesmaid to my uncle. I don't remember much of it, so I'm excited for today, and happy for Taryn, who is literally over the moon that her mum is marrying Dean. She loves him as if he's her dad, and I suppose, in most ways, he actually is.

Dad is home for the weekend but the tension between Mum and Dad is just horrible. I don't know what the hell is going on but I wish they'd get their acts together and make up. I asked Mum what the argument is about and she refused to tell me, which is really pathetic. Anyway, I'm going to ignore them both and be there for Taryn.

Dressed in smart clothes, Dad drives us into Beacham, parks the car, and we walk to the registry office, which is some ordinary-looking building in the middle of town. There's a group of people standing on the steps when we get there. Mum recognises them, so I assume they're some of her yoga groupies. And then a black limousine arrives with a ribbon attached to its bonnet and Taryn and Paige get out. Paige looks like a film star in her beautiful dress with her hair pinned up. She's carrying a posy of flowers wrapped with a blue ribbon, the same shade as Taryn's dress. I almost don't recognise her. Gone are the black clothes and black nail varnish, and although her hair is still black, she's got a flower behind her ear, and she's wearing a knee-length blue dress in shiny satin and flat pumps. She looks completely different and I think she's a bit self-conscious because her shoulders are rounded and she's not looking at anyone. I walk over to her and she smiles broadly.

'You look amazing, Taryn,' I say, and her smile widens even further.

We follow Paige and Taryn into the building. There's a reception area with a sign that lists all the weddings happening today. Six in total. It's like a conveyor belt, which is a bit sad. There's a wedding party leaving, and they're milling in the lobby, all chatty and laughing, and there are loads of them and very few of us. Eventually, a man in a suit arrives and whispers something to Paige. Then he ushers the guests into the room where the ceremony is being held. Mum, Dad and I sit together on the right-hand side of the aisle. We wait for ages, listening to dull, piped, classical music.

Mum leans across to Dad and says too loudly, 'Where's Dean? Shouldn't he already be here?'

'Perhaps they're going to walk up the aisle together,' he says. It's the first civil words they've said to each other all day. One of Mum's friends leans over from behind us and she and Mum start whispering. The registrar who is standing at the front of the room looks at her watch and frowns. The music stops and starts again, playing the same loop of classical music. After another couple of minutes, the registrar steps forward and walks down the aisle, her eyes on the back of the room, avoiding catching anyone's attention. This is weird. Very weird. She's gone for ages and still Paige and Taryn don't appear. Something must be wrong. Eventually, there are footsteps and the registrar is back. Her face is red and she appears ruffled, jittery. There must be about thirty people in here and everyone falls silent, but she has to raise her voice in order to be heard over the music, which still carries on.

'I'm afraid that the Smith wedding will not be taking place today. You will be contacted in due course should Dean and Paige decide to rearrange.' She looks at her feet and then mutters, 'Sorry for the inconvenience.'

'What the hell!' I say out aloud, and then I'm up on my feet, hurrying along the aisle and out of the room before the other guests can even process what's been said. I need to get to Taryn.

She's there, huddled at the side of the entrance lobby, her arms wrapped around herself, her face wet with tears.

'What's happened?' I ask.

'Dean hasn't shown up.'

For a moment I'm speechless. 'I'm so sorry,' I say, putting an arm around her awkwardly. She leans into me. 'And you look so pretty.'

She lets out another little sob.

'Where's your mum?'

'In the ladies'. She says she's staying there until everyone leaves.'

'I'll get Mum and we'll come and find you. Okay?'

She nods but seems reluctant to let me go. I manage to unpeel myself from her grasp and wriggle my way through the stream of people emerging from the reception room.

There are a lot of loud whispers and shaking of heads. And then I see my parents.

'Dean hasn't shown up,' I say to Mum. 'I've told Taryn we'll find them and take them home. Is that alright?'

Mum looks shocked. 'Of course it is, darling. But don't they have any other relatives here who they might prefer to lean on? It's not like we know them that well.'

'Taryn is my best friend,' I say indignantly. Why's Mum being a bitch?

She has a little conflab with Dad, who leaves along with the other guests while Mum and I follow signs to the ladies' toilets. We find Paige and Taryn both crying, their mascara running down their cheeks and Paige's hand-tied bouquet lying on the side of the sink. They look completely miserable and I feel so sorry for them. It's the ultimate humiliation, isn't it, being jilted at the altar? The sort of thing you read about in books.

'I'm so embarrassed,' Paige says, repeatedly, burying her face in her hands.

'I can't believe it. Dean wouldn't do something like this,' Taryn says. 'He was so looking forward to marrying Mum.'

'Could something have happened to him?' Mum asks.

'That's what I'm worried about,' Paige says with a sniff. 'I just want to go home and call around the hospitals, speak to his workmates, check who saw him last.'

'When did you see Dean?' Mum asks.

'Yesterday. We agreed to do the traditional thing and be apart the night before the wedding.'

Mum seems a bit lost for words but eventually says, 'Right. Let's get you home. Hudson can get a taxi home so I can take you in our car.'

'But what about the wedding venue?' Paige asks.

'We'll worry about that a bit later,' Mum says. She puts her arm around Paige and I do the same to Taryn. Half an hour later, we're at Paige's house.

Mum hasn't been here before and I can see her looking around, a bit surprised, I think. Their house is about a quarter of the size of ours and really not very nice. It's clean and quite tidy but the walls are all painted white and there are no paintings or photographs anywhere. The living room is crammed full of cream leather chairs and a sofa that is way too big for the room, making it feel even more cramped than it is. There's an old laptop with its lid open on the scratched glass coffee table.

'What's that doing there?' Paige asks, pointing at the laptop. She looks weird still in her wedding dress, bare feet poking underneath the dress, her face tear-stained.

Mum looks confused. 'Isn't that your laptop?' Mum asks.

'No, it's Dean's. He hardly ever uses it except to do his accounts, and generally, I help him do them.' She walks over to it, her dress catching on a chair leg. There's the sound of ripping but she doesn't even notice. Paige picks up the laptop and the screen lights up. I can see from here that there's a big crack across the screen.

'Oh'! she exclaims and drops the laptop onto the sofa.

'What is it?' Taryn leaps forward and grabs the laptop. 'No!' she exclaims.

Now Paige is out of the living room and running up the stairs. I can hear heavy footsteps above us.

'He's gone!' she shouts. 'The bastard is gone!'

I stare at Taryn, who is shaking. 'He's left a note,' she murmurs. 'Read it.'

She shoves the laptop towards me and Mum and I grab hold of it. A message is written all in capital letters.

SORRY, I CAN'T DO THIS ANYMORE. SORRY TO LET YOU DOWN AT THE LAST MINUTE BUT IT'S FOR THE BEST. WISHING YOU AND TARYN A GOOD LIFE. DEAN.

Taryn appears stunned, almost frozen, but upstairs Paige is wailing. Mum hurries out of the room and rushes upstairs to look after Paige, while Taryn sinks onto the leather sofa. I put the laptop back on the coffee table and sit down next to her. The sofa isn't leather at all, but plastic. It feels sticky and cold against my bare legs. Taryn seems to sink into herself, her shoulders hunched, her chin on her chest, her arms wrapped around her torso.

'I can't believe he's done this,' she murmurs. 'He's always been there for me. Dean is my dad.'

I don't know what to say, so I just sit there awkwardly. Eventually I ask, 'Why do you think he left?'

'It's probably because Mum loses her shit a lot. She goes from zero to a million in a nano-second, and it can be really difficult. She can be a complete psycho.'

'Have things got worse between your mum and Dean recently?' I'm wondering if something weird is going on with adults at the moment, because my parents are also at each other's throats.

'No. I thought everything was okay, more than okay, because they've been together for years and never bothered to get married, and now we were going to be a family.' Taryn buries her face in her hands again and I rub her shoulder. 'But Mum probably pushed him too hard,' she says.

'I'm sorry,' I say, because I'm at a loss how to make things better for Taryn. I can't imagine what she's feeling right now.

'Mum had a really difficult childhood. I never met my

gran but apparently she was a cow, really mean to Mum. And they never had any money and Mum had to go out to work when she was fifteen.' We're both silent for a long time. 'Do you think Dean left because of me?' Taryn asks.

'No, of course not. Why would he leave because of you?'

She shrugs. 'I don't know, but maybe he didn't want to adopt me.'

'Was he going to?'

'Well, it would have been more official with them being married. How can he leave me to be alone with Mum?' Taryn sniffs.

'Things are pretty crap with my parents too,' I say. 'Dad's away, and when they're together they're fighting all the time.'

'I'm never going to get married,' Taryn says. There's something really sad about the way she says that, as if no one would ever want her rather than her choosing not to wed.

'You'll find a man who will love you for you,' I say. Taryn is a good person and today, in her bridesmaid dress, she's looking really pretty.

There's a long silence, and although I know now probably isn't the best time to say it, I just blurt out what's been on my mind. 'I did something bad,' I admit.

Taryn looks up at me. Her eyes are dry now.

'I stole my mum's favourite bracelet and mailed it to Jax.'

'Jax?' Taryn frowns, her head bobbing back with surprise. 'As in the A&R Jax?'

'Yes. I thought he was my boyfriend. You know how friendly he was on Insta and then we arranged to meet up IRL.'

'God, Marnie. You didn't actually go to meet him, did you?'

'Yeah, I went.'

'But why didn't you tell me?'

'Because. I don't know. I thought you might try to talk me out of it, him being so much older than me. Anyway, he didn't show, so I don't know why I bothered.'

'Okay, no harm done then.'

'Except I'd sent him a load of photos.' I glance away, shame reddening my cheeks. There's a long beat before Taryn twigs what I mean.

'Oh, shit. You mean you sent him nude selfies?'

I nod. 'And then he started blackmailing me. Asking for money or for me to steal stuff.'

'And that's when you got caught and taken to the police?'

'Yup. I know it was stupid.' I finger the satiny fabric of my dress between my fingers.

'Stupid!' Taryn cries. 'I can't believe you did that! I thought you were cleverer than that, Marnie. What the fuck were you thinking?'

And now I wish more than anything that I hadn't told Taryn. I suppose I hoped she'd be supportive, understanding. But no. It seems she's judging me and that I'm a great disappointment to her and it makes me feel even worse, if that's possible. I know I was an idiot and I don't need my best friend rubbing it in. I stand up.

'I'm going to go now,' I say.

Taryn's hand darts forward and she grabs my wrist. 'Please don't.'

I pull away and hover at the door to the living room.

'What are you going to do? Did you give him money?' she asks.

'I sent him Mum's bracelet so he can sell it.'

'You've got his address then? You can report him.'

I sigh. 'No, it was a PO box. He isn't that stupid. It's

worth a fortune, that bracelet,' I say. 'And Mum thinks she's mislaid it when in fact I gave it away. It makes me feel really shitty.'

'Are you going to tell her?' Taryn asks.

'Dunno. Everything's a bit crap at the moment.'

'Yeah, it is.'

I rub the toe of my shoe against the side of my other shoe, unsure what to say, what to do. I can hear Mum and Paige's voices in the kitchen and they sound calmer now but I can't make out what they're saying.

'I've got something to tell you too,' Taryn says. 'Can you shut the door?'

I nod and close the living room door, returning to sit on the armchair opposite Taryn.

'I think I know why Dean has left us. I came out to Mum and Dean last week.'

'Came out?' I'm confused for a moment.

'I'm gay, Marnie. Hadn't you realised?'

And now I feel like a double idiot, because it kind of makes sense but it had literally never crossed my mind. I think back through the conversations we've had where I shared how much I like Ryan and then how excited I was about Jax, and with hindsight, Taryn never mentioned the names of any boys that she liked.

'Sorry, I hadn't realised. Not that it matters,' I say hurriedly. 'You can still be my bestie, can't you?'

Taryn rolls her eyes. 'But anyway, that'll be the reason Dean has vanished.'

'Don't be ridiculous, Taryn,' I say, edging towards her. 'He's been like your dad since you were how old?'

'Six.'

'That's pretty much the whole of your life. He's not

going to suddenly not love you because you prefer women to men.'

'He was kind of disappointed.'

'And what did your mum say?'

'That it made sense why I dressed like a dyke.'

'God, that's horrible.'

'Yeah, but that's Mum for you. I'd expect it from her, just not from Dean.'

'Isn't it more likely that Dean has gone because of your mum? After all, he left that note on his laptop.'

Taryn shakes her head slowly in agreement, but I'm not sure she genuinely believes it. 'We're a right pair of idiots, aren't we?' she says, for the first time a little smile edging at her lips. 'What are you going to do if Jax comes back for more?'

I can feel myself paling, because I'd convinced myself that now he has the bracelet, he won't bother me again. But the truth is he's got those photos and I guess he could blackmail me again at any time in the future. I could post something about him online, expose him for being the bastard that he is, but that's really dangerous as he might feel he's got nothing to lose and post the photos anyway. It's like I'm stuck between a rock and a hard place, and it's all of my own making.

CHAPTER SEVENTEEN

AMELIA

Poor Paige. I can't imagine how humiliating it must be to be stood up at the altar. And how devastating that what is meant to be the best day of her life has turned into the worst. I hate to think how much money she's wasted as well, and looking around her modest house, I very much doubt she can afford it. She's being remarkably stoic, all things considered. If I were her, I would be ranting about what a bastard Dean is. How cowardly he has behaved.

Paige isn't the only one with money worries. Every day, Hudson asks me if I've got the money back yet, and every day I have to say no. It leaves me with a constant sense of dread in my stomach. Hudson and I still need to thrash things out, particularly about him having an affair, and I'd hoped to have a proper chat with him after the wedding, when he would be mellowed from the alcohol and the bonhomie of love and hope following Paige and Dean's commitment to each other. Instead, he's gone home alone and the day has disintegrated. After plying Paige with several cups of tea, she tells me that she'd rather be alone with Taryn now, and would it be possible for me and Marnie to leave. The way she says it is curt and a little rude, but she must be hurting and I don't blame her for taking it out on the person closest to her, which at this moment is me. To be honest, I was surprised that she has turned to me for support today. I assumed she'd have parents, siblings or old friends rallying around her in light of today's events. But neither the doorbell nor her phone have rung. That makes me feel even more sad for her.

Back at our home, the door is locked. Marnie is being monosyllabic and I'm in need of a strong drink. Clover greets us joyously, nudging her favourite soft toy, a battered chicken, into my legs. Then she's whimpering, hovering around her food bowl, as if she hasn't eaten. I wonder why Hudson hasn't fed her, until that is, I see a note on the kitchen table.

Returned to Manchester early. Got loads of work. Speak later.

I am absolutely livid. On what level is it right that he's pissed off to Manchester? He's leaving me high and dry in the middle of a drama, uncaring and utterly selfish. It makes me think; has Hudson always been so selfish? When Marnie was sick, he couldn't have been more attentive, choosing to sleep on the floor next to her bed, giving me that bracelet. Hudson has always worked long hours, and it pays for my life, so I've never begrudged him when he wanted to go out for a drink after work with his mates. Perhaps I've been too easy on him.

But more recently, he's been so distant, unwilling to talk to me, and when we do, we're ducking and diving, not confronting the real issues. If he's having an affair, and has returned to Manchester to be with his lover, I just need him to tell me, to be honest. Perhaps I'm not enough for him, perhaps he wants out of the marriage. But if so, why not tell me? And then I wonder why he didn't send me a text message. Probably because he's avoiding direct confrontation. It strikes me that he's behaved a bit like Dean. Leaving a note rather than facing issues head-on. Are they both cowards?

And what about Marnie? She's barely seen her dad these last weeks. Talking of Marnie, she disappeared to her room the moment we got home, citing the need to revise. I don't have the energy to ask further questions.

Pouring myself a much-needed glass of Pinot Noir, I open my laptop intending to work on the programme for the yoga retreat weekend, which is now just three weeks away. I sent out emails to all ten of the ladies who have reserved places, requesting their fifty-percent deposits. My credit card is completely maxed out and I'm in desperate need of the money. I see that I've received emails from three of them. I open the first, from a woman called Maxine Thomson. She's been a regular in my classes since I started teaching.

Dear Amelia,

I'm very sorry but I'm not going to be able to make your yoga retreat weekend. Any chance I could have my 10% deposit back? If not, I understand.

Best,
Maxine

I feel a nugget of disquiet in my stomach. Maxine is always so friendly in class, and I would have thought she'd at least give me a reason for pulling out. I click on the next email. This one is much curter.

Can't make the retreat weekend now. Please give my place to someone else.

When I open the third email and it's in a similar vein, I know that something is very wrong. Just days ago, these women seemed so excited, committed, eager to have a weekend away from the mundanities of their lives, supportive of my new venture. I go onto my banking app to see if I have received any deposits, but no money has come in. All that remains is the huge bill that I need to pay the hotel. I let out a groan. What am I going to do? Several of them, including Maxine, attend my Monday afternoon class, so I can talk to them, ask why they've got cold feet. But it doesn't get away from the fact that I owe money. I could ask Hudson to loan it to me, but I know what his reaction will be. He'll go apoplectic.

Instead, I pour myself another glass of wine, close my laptop and try to watch some mindless television.

My regular Monday morning classes are normally full. Twenty eager women all looking to get fit and decompress. Except today, 10 a.m. comes and goes and I only have two attendees, both ladies new to the area and new to my classes. This doesn't make any sense. Normally, this room is bustling with low chatter. I wait for almost ten minutes, wondering if Vanessa accidentally cancelled the class. I check my phone but I haven't received any messages or emails, so I have no choice but to start. I find it hard to maintain focus. Afterwards, I hang around the coffee shop opposite alone before returning for my later class. Once again, it's almost empty. Just three women. There's a sensation of impending doom in my gut, something I don't understand. When the three ladies have left, and I'm tidying up, Vanessa pops her head around the door.

'Can you come to my office, Amelia?'

Before I got into the yoga world, I'd assumed that all yoga teachers would have an air of calm about them, be gentle in their practice of Buddhist principles, being part of a kind community. Of course, I was hopelessly naive. Vanessa has an aura of officiousness about her, all hard edges and no-nonsense, and even her voice is strident. I follow Vanessa in silence into her office. Once again, I wonder if she employed an interior designer because the space attempts to be zen but somehow misses the mark. Yes, she has the obligatory Buddha statue on the bookshelves behind her desk. There are two salt lamps which never seem to be switched on, and a scent machine that bellows air rather than aromatherapy scents. The faux wooden floor is covered with a jute carpet and she has two futon-type chairs to the side of her pale wood desk. On the few times I've been summoned into her office, we've sat on the futon chairs, but today Vanessa is behind her desk and she motions to me to sit on the wooden chair opposite.

'I'm going to come straight to the point,' she says. As if she never does. 'I can't have you working here anymore.'

'What?' I exclaim.

'As I hope you know, I'm not the sort of person to be influenced by rumours and gossip, but this is affecting my business, so whether it's true or not, I can't be associated with you.'

'What rumours?' I ask, perching forward on the edge of the uncomfortable chair.

'You mean you haven't heard?' She knots her eyebrows together as if she doesn't believe me.

She sighs. 'It's about your daughter.'

There's a long silence and bizarrely, Vanessa seems unable to meet my eyes. This isn't like her.

'What about my daughter?' I wonder if somehow she's found out that Marnie was cautioned for shoplifting, but is that really a reason to fire me?

'I believe she was taken out of school for a period a couple of years ago.'

'Yes. Marnie had meningitis.'

Vanessa extends her neck from one side to the other, causing it to crick. Why the hell isn't she getting to the point?

'What's going on, Vanessa?'

'I've been told on good authority that your daughter Marnie wasn't sick a couple of years ago but she was taken out of school by social services.'

'Social services?' I exclaim. 'I've never even met someone from social services.'

'They were investigating child abuse claims against you and your husband.'

'What?' I can't digest what Vanessa is saying. 'Child abuse?'

'That's what I have been told and what most of this town seems to believe. Your clients have been cancelling left, right and centre, asking to be moved to other teachers, some saying that they're taking their business elsewhere.'

'I'm sorry, but I haven't got a clue what you're talking about.' Blood rushes into my face, and if it was anyone else other than Vanessa telling me this, I'd think they were playing a sick joke on me.

'Is it correct that your daughter was off school for a couple of months?' she asks.

'Yes. As I said, she had meningitis and was in hospital for three weeks, followed by several weeks' recovery at home.'

'Except people are saying she didn't really have meningitis, that in fact you were being investigated for child abuse and that your daughter was in the care of social services.'

'That's ridiculous! It's on her medical records where she was, what happened.'

Vanessa shrugs her shoulders. 'I'm not passing judgment one way or another, but any whiff of child abuse and I have to step right away. I'm sure you understand how this looks.'

I stand up now and lean over Vanessa's desk, looking at her imploringly. 'But it's all untrue. This is a complete travesty; Chinese whispers based upon lies. You only have to ask Marnie, ask our doctor.'

'Except that isn't information I'm able to get hold of, is it?' Vanessa pushes her chair back and it scrapes on the floor. 'You're getting in my personal space, Amelia, and I don't appreciate it. I'll be following this up with a formal letter, but for now, I'd like you to leave. And please remember the clause in the contract you signed that states you are not permitted to solicit business from any of our clients.'

I don't know whether to laugh or cry. This is completely absurd, like I've stepped into some dystopian parallel life. 'And if I can prove that this is completely false,' I say. 'Will you reinstate me?'

Vanessa's mouth narrows into a thin line. 'If having you here is harming my business, then I'm afraid the answer is no. I'm sure you understand.'

Except I don't understand. Where has this rumour come from? And why are people believing something that is completely horrific? As if we didn't go through enough stress as a family as a result of Marnie's illness. I try not to think about those days when I wasn't sure if my beautiful daughter was going to live or die; how terrified we were that she was going to lose her hearing or her limbs, and the gratitude afterwards that she seemed to suffer no long-lasting effects. How can something so awful be turned into such a grotesque lie? And why?

I back out of Vanessa's office and stand for a moment in the corridor trying to catch my breath. This could be easily cleared up by asking Marnie to explain what happened, for her to tell Vanessa that she was genuinely ill, except how can I ask my fifteen-year-old daughter to explain to my employer that she wasn't sexually abused? Horrible thoughts of fake, implanted memories come to mind, how young people can be led to believe that something happened to them when actually it didn't. No, it's inconceivable that I can discuss this with Marnie. If only we had an old-fashioned doctor, someone who has known our family through the good and bad times, perhaps I could call on him or her to make a statement. Except we don't. We're part of a large surgery and never see the same doctor twice.

What I don't understand is why. Why has someone started such a vile rumour? What have Hudson or I done to warrant this? I straighten up, grab my coat and bag from the small kitchen where we yoga teachers leave our belongings, and walk through the foyer. There are a few women milling around, as always, dressed in yoga athletic wear. I can sense their strange glances, the whispering as I walk past them, my head down, the collar of my coat turned up in a futile attempt to shroud myself.

I walk quickly, almost running across the car park to my car, eager to get home. Whether he likes it or not, Hudson and I are going to have to talk. This affects us both.

Back at home, I go online, onto my Instagram account where I post yoga memes and photos of me in intricate poses. I've got a decent following and most of my new customers come through this channel. It's exactly as I feared. There are comments from strangers and even a few direct messages from people I know, asking if the rumours are true. Child abuse. Social services. Wicked mother. Investigation. The words make me want to be sick. I go onto other social media platforms and search for my name, and to my dismay, some anonymous posters have garnered a lot of traction, telling people to stay away from me, that I'm a child abuser, that there's no smoke without fire. This explains why I've had all the cancellations for the yoga weekend and why my regular customers at Vanessa's have deserted me. I don't cry easily but right now I want to sob, except the tears get caught at the back of my throat. I've worked so hard to get traction for my yoga business and overnight, it's all been destroyed.

CHAPTER EIGHTEEN

PAIGE

What's the saying: sticks and stones may break my bones but words will never hurt me. Well, that's not true. I've found that words are extremely powerful and can break someone easily. After I posted those online rumours about Dr Harrington, other women came out of the woodwork. I had no idea that my allegations were true, but they really got traction. A few times I've been described as brave for speaking out! It's made me feel so strong and powerful. And yesterday, I read in the Daily Mail that he's been suspended from practicing as a doctor while the allegations are being investigated. How cool is that! One of the many benefits of social media is that it's super-easy to start a rumour and for the rumour to take on a life of its own. You just need to know where to post, how to optimise posts, and whoosh, it's like starting a fire and letting someone else pour on the petrol.

So when it came to starting the child abuse rumour, it was really easy. I'm absolutely thrilled! A little post here, a whisper in a couple of clients' ears, and off it went. And now it's the talk of the studio that Vanessa has fired Amelia. I'm hopeful that her plans for the yoga retreat weekend will also be up in flames now, and I'm looking forward to getting a phone call where she sobs her heart out to me.

Oh dear, dear Amelia. I'm also hopeful that I'll pick up her old clients. I'm aware that I tend to go head-first into things, but with Project Amelia I've decided to be more systematic. I can destroy her business and her reputation easily – in fact, I've already pretty much ticked that box – but now I'm going to ruin her marriage. I've been thinking a lot about marriage the last few days and the ultimate humiliation I suffered. But my goodness, it was worth it. No one has suspected that I killed Dean; no one considered that it was me who left the note on his computer, that it was me who hid his van, or that it was me who chucked away some of his belongings, making it look like he'd upped sticks and left.

My day in the spotlight wasn't exactly what I dreamed of, but I enjoyed turning on the waterworks, lapping up all that sympathy, particularly from Amelia. Am I sad that Dean has gone forever? Not really. I knew it would happen at some point, that he would push me so far that I wouldn't be able to restrain myself, a bit like what happened with Mum. And I'm just relieved that I have the best cover story in the world.

The reality is that men are weak and I can't count on them. I'm stronger alone. I don't want Hudson either, but he is a bit of eye candy and I intend to take a big bite before letting him go. If I can't have a happy-ever-after, then why the hell should Amelia?

We didn't part on the easiest of terms, Hudson and me, but I think I've got a measure of the man. He thinks he's Mister Big Businessman so I'm going to put a proposition to him. I call him at his office, eventually persuading his idiot secretary that I *do* know him and that he *will* absolutely want to talk to me. Nevertheless, he sounds hesitant when he answers.

'I'm sorry about what happened... the wedding,' he says.

'Oh that,' I say dismissively. 'I'll get over it. Actually, I'm calling about something completely different. A business proposition that I think might interest you.'

'Okay.' There is hesitation in his voice and I curse myself for trying it on with him when we were last together. I should have taken my time. 'What exactly?'

'It's an opportunity in the luxury travel industry, a bit complicated to share over the phone. Could we meet up when I'm next in Manchester?'

There's a silence.

'Purely business, Hudson. Purely business.'

'Of course,' he says eventually. 'When are you next here?'

'I know it's rather soon, but tomorrow actually. My mum took a bit of a turn for the worse. Could I treat you to dinner this time? Tomorrow evening if you're free.'

He hesitates again.

'It's quite time-sensitive, this offer. I've been contacted by a contact in Cape Town.' This is a gamble because I've checked out Hudson's firm and he specialises in South America. Perhaps he doesn't want to get into Africa. But I had to choose a part of the world I'm hoping he knows little about.

'Actually, I am free tomorrow evening. Why don't we meet at Rothscoes at 7 p.m. I'll book us a table.'

When we finish the call, I do an arm pump. Men are so

predictable, so easy to manipulate, and I can't wait to have a little play with Hudson.

The next evening I make sure I arrive at Rothscoes ten minutes late. I'm wearing a smart suit – a navy jacket and matching skirt that sits just above my knees – and a pale pink silk blouse with a pussycat bow. Not my style at all and the outfit makes me feel constrained and awkward, but tonight I'm playing a part. I bought the clothes from an upmarket high street chain and I'll be taking them back in a couple of days, requesting a refund. The tags are neatly hidden and I have to make sure I don't sully the clothes. But I'm not going to waste my money on such tasteless items and as my plans are going so well, I don't want to risk shoplifting. Besides, I'll never wear this outfit again. Poking out of my tote bag is a folder housing about twenty pages of A4 typewritten notes. I found a standard business plan on the internet and printed it off.

The restaurant is large and noisy, with high ceilings and hard floors that make sounds bounce. There must be twenty or so servers hanging around, dressed in white shirts and black trousers. Faux green plants stand between tables and the kitchen area is open to view, with chefs hurrying around, dishes steaming and flames bursting upwards.

'Good evening, madam.' A server appears carrying a stack of menus.

'I'm here with Hudson Myers,' I say.

He glances at a computer screen and finds Hudson's name.

'Please follow me.'

Hudson is already seated on a bench seat in the centre of the restaurant. He stands up when I arrive and leans over to give me an air-kiss on both cheeks.

'Lovely to see you again,' I say, settling into the uncomfortable leather chair opposite him. I place my bag on the floor but not until I've ensured he's noticed the folder poking out. 'I'm sorry I didn't get to talk to you the other day. Amelia was so lovely to me.' We need to get the awkwardness of my non-wedding out of the way first.

'I'm very sorry that happened to you,' he says, twitching slightly, his fingers playing with the edges of the menu.

'It's going to take me a long time to get over it. Would you mind if we don't discuss it?' I tilt my head and stare at Hudson. He flushes slightly and looks away. I clap my hands together. 'So, have you found yourself a flat yet?'

'Yes, I have, actually. I'll be moving in next week.'

'It must be a relief knowing you're going to get out of that serviced apartment.' I wonder for a moment if he might mention the makeup pads I left in his bin and the earring under his bed, but he doesn't. No, of course he doesn't.

Instead, he laughs. 'It's not the nicest apartment, is it? How are things with your mother?'

We make chitchat for a while, skirting around the real reason I'm here, ordering food, a tuna dish to start with followed by steak for him, a salad and chicken for me. He selects us a decent bottle of red wine. I notice that he changes the subject when I mention Amelia, and I'm glad that things are not well in his paradise.

We're halfway through our main courses when he brings up the reason for our meeting.

'I'm curious about the business proposition you want to put to me.'

'Ah yes. I think you'll like it.' I lean down to my bag and remove the folder, very quickly flicking through the pages of the supposed proposal, pie charts and spreadsheets briefly visible. Then I shove it back in my bag. 'But not over dinner. Let's enjoy our food first, shall we?' I hold his eyes with mine.

'You're not even going to hint at what it's about?' He wriggles slightly, as if he's too hot in his starched white shirt, pulling the collar away from his neckline.

'It's a proposition in Cape Town,' I say.

He looks disappointed. 'We specialise in South American holidays.'

'I know that. I've done my research, Hudson. But you will need to see this. It's the most extraordinary expansion proposition regarding a South African holiday firm that's going to float. If you get in there now, you are guaranteed to make millions.'

'Millions of rand doesn't count for much.'

I shake my head slowly. 'I'm not that much of an idiot, Hudson. It'll make you millions of pounds. But it's quite a complex proposal so I suggest we go through it somewhere quiet, where we're not being listened to.' I glance at the table next to ours, where two couples are seated, in their thirties, deep in conversation and not remotely interested in us. 'You never know who might overhear things,' I add.

He seems to buy that and the conversation moves into more personal stuff; chatter about our girls, his worry that Marnie struggles with her education and how he's concerned she won't make university. I share the truth, that Taryn is ridiculously bright and I've no idea where her brains have come from. Hudson suggests from me, and I laugh raucously. He's right, of course. I didn't have a proper education but I'm certainly intelligent. Sometimes I wonder how my life might have turned out if I'd been born into a family such as the Myers. I would have attended good schools, been given extra coaching, gone to a first-rate university and then my parents would have contacted their friends to help me onto the careers ladder. I'd probably be the CEO of a multinational by now, or prime minister even.

We both decline a dessert, but Hudson orders coffee, so I do the same. I just need him to leave the table for a bit and I'm working out how to make that happen when he says, 'Would you excuse me for a moment. Just need to visit the bathroom.'

Since when did British people start calling the bog the bathroom? I smile at him and say, 'Perhaps I'll order us both a nightcap. Are you a whiskey drinker?'

'I am, actually, but it is a week night.'

'And how often does a lady treat you to dinner?'

He holds his hands up in defeat and laughs. 'Thank you,' he adds.

I watch Hudson as he weaves between the tables. Our coffees arrive and I order a double whiskey on the rocks for Hudson and a non-alcoholic cocktail for myself. And then I grab my handbag, placing it on my lap, remove the two pills that I've hidden in the pocket and drop them into Hudson's coffee. I give it a little stir and then sit back and wait.

He returns quickly and when our drinks arrive, he doesn't comment that he's got a double. He takes a sip and purrs with appreciation.

'It's the Glenfiddich 21 years,' I say.

His eyes widen and he licks his lips. 'Really?' he murmurs. 'That's very generous of you.'

I didn't order the 21 years. I'm not going to pay £35 for a small glass of whiskey, thank you very much. The 12 years was £15.50 and even that's a crazy price. He finishes his coffee quickly but sips at the whiskey slowly.

'Is the cocktail good?' he asks.

I lick my lips and hold his gaze. 'Delicious,' I say in a husky voice, as I play with the bow at my neck. He shifts slightly in his chair and I know that I'm having an effect on him. I lick my teeth with my tongue and part my lips.

'Tell me about your company,' I say.

He starts talking about his travel agency, how it's being bought by this larger firm, but the more he speaks, the more his words begin to slur. His eyelids start closing as if they're too heavy to stay open and I realise I need to get him out of here quickly.

I wriggle my fingers at a passing server. 'Could you bring us the bill as fast as possible, please. My friend isn't feeling so well.' The server looks concerned. The last thing the restaurant will want is one of their customers puking over a table.

She returns quickly, and I pay with my credit card, not even looking at the total because I know it'll sicken me. I don't leave a tip.

'I think it's time we got you home, Hudson,' I say.

His head jerks backwards and I can tell he's finding it hard to focus on me. Perhaps I shouldn't have given him the double dose. I stand up, fling my bag across my body and move to Hudson's side of the table. I whisper into his ear. 'You need to get up and lean on me, Hudson. You've drunk too much and we don't want to make a scene in the restaurant. Imagine what your new boss would think.' Momentarily, that seems to awaken him and I help push his chair back so he can stand up. He wobbles a bit, but I put my arm through his and manage to steer him through the restaurant.

'Concentrate on where you're walking,' I instruct him. 'And lots of slow, deep breaths.'

It's such a relief when we're outside and, fortunately, the cold night air seems to awaken him.

'I'll order you a taxi,' I say, holding out my hand as a cab passes, its orange light lit up. The taxi slows down a few feet from us and I steer Hudson towards the waiting car. I open the door and gently push Hudson so he fumbles his way inside.

'I think I'd better come with you,' I say. Hudson doesn't even glance at me.

'If he's pissed, I don't want him in my cab,' the taxi driver says.

'No, sorry. He's just had a bit of an adverse reaction to his medication. Nothing out of the ordinary.'

'If he throws up in the back, you'll have to pay for it to be steam-cleaned.'

'Don't worry, he won't,' I say, with more conviction than I feel.

The cabbie rolls his eyes but starts driving. Besides, it's less than five minutes to Hudson's serviced apartment block. I manage to get him out of the cab, but he's leaning so heavily onto me, I'm not sure I can hold him upright.

'Wake up!' I say, slapping his right cheek. That seems to rouse him. 'You need to walk properly, through the foyer and into the lifts. We don't want the concierge to see you in this state. Pull yourself together,' I say brusquely.

I put my arm around Hudson as we enter the building. The concierge stares at me, and I can't work out if it's a good or bad thing that it's the same man who saw me here last time.

'He's drunk way too much,' I say, with a false laugh. The concierge just nods as I scribble my name illegibly in his book.

In the lift, Hudson leans against the wall, his eyes closed. I slap his face again in order to rouse him so I can manhandle him towards his apartment.

'Where's your key?' I ask.

He fumbles half-heartedly in his jacket pocket, so I pat him down until I find the keys. Inside his apartment, I guide him to the bedroom and he literally collapses half-on, half-off the bed. His eyes are closed and his breathing slow and shallow. I take my time removing Hudson's clothes, first taking off his shoes and letting them slip to the floor. Then I remove everything else and scatter the clothes around the small apartment. Shoes and socks at the door, trousers, belt and shirt in the living room, and his boxer shorts near the bedroom door. When he's totally naked, I have a good look at him. Honestly, he looks better dressed than naked, with the beginnings of a paunch around his middle and white limbs covered in dark hair. I tug him up the bed and struggle to pull the duvet from underneath him. Eventually, I get him where I want him. His head on the pillow, his body underneath the duvet, one arm hanging off the side of the bed.

I spend a little while wandering around the flat, looking at his pathetic belongings. I hold his phone up to his face so that it opens and I look through the messages he's had with Amelia. They're curt and functional and ever so boring. What a shame that Hudson is so dull, and how lucky he is that I'm going to be spicing things up a bit. I open his fridge but there's little inside. I ignore the food and remove three cans of beer and a bottle of wine. I open them all and pour them down the sink, leaving the empty cans and bottle on the living room table. I then remove some cushions from the sofa and scatter them on the floor. It looks suitably messy in here.

Eventually, I wander back into the bedroom. Hudson is still fast asleep, snoring slightly. I use the bathroom, then strip off my clothes, scattering them across the flat alongside Hudson's discarded items. Finally, completely naked, I slip into bed beside Hudson. I run my fingers along his body, which feels so different to Dean's, softer, less enticing somehow, despite his better looks. But manhandling an unconscious person doesn't do it for me, so I turn over and eventually drift off to sleep.

When I wake up, the soft morning light is drifting into the small bedroom and Hudson is sitting upright in bed, rubbing his eyes.

'Hello, gorgeous,' I say in a husky voice. I also sit up and let the duvet fall away from my body so that my breasts are on show.

'Oh God,' he murmurs, looking at me and then glancing away.

'Hey.' I run my hand along his arm. 'That was quite the night.'

'I'm sorry... I don't... I'm just...'

I move my hand so it's pressed against his chest and I can feel his heart hammering. 'It's alright, Hudson. You were really drunk but it was still amazing. You're quite the Lothario, aren't you, performing like that after drinking so much.'

He buries his face into his hands. 'I'm sorry, Paige, but I can't remember anything.'

'Well, that's a shame,' I say. 'Because you are one hell of a lover. Do you remember how many times you made me come?'

He glances at me, his face deathly pale, eyes wide.

'Don't look so shocked. I was a lucky girl. Fancy doing it

all over again?' I let my fingers trail gently down his chest towards his stomach. But Hudson pushes me away and swings his legs out of the bed, his back towards me.

'Hey, babe. What's up?' I edge across the bed so my breasts are pushed up against his back, my arms circling his chest.

'I can't,' he says. He removes my arms and stands up, his back to me. 'I don't remember anything, Paige. It was a mistake. I'm sorry. In fact, I feel terrible.'

'Hey, look at me.'

He does as he's told, his hands in front of his genitals, and he looks so very pathetic.

'I'm married,' he says, forlornly.

'Except your wife is cheating on you.'

'What? No!' He walks across the room, finds his boxer shorts and tugs them on.

I lean back on the pillows, my arms above my head, my hair splayed out. 'Why do you think Amelia refused to move to Manchester with you?' I ask.

He swivels to stare at me, and this time I'm sure I can see longing in his eyes. I push the duvet down so that I'm fully exposed, my body ready for him.

'No,' he says, shaking his head vigorously. 'Please, Paige, cover yourself up.'

'Why?' I let out a sharp laugh. 'Because you can't restrain yourself?'

'Because I am riddled with guilt, that's why. I've never been unfaithful to Amelia.'

'We can't say the same about her. She's been seeing this guy for a few months now.'

And then, to my dismay, Hudson bursts into snivelling tears. This grown man, who no doubt prides himself on being strong and masculine, is a feeble wreck. He sinks onto the bedroom chair, cradling his head with his arms, and sobs. I'm not sure what to do. To comfort him, to ignore him? Eventually, I slip out of bed, wrap a blanket around myself and pad towards him. I kneel down in front of him.

'We had an amazing night, Hudson. I know you're feeling broken that you cheated on Amelia and that she's been cheating on you, but please don't regret it. We don't have to do it again if you don't want to.'

'Do you know who Amelia is seeing?' he asks, his voice cracking.

'He's a personal trainer who does occasional work at Vanessa's studio,' I say.

Hudson wipes his nose with the back of his arm. Gross. 'Do you know his name?'

'Yes, but I'm not going to give it to you. You and Amelia have a lot of sorting out to do. When you're ready, we can meet again. For now, thank you for the most amazing night.' I kiss the top of his head.

'I'm sorry,' Hudson says.

'Don't be.' I stand up. 'We never got around to discussing the business proposal, so let me know if you want to chat through it sometime,' I say. 'Is it alright if I use the bathroom?'

By the time I've showered, put on my makeup and dressed, Hudson is also dressed and more composed. He's made me a cup of coffee, except I don't want it.

I walk up to him so we're just centimetres apart. 'A final goodbye hug?' I ask, holding my arms wide open. He nods. I squeeze him tightly, my body pressed hard up against the whole of him. I stay there for a long moment, my fingers gently caressing the back of his neck, that is until I feel him beginning to harden. Then I pull away, stand on tiptoes and gently brush his lips with mine.

I turn and stride to the front door, opening and closing it behind me without so much as a backwards glance. As I walk along the corridor to the lifts in yesterday's clothes, my bag swinging off my arm, I feel pleased with myself. Very pleased with a job well done. Now for the next step.

CHAPTER NINETEEN

MARNIE

Things are really weird at school today. I sense it the moment I walk in through the gates, as if people are staring at me, whispering behind their hands. It happened before, when I returned to school after having meningitis. But that was ages ago and I get why people stayed away. I think they thought I was contagious, that even though I was better and no one else at the school had it, I was somehow a pariah. But that passed quickly enough. A week later and I was just another ordinary kid.

I'm at my locker collecting my books when Olivia sidles up next to me. She blows so hot and cold. Sometimes she's my friend, other times she's bitching about me. She's having a sixteenth birthday party tonight and I haven't been invited. I'm pissed about that.

'Hi,' I say. 'Happy birthday.'

She's wearing a Sweet Sixteen badge. She stops still and stares at me, then shakes her head with an expression of disgust and walks away. *What the hell was that?*

It's the same in all my morning classes. People move

away from me, they stare, mutter behind their hands, and I haven't got a bloody clue what I'm supposed to have done wrong. I message Taryn.

> U know what's going on today?

She sees my message but doesn't respond. At lunchtime, I wait until she appears, her head down, her spiky black hair the same as it was before her mum's non-wedding.

'Hey,' I say, nudging her in the ribs. For one horrible moment, I wonder if she's going to be acting strange towards me too. Taryn, my only real friend. But no, she looks up and smiles, removing her earbuds from her ears and shoving them in the pocket of her skirt. 'Do you know what's going on?' I ask.

She frowns.

'Why people are acting weird towards me today.'

'Oh that,' she says, as her shoulder slump. 'You really don't know?'

'I wouldn't be asking if I did,' I say a little too sharply.

'It's the rumours about the abuse.'

I stop still in the corridor and a boy from the year below slams into me, cursing under his breath.

'What rumours about abuse?' I ask, hurrying to catch up with Taryn, who is galloping towards the cafeteria.

'People are saying that you weren't really ill but your parents were suspected of abusing you and they were reported to social services and you were put into care for a couple of weeks.'

'What!' I exclaim. I've never heard such nonsense. 'But I did have meningitis. I was in hospital! I didn't go into social services.'

'You don't go into social services, Marnie. You're under their care,' Taryn corrects me. 'But never mind. I believe you.'

I can't get my head around this. 'Why would anyone think that my parents abused me? And three years later, too.'

Taryn shrugs her shoulders. We're at the front of the cafeteria queue now, but I'm not hungry. I grab an apple and a Mars bar and pay for them.

'Look, I know it's a load of bull,' Taryn says. 'Your parents are the nicest and there's no way that they'd do anything like that to you, but people talk. And this is one of those rumours that has got out of hand.'

We sit down opposite each other at the end of a long table. I notice that no one else comes to sit anywhere near us, even though there aren't any free spaces elsewhere.

'What am I going to do about it?' I ask.

'Talk to your parents. I dunno.' She takes a mouthful of baked potato. 'At least you've still got parents,' she mutters.

'I'm sorry,' I say. 'Any news on Dean?'

'None. I'm so worried about him.' She talks with her mouth full. 'It's one thing walking away from Mum, but I really thought that he'd be in touch with me. Dean has always been there for me, even when he and Mum were at each other's throats. He'd come up to my room before bedtime, sit on the bed and apologise for their fighting. When I was sick, it was Dean who looked after me, and even though he didn't understand most of what I was learning, he'd help me revise for tests. Other than the fact he wasn't my biological dad, he was my dad, if you know what I mean. I just know that he wouldn't disappear like this.'

'You're right, it doesn't make sense,' I say, thinking how

both Taryn and I have been so mucked up by our parents. 'Do you think he's gone off with someone else?'

'If he has, he'd tell me, I'm sure. I'm worried he's sick, or something worse.' She shakes her head as if to dismiss the thought. 'Anyway, what are you doing about getting your mum's bracelet back?'

'Not much I can do. The number Jax used is out of service now.'

'You could go to the police,' Taryn suggests.

I look at her in horror. 'And then I'd have to tell them that I took nude pics of myself and they'd want to see them and I'd look like a complete prat. No way.'

Suddenly it hits me. Maybe the photos have already been shared; maybe that's why everyone is staring at me and laughing. Maybe the abuse rumour is somehow related to that. I think I'm going to throw up.

'You haven't seen the photos, have you?'

'What, your nudes?' Taryn wrinkles her nose.

'Yeah.'

'Of course not. Why?'

'I was just wondering if Jax might have put them up somewhere and people have seen them.'

Taryn shakes her head vigorously. 'No, it's the abuse rumours that are making people talk about you. The two things have got nothing to do with each other. Anyway, have you been invited to Olivia's party?'

'No. And you?'

'She asked me this morning but I'm not going to go.'

I feel a stab of envy. Olivia used to be my friend and she's never been nice to Taryn, always mocking her behind her back. Why would she invite Taryn and not me?

I keep my head down for the rest of the afternoon and

am relieved when the final bell goes. I'm hurrying along the main corridor, when a boy shouts my name. I turn around to see Ryan. Gorgeous Ryan with his floppy blond hair and green eyes. My heart sinks for a moment, and I'm fearful of what he's going to say to me. I'm relieved, at least, that he's alone and not with his posse of yobbish mates.

'Hey, Marnie. How are you doing?'

'Okay,' I say cautiously.

'Are you going to Olivia's party tonight?'

I shake my head.

'That's a shame. I was hoping you'd come with me.'

'With you?' I ask, unable to keep the surprise from my voice.

'Yeah, why not?'

'Um, yes. I'd love to. Thanks.' My heart is thudding and I can feel my cheeks flushing. I can't believe that Ryan is asking me to go to the party with him.

'Meet you there, then,' he says. 'Olivia's house at eight.'

'Sure,' I say, but he's already walked away. I feel giddy with excitement. Perhaps today isn't as bad as I thought it was.

Mum picks me up as usual. She's stony-faced and quiet and I wonder if she's heard about the abuse rumour too. I so nearly ask her but then change my mind. If she knows about it, she definitely won't let me go to the party.

'I've been invited to Olivia's birthday party tonight,' I say, as casually as I can. 'Can you drop me off?'

'No, Marnie. You know perfectly well that you're not allowed out on a school night.'

'But it's Friday tomorrow, so there's only one day left, and I don't need to stay out late.'

'The answer is no.'

I glower at her. It's so unfair. Just because we live out in the sticks means I'm always penalised, because I can't just catch a bus from the next street or hitch a lift with a friend. If I need to go anywhere, it's such a convoluted process, like when I lied that I was going to London with Olivia's mum. I didn't get caught that time, so I just need to come up with a way of getting to the party without Mum knowing. Annoyingly, I can't ask Paige to collect me because Taryn's not going. But that isn't going to stop me because I am absolutely not going to let the chance to have a date with Ryan pass me by.

After supper, where Mum tries to engage in conversation and I refuse to say a word, I disappear up to my room. I count out all of my pocket money and check my bank account. I've got twenty-three pounds and fifty pence. Speaking quietly, I order a taxi and ask for it to wait at the end of the lane. I then put on the bandeau dress that Mum doesn't know I own and cover it up with a thick jumper. I shove the skirt up, bunching it around my waist, and tug on a pair of joggers. What Mum hasn't worked out is that if I climb out of my bathroom window, I can hop down onto the flat roof below and then shimmy down the drainpipe. I've done it a few times before but never to actually run away. I can hear her downstairs. She's got the television on and she's clattering plates in the kitchen. Quickly, I climb out, jump onto the flat roof but then Clover starts barking. I almost slip coming down the drainpipe and land heavily on my right ankle. It hurts, but I haven't got time to recover. I can hear Mum talking to Clover and then she opens the back door and the dog comes out. But I don't wait. I pelt along our drive, keeping close to the hedge on the right, trying to ignore the pain in my ankle, running as fast as I can. I emerge onto the lane at the bottom just as a silver taxi indicates to the left. I wave maniacally. He winds down his window.

'Are you Marnie?'

'Yes,' I pant, and climb in.

He eyes me suspiciously but doesn't say anything. Fifteen minutes later, I've tugged off my joggers, pulled down the skirt, which was awkward on the back seat, trying to do it without the taxi driver seeing in his rearview mirror. I remove my sweater and stuff my clothes into a canvas bag, and then we're pulling up outside Oliva's house. I've never been here before. She lives on a small estate of executive homes, big houses with small gardens, and lots of cars parked everywhere. There are balloons hanging on the fence and on the porch of her house and a big banner that says, 'Sweet Sixteen!' I pay the taxi driver, although I've got literally no change and I haven't got a clue how I'm meant to get home. As he's seventeen, perhaps Ryan has a car and will drop me off.

With a pounding heart, I walk up the path and push open the front door. The noise is deafening. Kids shouting, laughing, loud music blaring. I pass several of my classmates who are gathered in small groups of threes and fours, drinking from plastic glasses. A lot of them glance up and stare at me. I know they're whispering about me, making jibes, but I ignore them. I'm just focused on finding Ryan.

'What are you doing here?' Olivia stands in front of me, flanked by Rosie and Emily. They used to be my good friends until they dropped me for no obvious reason.

'Ryan invited me.'

'Actually, it's my party and I didn't invite you,' Olivia says. She puts her hands on her hips. She's wearing a silver sequinned mini-skirt and a black figure-hugging top. Her skin is really bronzed and it looks like she's had a fake tan.

I'm not sure what to say and just look around, desperately trying to seek out Ryan.

'Did you hear me?' Olivia asks, stepping aggressively towards me.

'Yes, I heard you,' I say. 'And what are you going to do about it?' A surge of anger passes through me and I cross my arms over my chest. 'Are you going to get one of your bouncers to chuck me out? Anyway, why are you being such a bitch towards me? I've done nothing wrong.'

'Other than the fact you're gross and disgusting.'

I stare at her, my mouth slack, not understanding.

'Come on,' Emily says, grabbing Olivia's arm. 'Don't let her ruin your party. Let's get some more drinks.' She tugs Olivia away from me and I've never been so relieved to see anyone go. What the hell does she mean, you're disgusting?

'So you came.' Ryan appears in front of me. He looks me up and down and I hope he likes what he sees. I smile inanely at him, thoughts of Olivia already banished. 'You haven't got a drink. Come on, let's get you one.' A couple of his friends appear, boys from the year above whose names I don't know. 'Get Marnie a drink, will you,' he asks one of his mates. He runs his eyes up and down me. 'You're looking very, um, dressed up,' Ryan says. I'm not sure whether that's a compliment or not. We stand in the hallway awkwardly. He takes a swig from a beer bottle. I'm surprised that people seem to be drinking alcohol and wonder if perhaps Olivia's parents aren't here. His friend arrives and hands me a white plastic cup. I can't tell what the drink is so I take a quick sip. It's disgusting, really strong, like drinking diesel. I grimace.

'I've got something I want to show you,' Ryan says. He

grabs my left wrist and for a moment I hesitate. 'Don't you want to see?' he asks. His eyes sparkle and his pupils are wide and dark. A flutter of nerves batter my chest as he pulls me towards the staircase. I can see a few kids upstairs, mingling in the corridor, chatting in excited little groups, so I should be all right. We run up the wide curving staircase that leads to a hallway of white doors. He hesitates in front of one of them.

'Drink up,' he says, looking at the plastic cup in my hand. He takes another swig of beer and I follow suit, but the drink is really gross. He pushes the door open with his back and then we're inside. It's a large bedroom, with a giant bed neatly made up with plump cushions and a pale, floral duvet cover. The curtains are drawn and they're in a matching floral design.

'What are we doing up here?' I ask, nerves flickering, but at the same time, I can already feel the alcohol warming my veins. This isn't right. Ryan places his bottle on a chest of drawers and steps towards me. He takes my left wrist and grabs the plastic cup from my hand, placing it on the chest of drawers next to his beer bottle. I think he's going to kiss me but then he pushes me in the centre of my chest. The backs of my knees give way against the bed and I can't stop myself from falling. Before I know it, Ryan is on top of me, his hands under my top, kneading my breasts so hard it hurts.

'Stop!' I shout, but he's so much stronger than me, and then his hot, wet lips are on mine, a strong tongue trying to probe them apart. I hear male voices behind him, and they're chanting. 'Go, Ryan, go, Ryan.'

I summon all the strength I can to push him away.

'No!' I yell. He pulls back briefly, giving me just enough time to knee him in the balls. He gasps and I manage to wriggle out of his grip, tumbling to the floor. His mates are laughing now, one of them doubled over, as if this is the funniest thing he's ever seen.

'Leave me alone!' I say, using the duvet to pull myself upwards.

'You're such a fucking tease,' Ryan spits, sitting up now, his hand clasped around his balls.

What the hell? I've done nothing to provoke him, literally nothing. And then with a horrible thought I realise he must have seen the nude photos. Jax must have circulated them.

'We know you've done it,' Ryan says.

'Yeah. You did it with your dad,' his friend says from behind me.

'Fucking little daddy's girl, that's what you are,' Ryan snarls.

I don't wait a second longer. I dart between the laughing boys and race out of the bedroom, literally falling down the stairs, my ankle screaming in pain, tears pouring down my cheeks, tugging at my dress, which I wish with all my heart that I'd never worn. The words they said are ringing in my ears. Do they really think that I did it with Dad? How can they say such disgusting things, especially when they're not true. Dad's the best dad; he really is.

Somehow, I find myself downstairs and in the hallway, rummaging through a pile of bags and coats to find mine. When I do, I pelt out of the front door, into the cool, dark night, tears blinding me, not caring that my ankle feels like it's broken. Because that's not the only thing that broke tonight. My heart feels like it's shattered into a million pieces.

I slow down as I turn around the corner at the bottom of

the close, now not sure which way to turn. And then there are blinding headlights and a car pulls up alongside me. I cower against the hedge, terrified.

'Marnie!'

'Mum!' I exclaim, never, ever so happy to see her, but at the same time completely horrified that she's here.

'Get in the car now,' she says, her voice taut with anger. I don't need asking twice. I open the rear passenger door.

'In the front,' she says, and I realise that she's going to see what I'm wearing and she's going to be so angry. I do as she says and hurry to the front passenger door, opening it and climbing inside, trying very hard to tug my dress downwards, holding the bag over my lap. I glance at her but she's not looking at me. Her jaw is set and her knuckles are white in the dark as she grips the steering wheel. She puts her foot on the accelerator and drives forward, slowly. I expect her to say something, to shout, to do her normal 'I'm so disappointed in you, Marnie.' Except she says nothing, and somehow that's even worse. The words that Ryan said, 'Fucking little daddy's girl,' go around and around in my head and I let the tears trickle down my cheeks.

At home, Clover welcomes us as she normally does, except even my favourite being in the whole world doesn't make me feel better. I make for the staircase.

'Oh no you don't,' Mum says.

I pause with my back to her.

'In the kitchen, now,' she says, her voice low and almost trembling.

With slumped shoulders and my ankle throbbing, I turn around. I stand in the doorway, looking at my feet, wondering if my ankle is swollen.

'How dare you leave the house without my permission.

No, worse than that, Marnie. I specifically told you that you couldn't go to Olivia's party but you ignored me. You are fifteen years old and dressed like a...' She clearly can't bring herself to say the word *slut*. 'We brought you up better than that, didn't we?'

'Do you know what they're saying?' I snap back at her. 'The rumours about Dad and me and you?'

She goes very white and clutches the back of a chair. So she knows.

'Do you know what all the kids at school are saying about me, what a boy tried to do to me tonight?' And still Mum doesn't say anything. 'They're saying that you and Dad sexually abused me. This rumour is about you. It's because of you!'

'What did a boy try to do to you tonight?' she asks eventually.

'That's not the point, Mum! It's the rumour that's so terrible, and that's on you.'

'I'm sorry,' she says, but I interrupt her again.

'Why aren't you protecting me, Mum? What are you doing about it?'

An expression of deep sadness crosses her face and I think she's going to step towards me, try to take me into an embrace, when that's the very last thing I want. I turn on my heels, slam the kitchen door behind me and haul myself up the stairs. When I'm in my bedroom I pull a chest of drawers in front of the door so she can't get in and then I collapse onto my bed.

CHAPTER TWENTY

AMELIA

I played it all wrong. I should have realised that the child abuse rumour would be circulating around Marnie's school, except I'd hoped it wouldn't, that I could protect our daughter from it. I failed. Hudson and I failed; he because he's not here when we're facing a crisis, and I because I tried to bury my head in the sand. When I went up to say goodnight to Marnie and realised that there were piles of clothes under her duvet rather than my child, I knew straight away that she must have gone to the party I forbade her to attend. It only took a couple of phone calls to get Olivia's address and I headed straight over there. What I wasn't anticipating was Marnie running down the street in distress. At least that spared both of us the indignity of me marching into Olivia's parents' house seeking out my daughter. After she slammed the kitchen door in my face, I thought about going to her, trying to console her, attempting to come to an uneasy truce, but I remembered how I was at that age, and how I needed to calm down in my own time, away from my overbearing mother. So I left Marnie alone.

Hudson didn't call me and I didn't call him, so I guess we all went to bed angry and lonely, although perhaps Hudson was in the arms of his other woman. We have so much to sort out, Hudson and I; the infidelity, the money, our future, if we have one. Yet I can't muster the energy and I certainly don't want to have such a conversation on the phone.

After a restless night, I'm downstairs in the kitchen, making conciliatory pancakes. 7.30 a.m. comes and goes and Marnie doesn't appear. I shout up the stairs for her, but there are no creaking footsteps or the sound of water running in the taps. I head upstairs and knock on her door. When there's no answer, I turn the handle, except the door doesn't budge. Feeling a tightening in my stomach, I push against the door with my shoulder and realise that she's moved a piece of furniture up against it to stop me from easily entering.

'Come on, Marnie,' I say. 'We need to talk.'

I'm met with silence. I give a huge shove and the door opens. Marnie isn't there and this time she hasn't even pretended to be in bed. I stride into her en-suite bathroom and glance around, noticing that the window is half open, the cold air causing me to shiver. Marnie has gone. Again.

Except this morning I feel a knot of terror in my sternum. Last night, I knew where she was, who she was with. Today, I have absolutely no idea where she's gone. I try to stay calm, except my hand is gripping my throat and dread mounts as every second ticks by. I glance around and notice that her rucksack isn't here. In the bathroom, her toothbrush and toothpaste aren't in the cup holder and her lipstick, that I constantly deride her for wearing, is also missing. Marnie hasn't gone to school early; she's run away.

I hurry out of her room and back downstairs, grabbing my phone. I try calling her mobile, except it goes straight to voicemail. I leave a message. 'Darling, I'm not angry, I'm just worried about you. Please call me. I promise I won't tell you off. I just need you to be safe.'

I stalk the kitchen with Clover at my feet, who stays so close, I practically fall over her. She must be picking up on my nervous energy. Perhaps Marnie has taken it upon herself to go to Manchester, although with no money, I've no idea how. The thought of my naive fifteen-year-old hitchhiking up the spine of England fills me with horror. Or perhaps Hudson has sent for her? But surely he wouldn't be so cruel as to not tell me? I call him. The phone rings out. I call again and leave a message.

'Hudson, Marnie has run away. It's possible that she's on her way to Manchester to stay with you. Please call me as soon as you get this message.'

Maybe I'm overreacting here. She's angry with me for discovering that she went to the party, and she's angry about the rumour. Goodness knows how badly she's been bullied as a result of it, and I wish I'd pushed her for an explanation when she made that throw-away remark about what a boy did to her. In a way, she's right about the rumour. We should have protected her better. We did such a good job when she was sick, physically nursing her to health, but have Hudson and I been such good parents from an emotional and psychological perspective? Perhaps not. Marnie's only fifteen and so vulnerable.

The next person I call is Paige. I'm hopeful that Taryn will know where Marnie is.

'Good morning,' she says chirpily, as if it's completely normal for me to call her before 8 a.m. 'How are things?'

'I think Marnie has run away. Can you ask Taryn if she knows where she is?'

There's a long pause. 'Goodness, how awful. Hold on two ticks and I'll ask her.' I hear her put the phone down but then there's silence and I wonder if she's muted the phone. It seems like ages before she's back on the line. 'I'm afraid not. She hasn't heard from Marnie since they talked at school yesterday lunchtime.'

'If she hears from Marnie or she tips up, please can you ask Taryn to give me a call. I'm so worried.'

'Of course, Amelia. What's happened?'

'Have you heard the rumour?'

There's another long silence and I can imagine Paige searching for something appropriate to say.

'Yes, I have. Look, I need to go as I'm teaching this morning, but let me know if I can do anything. I'll leave my phone on so that it buzzes.'

Neither of us articulates what we're no doubt both thinking. Paige has taken over my morning classes.

I try calling both Marnie and Hudson every few minutes, but neither gets back to me. Unsure what to do next, I leave a scribbled handwritten note on the kitchen table asking Marnie to call me the moment she gets home, that I'm not angry, that I'm out looking for her. I remember the tracker I secretly put on her phone and with trembling fingers navigate through the app. Except when I click on her name, it says the last known location was here, at our home. Does that mean the app isn't working or that her phone is off? I grab my handbag and car keys, reverse the car out of the garage kicking up gravel as I do so, then I head to the end of our drive. I vacillate, wondering whether to turn left or right, but in the end turn left, the way we go to school. I drive slowly, scouring the side roads, the pavements, my head bouncing from left to right, except Marnie has vanished. I go into the centre of town, driving too slowly and getting hooted at by impatient drivers. And every few minutes I call both my daughter and husband.

When my phone starts ringing, I almost crash the car.

'Yes,' I say hurriedly.

'Good morning, Mrs Myers. This is the school secretary speaking. Marnie's form teacher has told me that she hasn't come into school today. Is she sick?'

'No, she's... I think she's run away. I don't know where she is.'

There's an audible intake of breath and a long pause. Eventually, the woman says, 'Well, please keep us posted, and if she turns up at school we'll let you know.'

'Thanks,' I say automatically. She ends the call.

Eventually, I head back home, hoping – no, praying – that Marnie will be there, apologetic for her little misadventure, and that we can hug and make up. Except the only being greeting me is Clover. I return to Marnie's bedroom and search through her drawers, under her bed and in her wardrobe, but I find nothing. It isn't until I lift the duvet off her bed followed by her pillows that I find it. Her mobile phone, which is switched off, is under her pillow. Why? Marnie never goes anywhere without her phone. Did she leave it here on purpose knowing that I might try to track her? My whole body clenches with fear.

I spend the next hour on the phone and it's definitely the worst hour of my year. People who I once considered friends are curt, even rude, unwilling to spend any time talking to me. It's obvious that the rumour about Hudson and me being investigated for child abuse is rife. Women I've known for years through Marnie's school promise to let me know if they see her, but the undertones are there. Judging, dismissive, and I imagine them thinking, this serves you right. There's no smoke without fire. Perhaps Marnie is better off without you.

I call Hudson's office, his new office. I'm put through to a woman on his team.

'How can I help you?' she asks cheerily.

'I'm Amelia, Hudson's wife,' I explain. 'Please can I talk to him. It's a family emergency.'

'Oh goodness,' she says, with a strong Mancunian accent. 'But I'm afraid he's not in the office today.'

'Where is he?' I ask, a little too curtly.

'I'm sorry, but I don't know. He just said he wasn't coming in today.'

Of course he did. The one day I actually need him, he's not contactable.

'And is it normal just to take the day off?' I ask.

There's an audible intake of breath. 'Mr Myers is my boss. I don't question him when he says he's taking the day off. I'm sorry I can't help you.'

By lunchtime, I'm feeling physically sick and dry-heave into the toilet. Nothing comes up and I don't feel any better. I imagine scenes of devastation, horrific things happening to Marnie, and I know there's only one place left for me to visit. The police station.

We have a small police station in Beacham. It's not manned all the time, but I'm hopeful it will be today and it'll save me the drive to Shoreham. I debate calling 999, but I need to look into the eyes of a police officer and not be fobbed off by a faceless person on the end of the phone. I drive too quickly and when I get there, I park on a yellow line, happy to accept the fines and any other consequences. I just need to find Marnie.

I'm in luck. The police station is open and there's a uniformed officer sitting behind a Plexiglass screen. He's typing something into a keyboard and takes a long time to look up despite clearly having seen me.

'Yes,' he says eventually. He's rotund, with a white beard and balding head. There's something Father Christmas-like about him, comforting even. 'How can I help?' His eyes crease as he looks at me.

'My daughter has gone missing. She's probably run away but she's only fifteen and she doesn't have any money or her mobile phone. I don't know what to do.'

'Oh dear. Teenagers,' he sighs, as if this is a regular issue for him. Perhaps it is. 'How long has she been gone for?'

'She left our home sometime in the night. It could be twelve hours or longer.'

'And you've tried friends and family, everyone you know?'

'Everyone,' I say, although that is patently not true. 'I've called her, left messages, but then I found her phone hidden under her pillow, switched off. Are you going to make me wait twenty-four hours before officially reporting her missing?' Horrible images flash through my head of her motionless body lying in long grass at the side of a road, cars dashing past.

'You say she's fifteen?' he asks, cupping his chin with his hand and leaning forward on his elbow.

'Yes. Still a kid.'

'No need to wait. She's a vulnerable young person. We'll file a report and put out an APB bulletin to all the cars.'

'An APB?' I ask.

'It's a broadcast to all the police officers in the area to keep a look out for her. Let's have a sit-down and I'll take some more details from you.' He gets up from his chair and appears in the doorway to the right of the reception area. Leaning against the door, he motions for me to walk through. The building is small and he takes me straight through to a room with a view onto the street. There are two wooden chairs and a computer standing on a desk.

'I'm PC Bruce Newlands, and you are?' He places a notebook and biro on the desk.

'Amelia Myers, and my daughter is called Marnie.'

'Has she been in trouble before?' he asks.

'No,' I say, before remembering the shoplifting caution just a couple of weeks ago. 'She was cautioned for shoplifting in Shoreham, but it's very out of character.'

'Things been going on at school lately, have they?' he asks. I wonder how many children he has; he gives the air of having seen it all.

PC Newlands asks me lots of questions about Marnie and I explain that her dad is currently in Manchester, working. I share a couple of recent photographs and he promises me that he'll be taking this very seriously, but conversely, the vast majority of missing kids turn up within a few hours. 'She's probably just annoyed with you over something very trivial,' he says, scribbling in his notebook. I wonder if I should mention the child abuse rumours, the fact that Marnie went to Olivia's party last night and I found her running away, down the street. For now, I don't. I decide not to muddy the waters because I just want this man to focus on finding her.

'What will you do?' I ask, desperation in my voice.

'We've got set procedures in cases like this, so in addition to putting out the APB, we'll start with house-to-house enquiries, send an officer around to her school, check local

CCTV. We'll do everything we can to find her, Mrs Myers.'

I smile weakly.

'Now, I want you to go home and stay there. I'm going to speak to my bosses, but we'll likely be sending a family liaison officer out to wait with you. And when young Marnie tips up, just give me a call.' He stands up, hands me a business card and then shakes my hand, and for a moment I don't want to leave this room where this kindly man is being so positive.

'When will I hear from you?' I ask.

'As soon as we have any news. Just try not to worry too much. Teenagers go walkabouts all the time.'

It's easy for PC Newlands to tell me not to worry, but I have a terrible sense of dread in my stomach and a tightening around my throat. Of course I'm going to worry about my only child, especially as our last words were an argument. I just pray that Marnie knows how much I love her, how I have a secret admiration for her Houdini escape and her ballsy decision to attend Olivia's party despite me forbidding her to go. I'm lost in thought as I head home, peering from side to side in the vain hope of seeing Marnie loping along a pavement. As I turn into our drive, I see there's a black car parked outside the front door. Two men climb out as I park up alongside them. Are they plain-clothed police officers, or the family liaison officer PC Newlands was talking about? But how did he organise this so quickly? The way they stride towards me sends another wave of fear through my veins. There's something about them that suggests they're not police. Both men are big and burly, one wearing a shirt that's too tight for him, the other displaying thick-set tattooed arms protruding from a short-sleeved T-shirt. They have matching buzz-cuts and the taller man looks as if his nose has been broken on multiple occasions.

'Mrs Amelia Myers?' the man in the shirt asks.

'Yes,' I say cautiously, clutching my handbag in front of me. 'Is this about Marnie?'

'Marnie?' He frowns.

I don't answer.

'We're bailiffs,' he says, producing some pieces of paper and waving them in front of me.

What? I can't take this in. It doesn't make any sense, not today of all days when Marnie is missing. Why would bailiffs be asking for me?

'I'm sorry, I don't understand,' I say. I can hear Clover barking from inside the house. It's started to drizzle and the droplets tickle my head.

'You and Mr Myers defaulted on various loans, I believe. We're High Court enforcement officers, otherwise known as private bailiffs. The paperwork's all here.'

'That can't be right,' I say. 'I don't understand.'

'Mr Myers home?' the man asks.

I shake my head.

This doesn't make any sense. I've never owed money, never defaulted on a debt. I've paid off my credit card dutifully every month, until that is, this last month after my account was drained. Has all this come about because of the Chinese scam? But what has Hudson got to do with it? With a sinking feeling, I wonder what he's been keeping from me. As he pays the mortgage and settles our utility bills, I wouldn't actually know if he's defaulted.

'You'd better take these and let us in.' He hands me the sheets of paper and I glance down at them. They look official, with stamps and dates, but the words are swimming and I can't concentrate.

'I need to talk to my husband,' I say, hoping, desperately hoping that Hudson will actually answer his phone, hoping that this is all some terrible mistake.

'Haven't got long until the van turns up,' the man says, glancing at his watch, which looks suspiciously like a Rolex. I swallow hard. How much stuff are they planning on taking?

I call Hudson. Yet again. And yet again, it goes straight to voicemail. This time the tone of my voice is furious. 'Call me immediately. It's a matter of life or death.' It hits me then that Hudson must have known about this. He must have known that we – or at least he – has been accumulating debt and that at some point the bailiffs were going to turn up. They don't just appear without any prior notice. And I suppose that's why he has done this disappearing act on me. A huge sense of injustice and anger sears through me. The bastard! Why didn't he talk to me? And then I wonder. Did Hudson take the money out of my savings account? Have I been erroneously assuming that I've been scammed? Has my husband been accumulating debts and using my money to pay them off without letting me know?

As I'm trying to process all of this, I hear the low rumble of an engine. A large transit van is indicating to turn into our driveway.

I stare at it in horror and then turn to the two men. 'What are you going to take?' I ask.

'Any goods that we believe are to the value of seventy grand. And between you and me, I believe your lender is looking at repossessing the house, so you might want to pay up on the mortgage.'

I'm not sure whether to laugh or cry. Can today actually get any worse?

'What happens if I don't let you in?' I ask.

The men raise their eyebrows at each other. 'Not a good idea, love. Not unless you want to be hauled up in front of the courts.'

Slowly, I turn around and open the front door. Clover comes bounding out, barking viciously at the bailiffs. At least the dog is on my side.

'Can you get her out the way,' the larger man says, his steel-capped boots edging closer to Clover. I grab her collar and walk her inside, the heavy footsteps of the men behind us. I watch helplessly as they walk into the living room and survey it, their presence too large, just wrong in my carefully curated space. What do they see? The cream sofas, the pastel-coloured curtains, the photos of Marnie on the top of the upright piano? They walk towards the large television in the corner of the room, and the ugly leather chair where Hudson has spent hours watching the football. I turn away just as a female voice rings out.

'Mrs Myers?'

Dear God. What now? I edge out into the hall. There's a woman wearing a black trouser suit standing in the doorway, her hair tied back in a ponytail, freckles covering her nose. 'Mrs Myers?' she asks again. 'I'm Connie Mattman, the family liaison officer. I'm a police officer, here to support you whilst the team look for Marnie. Can I come in?'

She doesn't wait for an answer and steps into the hallway. 'Would you like me to take my shoes off?' she asks. I almost laugh with the absurdity of a question which only a couple of hours ago would have sounded perfectly normal. I shake my head.

'We'd better go through to the kitchen,' I say, my head buzzing.

'You're having a delivery?' she asks.

'No.' I wonder if I need to tell her, because it's humiliating, but then the words just slip out with a sob. 'It's the bailiffs. The bailiffs have turned up right in the middle of this horrific day. Have you got any news on Marnie?'

'Oh dear,' Connie Mattman says, her nostrils flaring. 'I'm afraid there's nothing on Marnie yet, but I don't want you to worry.'

'Not worry!' I exclaim. 'Clearly, my husband has got us into terrible debt and he hasn't even had the decency to tell me about it. I've just got home to find these men taking away our possessions. And worst of all, by far the worst of all, my fifteen-year-old daughter has disappeared.' My voice is on the edge of hysterical.

'I'm sorry you're going through this. It does sound very miserable.' Quite the understatement.

'Hudson isn't answering his phone and for all I know, Marnie might be with him.'

'That would be a good starting point for us. Where is Mr Myers?'

'In Manchester, I think. He's moved there for work but he's not in the office today. I explained that to the police officer at the station.'

'Right. Leave that with me, and I'll ring a colleague. We'll get the Manchester Constabulary to call in on your husband. Can you give me his address at home and at work?'

With shaking fingers, I scroll through my phone's address book and give Connie Mattman Hudson's new addresses. She turns her back to me as she calls a colleague, talking in a low whisper. When she's finished, she says, 'I think we both need a cuppa, don't we? Show me where your mugs are and I'll make us a nice cup of tea.'

'I don't want tea!' I exclaim, realising I'm biting the head off the one person who is being kind to me today. 'Sorry, it's just I want you to find Marnie, to get these men out of my house, and tell my husband to sort the bloody mess he's got us into.'

'Of course, love,' she says. It strikes me that she's too young to be calling me love. 'Have a seat.'

Except I don't. While Connie Mattman is rifling through my cupboards, I pace the kitchen, rage, humiliation and a terrible fear, all knotting together inside me, until my stomach clenches so painfully, I have to grab onto the back of a kitchen chair and bend over with pain. In my twisting gut, I realise that today is a turning point in my life. That today there will be the before, when life was rosy, and the after, which right now is a black gaping hole.

CHAPTER TWENTY-ONE

PAIGE

'Here you go.' I've made the girls hot chocolate with piped cream on the top, a big swirl that's come out of the spray can of cream. They're curled up either end of the sofa, both with blankets wrapped around them, their feet touching. It's rather sweet, actually. God knows what they're watching. Some reality rubbish on Netflix. Not that I mind. It'll do Taryn good, taking the day off school, getting her nose out of those books. And as for Marnie, well, I was hardly going to turn her away, was I?

The poor kid walked all the way to our house, traipsing along country lanes in the dead of night, her way illuminated by a torch. She's lucky she didn't get hit by a car or picked up by some weirdo. The knocking on our front door startled me, and when I glanced at the clock and saw it was only 5.46 a.m., my first thought was, *Dean's back.* Except Dean has a key, so it wouldn't have been him. Then I thought of the police, but I've been so careful, haven't I? I tiptoed to the window and pulled back the curtain, peering out into the murky light. And there was young Marnie, standing at our door, a small rucksack on her back, her shoulders hunched and her hair damp from the rain. I pulled on my dressing gown and hurried downstairs, unlocking the door. She took one look at me and burst into tears.

'What's going on?' I asked.

'I'm sorry,' she sniffled. 'Things are really bad with my mum and I didn't know where else to go. Can I come in?'

'Of course you can, you lovely girl,' I said, putting my arm around her shoulders and pushing her into the hallway. I took a quick glance at the street, but there was no one around and I'm hopeful none of my neighbours saw her. I was horrified when she told me that she'd walked the five or so miles to get here. 'I'd have picked you up if you'd called,' I said.

'I tried Taryn but her phone is off, and I've left mine at home in case Mum tries to track me.'

'Let's get you dry and warm and then you can tell me everything.' Honestly, I felt on top of the world knowing that Amelia and Hudson's daughter had rejected them in favour of me.

By the time Marnie emerged from the bathroom, Taryn was up, wondering what all the clattering was about. I was in the kitchen making the girls a full English breakfast along with pancakes. Taryn seemed bemused that Marnie was here, but that's my girl. Sometimes she looks at me as if I'm the crazy one when it's actually her who's on the spectrum.

'Tell us what's happened,' I said to Marnie as she sat at the kitchen table and stared at the feast I made.

'Mum went apeshit because I went to Olivia's party when she told me I couldn't go.'

'And?' I said.

She just shrugged her shoulders. 'I couldn't stay at home

any more, not with Dad in Manchester and Mum acting like I'm a baby.'

'You have a bed here for as long as you want one,' I said, patting her arm reassuringly. 'You can share with Taryn or you can have my bed and I'll bunk down with Taryn on the pull-out mattress.' Taryn threw me a quizzical look, but then she doesn't know about Project Amelia. She's probably assuming I'm happy that she has a best friend at long last. Or perhaps they're more than that? A girlfriend, maybe?

'Thank you,' Marnie muttered, her mouth full of egg and bacon.

Amelia called me shortly after 7.30 a.m., as I knew she would. There was desperation in her voice.

'I think Marnie has run away. Does Taryn know where she is?'

I hurried up the stairs and into my bedroom, away from the girls, and then waited for a long time before answering, working hard to suppress my smile in case it showed in my voice. 'Goodness, how awful. Hold on two ticks and I'll ask her.' I closed my bedroom door just in case she could hear Marnie's voice in the background. I told her no, that Taryn hadn't heard from Marnie and that even though I'm teaching she should reach out to me. I laughed when I finished the call.

A couple of hours on and the girls are enjoying some relaxing time and I am on cloud nine. Of course, I'm going to keep Marnie hidden, because I know that Amelia will be frantic. To be fair, I would be too if Taryn disappeared, but that's not in Taryn's nature. Then again, I give Taryn a freer rein, but it's not in my daughter's nature to rebel. She'll choose a herbal tea over a cocktail and a book over a computer game. Heaven knows she doesn't take after me.

Anyway, now I'm going to add to the stress of Amelia's morning. While the girls are watching the TV, I'm at the kitchen table flicking through the photos I took of Hudson and me in his bed. I select my favourite, a photo of him splayed out on the mattress, his arm flung over my bare breasts, his penis flaccid and legs apart, the duvet crumpled to the side of the bed. You can see my torso but nothing more. I crop the photo so my hair isn't visible and when I'm happy with it, I send it to my burner phone. Then I input Amelia's phone number. I take a while to decide on the perfect message to accompany the photo and eventually just say, 'Hudson having fun in Manchester. Doubt he'll be home any time soon...'

As soon as I press send, I turn the phone off and remove the SIM card and then I burst out laughing.

'What's up with you?' Taryn asks as she pads barefoot into the kitchen carrying the two empty mugs.

'Just having a bit of fun,' I say. 'Hope you are too.'

She throws me a scowl and puts the mugs in the dishwasher, before returning to the living room. I can hear her talking in a low voice to Marnie. I wonder what Amelia is doing, whether she's frantically scouring the streets and at what point she will go to the police. Knowing her, she's probably already got a SWAT team out searching for precious Marnie.

I scour the local news and all the social media platforms but there's nothing yet about a missing teenager. But then a message comes through on the school WhatsApp asking if anyone has seen Marnie Myers today and I let out a whoop. A few minutes later, Amelia sends another message, clearly to all of the contacts on her phone, saying that Marnie is missing and she's reported it to the police.

I consider waiting all day, but at some point in the future

Marnie will tell her mum that she was here all along, and that could really backfire for me, so just after midday I go out to my car and telephone the police.

'I'm calling about a young woman called Marnie Myers,' I explain. 'It's possible that she's been reported missing.'

The police officer doesn't elucidate one way or another, so I carry on.

'She's running away from an abusive environment. She hasn't told me much and I don't want to push her, but she's really upset and I believe she might have been sexually abused by her parents.'

'Right,' the officer says.

'I actually hadn't realised that she's been reported missing, except then I got a message from her mother, Amelia Myers, and thought I'd better tell you that Marnie is at our house. There is no way that I'm letting her go home and I'm hoping that you could send an officer round here, or social services perhaps.'

I give the officer further details on Marnie and on my relationship with the Myers, and also direct him to the rumours online. When I finish the call I lean my head back and grin. I hope that I've just opened the sluice gates and that the consequences for Amelia and Hudson will be devastating.

CHAPTER TWENTY-TWO
AMELIA

My phone pings with a message and for a millisecond I'm hopeful that it's someone saying they've found Marnie. It isn't. The message comes from an unknown number and it's accompanied by a photograph. I snort out aloud when I see the photograph of Hudson splayed across a bed naked with a woman who most certainly isn't me.

> Hudson having fun in Manchester. Doubt he'll be home any time soon…

So that's why my bastard of a husband is ignoring me. He's gone off with another woman and has frittered away all of our money. A surge of fury pounds through me and I chuck my phone onto the table with such force, I wonder if I've broken it. I realise with dismay that Connie Mattman is standing in the doorway and has just seen me do that.

'Everything alright?' she asks.

'No.' I can't stop myself from letting out a little sob. 'I think today is the worst day of my life.' I point to the phone and she steps across the room to pick it up. Her thin eyebrows rise upwards as she looks at the photo and caption.

'Things a bit rough with your husband?' she asks.

'You could say that.' I sink down into a kitchen chair. 'But the only thing that matters is finding Marnie.' And I genuinely mean that. I couldn't care less whom Hudson is sleeping with and I can live without all his fancy televisions and gadgets. Hudson has shown no support or interest in me or Marnie since he moved to Manchester, and now I'm thinking about it, he was pretty distant for months beforehand. He let the bailiffs turn up here without giving me any warning, so if he's sleeping with some whore, then let him. I'm well rid of the man.

'Right, we're done.' The bailiff seems enormous standing in the kitchen doorway. And then he adds, rather ominously, 'For now. Suggest you get those debts paid off, Mrs Myers.' He produces a piece of paper on a clipboard that has a biro attached to it with a piece of string. 'Sign here, please.'

I think about saying no, but what will that achieve? Perhaps Connie Mattman would have to arrest me and the police focus would be diverted from finding Marnie. Except the police don't get involved in such matters, or do they? My brain, which normally works well enough, seems to have seized up in a fog of confusion and panic. I can feel the bailiff and Connie's eyes on me, so I sign in the allocated box.

'Thanks,' the bailiff says. 'We're off for now.'

I stay seated at the table, stroking Clover, listening as the vehicles leave our property, repeatedly making silent pleas to whatever higher being there is up there, begging them to bring Marnie home safely. My phone rings and my heart pounds when I see Hudson's name pop up on the screen. Should I answer? I want to scream and shout at him, but the policewoman is still here, listening to every word I'm saying. What will she think of us and the disaster that is our lives? I vacillate for too long and my phone goes to voicemail. It pings with a new message.

After a long few seconds, I listen to it. Hudson sounds frantic. 'What's this about the bailiffs? About Marnie being missing. I'm on a train south. I was in London last night so I'll be with you within the hour. Call me.'

Me call him? He's the one who has been ignoring my calls, who has been quietly unpicking my life without so much as a hint of a warning. I don't want Hudson here; in fact, I don't think I ever want to see him again.

I send him a message.

> You should be in Manchester. What if Marnie turns up at your flat and you're not there???

He rings me again and once more, I let it go to voicemail. A couple of seconds later another message arrives.

> The concierge will keep an eye out for her.

If I was angry before, now I'm livid. How will darling Marnie feel if she makes it all the way to Manchester to discover that her father isn't there? He has completely let us both down. No, more than that. He's been knowingly evil towards us and I don't think I can ever forgive him for it.

As I'm pacing the house in fury, my eyes are drawn to blanks in all of the rooms. The places where the televisions used to hang, the painting above the fireplace that Hudson overpaid for by an American artist I'd never heard of, two silver jugs that his parents gave us for our second wedding anniversary, the living room sofa and Hudson's leather chair. But worst of all, I look outside and realise that my car is gone. I hurry to the key holder on the wall by the back door and see that my car keys are missing. They've taken my Volvo XC60! How the hell am I meant to get around? I can't even go to a local shop without driving. But then I remember that we still have the little Fiat in the garage that used to belong to Mum, that we've kept for Marnie's use when she passes her test. Assuming they haven't taken it, I'll have to use that.

Connie Mattman's phone rings and she leaves the room to answer it. I can hear her speaking in a hushed tone in the living room. I'm tempted to tiptoe out into the hall to try to hear what she's saying, except I'm too late. She's already back in the kitchen, the expression on her face unreadable.

'Good news, Amelia. Marnie has been found and she appears to be safe and well.'

'Oh my God!' I exclaim, the relief making tears spring to my eyes. 'Where is she?'

'I can't give you any more information at this stage but rest assured, she's safe.'

'When is she coming home?'

'I suggest you stay here and we'll be in touch as soon as we have more information.'

'Can I talk to her? Is she at the police station?'

'I'm sorry, but I can't give you further details.' There's something in the tone of her voice that suggests she's keeping something from me, and despite the great news, I feel a shiver of discomfort. 'My job is done here for now,' she says, gathering up her jacket and handbag.

'For now?'

She gives me a sideways glance. 'Just a manner of speaking.'

With the house empty, the enormity of the morning hits me. Every bone in my body aches as if I have been pummelled, yet it's my heart that is the most broken. I sink to the living room floor and bury my face in Clover's velvet-soft, black coat. I think back through the years of our relationship. Hudson and I were strong for so long. We had our hiccups as every couple does. I'd desperately wanted another child and when, month after month, I failed to get pregnant, we did a round of IVF. And another. But I didn't have the emotional or physical energy to do a third round. I quit work, we moved here, to our lovely house, and I spent ages renovating it, doing much of the painting and sewing of curtains myself. Meanwhile, I was there for Marnie and for Hudson, supporting him as his business grew and then floundered when Covid hit. And I thought we got through the horror of Marnie's illness, even though we dealt with it in such different ways. I wanted to talk about it, to face the fear. Hudson refused. His way of dealing with difficult emotions is to bury them, repress them completely in the hope that they'll never pop up again. I thought we had honesty in our relationship, except now I know we didn't. Hudson has betrayed me and Marnie in the worst possible way.

There's the sound of wheels on the driveway, but this time I can't muster the energy to get up. Clover runs through the house and starts barking and then I hear the sound of a key in the lock and Hudson's low voice. His footsteps get louder until I can sense he's in the living room staring at me.

'What's up?' he asks.

And that triggers a tsunami of fury. I jump to my feet. 'What's up!' I exclaim. 'You ask me what's up when our daughter has gone missing and you've defaulted on goodness knows how many debts, so much so that I've had the bailiffs here this morning clearing out our house, taking my car. Oh, and then there's your mistress and all the lies you've been telling me.'

I don't know what Hudson expected but he goes very pale and takes a step backwards. He steps on Clover's paw and she lets out a little yelp. He can't even stop himself from hurting the dog.

'I'm sorry,' he says, in a quiet voice. 'I should have told you about the debts.'

'You're a coward, Hudson.'

He flinches. 'What did they take?'

'It doesn't matter what they took. What matters is, you didn't tell me! How do you think it felt to have the bailiffs here and then the police turn up because of Marnie and now we're in the most terrible mess?'

'Marnie... Where is she?'

'I don't know but she's with the police. She's safe.' There's a long silence before I say, 'You've ruined us, Hudson.'

He nods and seems so pathetic that I have this overwhelming urge to slap him around the face. Except I don't. I go to sit down on the sofa, but all that's left is a cushion lying discarded on the floor. I sink onto it, my hands underneath my buttocks, to stop them from shaking, from whipping up and slapping him. Hudson leans against the mantlepiece.

'The business never recovered, not after all the hits with Covid, the economic downturn, Brexit.'

'Excuses, excuses,' I say, sarcastically. He ignores me.

'I tried really hard to fix things, to take out more loans, to get investment, except it didn't work. I know I should have told you but I didn't want to worry you, to disappoint you. And then Globus Planet offered to take over the business.'

'So what's happened to the money for that?' I ask.

'They... They haven't actually paid me anything. We've written off the debts and after I've worked for them for a year, they'll start paying me a salary. And commission.'

I stare at him wondering if I've heard him properly. He's got debts and no income for a whole year.

'Why didn't you just put the business into voluntary liquidation?' I ask.

'Because you're a director and I wanted to keep it from you. I thought this was a better way out.'

'You're a lying fool!' I say, the anger returning with a vengeance as I jump back to my feet.

'I thought we could use the money in your savings account except you lost it, didn't you?'

'This is hardly my fault, Hudson! Besides, my savings wouldn't have stopped all of this.' I wave my hands around our empty living room. 'Have you been paying the mortgage?' Are we going to lose the house?'

Hudson slumps even further. 'I thought I could use your savings to pay off the mortgage arrears. I thought you wouldn't mind.'

'You were just going to take the money?'

He can't bring himself to look at me, this pathetic man I've wasted the past two decades on. How has he withered to such foolishness? How could I have not seen him sinking in front of my eyes?

'So where is the money?' he asks.

'Did you take it?'

His jaw falls open. 'Of course not.'

Do I believe him? Actually, yes. So here it is. I have to admit that he's not the only idiot in our relationship. I've fallen victim to fraud, but was that my fault or something that could happen to anyone? At least I haven't consistently lied.

'You'll have to look for a job,' Hudson says. 'A proper job. Not just teaching yoga.'

'I've lost my yoga teaching anyway,' I say. I debate telling him about the deposit I lost on the hotel where I was going to run a yoga retreat, and decide that it's pittance in comparison to the debts that he's incurred. 'So, to get this straight, you've lost us the house and the business, and you're a lying, cheating coward, having an affair in the midst of all of this chaos!'

His head jerks upwards. 'What? I haven't been having an affair.'

'Stop with the lies, Hudson.' I pull my mobile phone out of my pocket and show him the photo I received of him lying on a bed, in the nude, with a female draped over him.

'The evidence is all here, Hudson, so stop with the bloody lies! And where have you been when Marnie needed you? In Manchester, sleeping with your mistress.'

'That's not fair!' He's shouting now too. 'Marnie ran away from you, not me.'

'Only because you weren't here.' I'm crying; I just can't help myself, yet I don't want Hudson to see me like this, weakened by all of his blows.

'I want a divorce,' I say, angrily rubbing the tears from my cheeks. 'And I want sole custody.'

Hudson loses it now. He grabs the cushion off the floor and hurls it towards me. For the first time in our marriage, I'm actually scared that he's going to be violent towards me. He grits his teeth together, a vein in his forehead bulging and beating furiously, a flush creeping up his neck.

'Sole custody!' he says. He's clasping and unclasping his

fingers, bouncing on the balls of his feet, and I take a step backwards, worried he's going to charge at me. 'You are never going to get sole custody of our daughter,' he spits.

And then the doorbell rings.

We both freeze. Clover barks from the hallway.

'Who's that?' he asks.

I walk to the window and glance outside. It's a dark saloon car.

'They've probably brought Marnie home. I want you out of this house. Go out through the back door and don't come back.' I storm past him, into the hallway, and fling open the front door.

Except Marnie isn't there. There are two men on the doorstep, both wearing dark suits. The shorter man holds out his warrant card.

'Mrs Myers?' he asks.

'Yes,' I say cautiously. His colleague appears to look over my shoulder but I don't turn.

'I'm DC Craig Cooley and this is my colleague DC Arjan Singh. We're here to talk about your daughter, Marnie. Can we come in?'

'Is she alright?' I ask, suddenly panicked that Connie Mattman might not have told me the truth.

'She's fine,' DC Cooley says, 'but we need to explain what's going on.' I step to one side and let the two men in.

'I'm Hudson Myers.' Hudson steps forward and shakes both of their hands, a little too vigorously I think, as if he's trying to prove a point. So he ignored my instructions to leave the house. Instead, he leads them into the living room where the cushion he threw at me is on the floor and where there are ugly blank spaces, scarred with a lighter-coloured paint where the picture and television used to be.

'Oh,' Hudson says. 'We'll have to go into the kitchen.' I want to shout at him, to say that he threw away our home and no longer has any right to invite people in. The two men follow him into the kitchen and Hudson indicates for them to sit down. I bite the side of my cheek and choose a seat as far away from my husband as possible.

DC Singh speaks first. 'Marnie is safe but I'm afraid that your daughter will not be coming home.'

'What?' I ask.

He carries on talking. 'She's in the care of social services while we investigate allegations of child abuse.'

'What allegations?' Hudson asks, his face white.

It feels as if my world has truly dropped into hell. With the terror of losing Marnie, the horror of the bailiffs and the arguments with Hudson, I have completely forgotten about those horrific rumours.

'But they're not true!' I exclaim.

'What allegations?' Hudson asks again, and I realise that perhaps for the first time in a long time, Hudson is being honest. He genuinely doesn't know what we're talking about.

CHAPTER TWENTY-THREE
MARNIE

Two women turned up at Taryn's house and talked to Paige in hushed whispers in the kitchen for ages. Then one of them came into the living room and told me that I was going to go with her.

'Why?' I asked. Paige came into the room and tried to pacify things, saying that these ladies were from social services and that although she'd explained I could stay with her, unfortunately there were rules and I had to go with them.

'But I don't understand,' I said repeatedly. Why couldn't I go home? Where was Mum?

'It's to do with some rumours,' the taller woman said. She introduced herself as Candice and said she'd be looking after me.

'I don't need looking after,' I said. 'I just want to go home. I'm really sorry I ran away. I should never have done that. It's my bad.'

But the two women just glanced at each other, as if silent words were being passed between the two of them.

'We're here to keep you safe,' Candice said.

'But I am safe.'

'I'm sorry, love,' Paige added. 'But you need to go with these ladies. There's no choice because you're underage.'

'I'm nearly sixteen,' I said, but apparently that didn't count. I looked at Taryn, appealing for her to say something, but she just shrugged, a frown on her forehead. She didn't understand any more than I did.

When Candice opened the rear door to a small silver car, I thought about running away, because I'm sure I could have outrun these two, but I reckoned I was already in enough trouble as it was. Besides, I stupidly left my mobile at home, worried that Mum was going to track me through it. If I'd known I was going to be reported to social services for running away, I would never have done it. Never.

We drove through town and into another town about twenty minutes away.

'I'm sorry if I've done something wrong,' I said when we stopped at some traffic lights.

'Sweetheart, you've done nothing wrong. We're here to protect you.'

For a moment I wondered if they were abducting me and if I was going to be tied up in some basement somewhere and held for a great big ransom. But I trust Paige, and I don't think she'd have let me go if she thought it was dodgy. We stopped in front of a Victorian brick house. It was large, double-fronted, with a black front door and overgrown grass at the front. Candice got out and opened the door for me. I climbed out of the car carrying my backpack. Candice leaned back into the car and said something to the other woman, who then drove away.

'Welcome to your new home for the next few days,'

Candice said, beckoning me to join her as she walked along the path.

'I don't understand why I'm here,' I said. My knees were knocking together and I wished I hadn't drunk that hot chocolate at Taryn's because now I felt sick.

'I'll explain everything when we're inside.' She smiled at me, but there was a pitying look in her black eyes that I didn't like.

The hallway was narrow, with lots of hooks on one wall, anoraks and coats hanging in different sizes. Rows of trainers and boots stood underneath. I could hear voices from further inside the house. She led me into a kind of living room with a bow window that looked out to the front. The sofas were shabby and there was a brown wooden table in the window and a bookshelf with leaflets on it, the type that you see in a doctor's surgery.

'Have a seat, love. Would you like a drink?'

'No, thanks,' I said. 'I just want to know why I'm here.'

'Of course you do. I can tell you're a bright young lady.' Her chair creaked when she sat in it. I sat as far away from her as I could.

'There have been some rumours that things might not be as safe at your home as they should be. That your mum and dad might have hurt you in the past.'

'But that's not true!' I exclaimed. 'It's horrible stuff that's completely untrue.'

She tilted her head at me and nodded slowly. 'When there are rumours like that, we have to investigate properly to make sure that young people are being kept safe, and that's why you're here. So my colleagues can investigate and in the meantime ensure you're well looked after.'

I shook my head vigorously. 'It's all a big misunderstanding. I had meningitis, was in hospital, it's not–'

She interrupted me. 'Look, love. You'll have plenty of time to tell all of this to the police and the psychologist. I'm just your assigned social worker. Have you got a mobile phone?'

'I left it at home.'

She hesitated for a moment. 'Can I have a quick look in your backpack?'

'You think I'm lying!' I exclaim.

'It's not in your best interests to have your devices today,' she says, before adding, 'This is for your own good, Marnie.'

Except it wasn't. It isn't. She held out her hand and I felt like swatting it away. I stared at it, her big, brown palm with deep lines, and I looked up at her and her kindly face. I remember once, years ago at junior school, when I got really angry with a friend who had told me that our teacher wanted to see me. I don't even remember what I did wrong. I'd shouted at her and reduced her to tears. Mum was called into school and she told me that I shouldn't shoot the messenger. I'm not sure I fully understood back then what she meant, but now I do. Candice isn't the person making up the rules here, she's just the messenger. Reluctantly, I hand over my backpack.

'Thanks, Marnie. If you keep your head down and do as you're told, things won't be so bad for you here.'

After that, a man appeared wearing a T-shirt advertising some band I'd never heard of, which is weird because I really know my music. He took me to a room which was going to be mine. It's a small room, narrow, with a single bed and a big pinboard on the wall that's covered with little lumps of old Blu Tack. There's a sink in here too and a wardrobe with two plastic coat hangers. It smells weird and has a bad feeling to it. I remember Taryn and me watching a YouTube video about Feng Shui and I'm pretty sure that this room is all wrong. Connie walked in a couple of minutes later and handed back my rucksack.

'Go and meet the others when you feel like it. There's a television room and kitchen downstairs, which you're welcome to use.' She gave me a sad smile, hesitated for a moment and then left.

YESTERDAY EVENING, I was starving, and I could hear voices in the dining room and the scent of cooking. I made my way downstairs.

The door was open and there was a bunch of kids seated around a huge table, I guess ranging in age from seven to sixteen. A girl with short hair and ripped skinny jeans was helping herself to food from dishes lined up on a side table.

'Hi,' I said, feeling awkward. She ignored me.

'Do I just help myself?' I asked.

'Ooo, do I just help myself?' she mocked me in a faux-posh accent. 'Up to you. Eat or starve. No one gives a shit.' She picked up her plate and headed back to the table. I did the same, sitting at the far end. The stew was disgusting and I barely touched it as I glanced up at them all whilst pretending not to look. Most of them have no table manners, talking with their mouths full and picking up food with their fingers.

The man who runs the place is called Jim and he pretends to be cool, but I don't think he really is. After supper, I went straight back to my bedroom. Thank goodness I had a few school books in my bag, along with my laptop, which I was surprised was still there. I'd expected Connie to confiscate it. Except then I realised why she didn't. I couldn't get online. There is Wi-Fi here but Jim said he couldn't give me the password. All the same, I wrote a long email to Mum and Dad, telling them how sorry I am for running away, and when I'm home I'll send it to them.

I didn't sleep much. The pillow is thin and lumpy and the sheets smell stale. There's a blind at the window but it's too transparent and the light from the streetlamps pours in. Instead, I sobbed for Mum for hours, the first time I've done that since I was about five years old. It's like I've been caught up in some alternative reality nightmare, and I think it's all because I ran away. I'm such an idiot. I don't belong here.

AND NOW IT'S morning and I'm eating a bowl of coco pops and a slice of white bread, trying not to catch anyone's eye. The mean girl keeps throwing me looks and I have to pretend I don't notice.

Jim appears in the doorway. 'Right, everyone. Time to get ready for school. The mini-bus will be out the front in ten minutes.'

I jump up, relieved to be able to get out of here, to get back to my normal life. Except Jim holds up his hand.

'Not you, Marnie. You won't be going to school today. You've got an appointment with Jemma.'

I don't know why, but I thought with the name Jemma, she'd be young. Except she's not. She looks almost as old as my gran and she's got grey hair with white strands in it and wears bright red glasses that she probably thinks look trendy but make her look absurd. We're sitting in another small room. There are two sagging armchairs and a coffee table between us that has a box of tissues on it, and a jug of water with two glasses. She offers me a Coke but I say no.

'Do you know why you're here, Marnie?' she asks me, crossing her legs. She's wearing really baggy trousers that look like a skirt and thick black boots that belong on the feet of someone half her age.

'Because there are some false rumours going around that Mum and Dad have abused me. It's not true.'

She stares at me through those glasses and scribbles something on a lined pad of paper.

'I'm a psychologist, Marnie, and I've been appointed by social services and the police. I'll be reporting back to them after our chat today. I specialise in talking to young people. Tell me why you think you're here.'

'I've already told you. Someone at school has spread rumours that I was abused and that my parents were investigated, except that's not true. I had meningitis and was in hospital and then had to recover at home. That's why I missed so much school. Surely you can check that with my doctor, can't you?'

'Yes, that's something we'll be double-checking. So why do you think these rumours were started?'

'I've no idea.' This woman is a complete idiot and she's really annoying me. 'You need to ask Mum or Dad that. It's nothing to do with me. I'm the victim here!' Immediately I wish I hadn't said that, because I'm not a victim. Not in the way she thinks I am.

'Do you understand what abuse is? Sexual abuse in particular?'

'I'm not an idiot!' I exclaim. 'I said I haven't been abused.'

'Repression and denial are perfectly normal responses to

trauma, Marnie. What we have to uncover is why you're reacting like this.'

I stare at the woman as if she's a fool, which she must be, because she's talking bullshit.

'Tell me what happened yesterday and the day before. What prompted you to run away from home?'

'I had an argument with Mum. Just a normal teenager argument because she didn't want me to go to a party and I went anyway. And then I discovered she'd known about the abuse rumours but hadn't told me, and I got really mad at her. We had a big argument and that night I decided to go to my friend Taryn's house. Her mum Paige is really cool and I knew she wouldn't sneak on me.'

'You seem to have thought this through very carefully, Marnie. You're an articulate young lady. So let's go back a bit further. What physical contact do you have with your parents? Are they the hugging types?'

I wonder if this is a trick question. 'Mum is, Dad less so. Anyway, Dad's been living in Manchester the last few weeks so he hasn't been around.'

'What's it been like having your dad living away?'

'Honestly, crap. Dad's fun and it's better when he's at home.'

'Better in what way?'

She's giving me a knowing look. I hesitate.

'Do you feel safe around your dad?'

And then I realise what she's asking me and it makes me want to puke.

'Are you asking if he touches me inappropriately, because if that is what you mean, then you've got it completely wrong. Dad is a good dad, he's never done anything disgusting, never.' I feel tears rising from the back of my throat.

'I'm glad to hear that, Marnie. And your mum? What's your relationship like with her?'

'You're gross!' I say, standing up now. 'How can you even think things like that? Mum and Dad are the best and I just want to go home.'

'Please sit down, Marnie. It's admirable that you want to protect your parents, but it's my job to make sure that your memories and feelings about your family are accurate. Sometimes when bad things happen, we repress those memories and replace them with happy memories to protect our own brains.'

'But that's not the case with me!' I say. This woman isn't listening. She's trying to impose a narrative on me that suits her. She must think I'm really thick. 'Why won't you let me go home?'

She rubs her eyes and looks at me with an expression of pity.

'We need to fully understand what has been going on first.'

'I hate it here,' I say. My throat feels raw and I want to cry, but not in front of this woman.

'I understand that. You won't be here for much longer. My colleagues are trying to find you a foster place until things are sorted out.'

'A foster place?' Orphans are sent to foster homes, aren't they? Or kids with druggies or convicts as parents, not people like me.

'Foster parents will look after you as an interim measure. They're lovely people who have been carefully vetted.'

'But I just want to be with my parents,' I say, quietly

now, because what's the point of wasting my breath on this woman?

She glances at her watch. It's plastic and white. 'Let's call it a day for now, Marnie, but we will talk again soon.'

'Can I go back to school?' I ask as I stand up.

'I'll have a word with my colleagues.' She smiles at me and it's such a fake, sickly sweet look, it makes me want to hit her. I scrunch my hands up into fists and turn away from her.

On the second day of my incarceration, I'm allowed to go to school. I don't go in the minibus with the other kids. Instead, Candice picks me up and gives me a little pep talk in the car.

'Now, I don't want you to listen to the rumours, Marnie. Just keep your head down and get on with your lessons. I'm going to have a little chat with the head teacher and your form teacher to explain what's going on.'

'Can you get my phone off Mum? I hid it under my pillow.'

'I'm afraid not. You might be tempted to borrow a friend's phone and call your parents, but I urge you not to. It could impede the investigation and mean that you're kept away from them for longer. I also suggest you don't go online. It's for your own benefit. Do you understand?'

I nodded, even though I didn't understand. Taryn will tell me what's going on anyway.

She accompanies me up the school path and I keep my head down because I know everyone is staring at me. At the entrance, I dart off in the opposite way to Candice and head for my locker. I pretend I don't hear the vile whispers, but I do.

Ryan and his pals saunter past me, sniggering, saying words like slut and paedo and daddy whore.

'Hey!' I jump as an arm snakes around my waist. 'It's only me.'

I've never been so pleased to see Taryn and I give her a huge hug. We rock together but then Ryan walks past us again and says, 'Lesbian sluts.' I bristle and pull away from Taryn.

'Don't let him get to you,' she says.

The bell goes and Taryn says, 'I've got to go but I'll catch you at lunch.' She gives me a wave and hurries away.

How I wish we were in the same classes.

The morning drags by. I try my hardest to ignore the whispers and to concentrate in class but I find my mind wandering and I spend most of the time doodling in my notebook. At the end of maths, during which I understood nothing, as normal, Miss Eisner beckons me over. I tense, waiting for her to tell me off for not completing my homework.

'How are you, Marnie?' she asks.

'Fine,' I say, crossing my arms.

'I heard you're not staying at home.'

I can't meet her eyes. This is so humiliating.

'You know you can talk to me, if you'd like.' There's warmth in her voice and I swallow hard.

'It's not true, what they're saying.' I look up at her and she's the very first adult who I think might believe me. 'They're making up stories about me and my parents and it's not fair. Will you help me?'

'Of course I will,' she says. 'Have you got any friends you can turn to?'

'Taryn. She's my best friend.'

'Well, I'm glad you've got someone.'

'Can you tell social services that they're making a huge mistake and that I think someone from school has been spreading false rumours about me? Or it might be Jax, a guy I met online, except I didn't tell the psychologist about him.'

'Why don't you come and see me after school, and I'll see what I can do to help?'

'Thank you,' I say with a watery smile. If she wasn't a teacher and an adult, I'd throw my arms around her.

At lunch, Taryn is waiting for me. She links her arm into mine and says in a low voice, 'Don't catch anyone's eye and only look at me. You need to ignore what they're saying.'

'Don't know what I'd do without you,' I murmur, and nudge my head into hers.

'Here come the lesbians!' Ryan's best friend Matt is dancing in front of us. 'Has your daddy turned you into a dyke, Marnie? Or has Taryn's butchness rubbed off?'

'Ignore him,' Taryn says through gritted teeth.

But I can't. 'Fuck off, Matt,' I say, but he just laughs and is joined by another few mates. My cheeks are flaming and I'm upset not just for me, but for Taryn too.

Eventually, we make it to the dining room and sit at a table as far away from anyone we know as possible.

'I'm sorry,' I say. 'For dragging you into this too. Sorry they called you a dyke.'

Taryn shrugs her shoulders. 'I don't mind. I'm gay and don't care who knows.' She pauses for a moment, a flush creeping up her neck. 'You know that I like you.'

I'm about to put a forkful of potato in my mouth and I let it hover mid-air. Taryn likes me *that* way?

'Have I shocked you?' Taryn asks. 'I mean, you're really pretty and you're my best friend.'

'I like you too,' I say, because I do, but not in a sexual way. 'The boys are all so horrible.'

'They're a bunch of pathetic dicks.' There's a knowing grin on her face.

CHAPTER TWENTY-FOUR

AMELIA

It's been the two longest days of my life. After our blazing row, Hudson stormed out, and I'm assuming he's back in Manchester in the arms of his lover, or perhaps he's in a hotel somewhere local to here. I don't care. I want a divorce. How can I ever trust him again? He had to speak to the police and probably social services too. Perhaps I shouldn't have told DC Singh that Hudson and I have split up, perhaps we should have sat down after the police had left and hammered things out, but I was too angry. And I still am.

I'm desperate to see Marnie, to listen to her loud music, to know that she's safe and happy. I simply can't fathom how these rumours have come about and why the police are giving them any credence. I'm sure they must have checked Marnie's health records by now and seen that she really did have meningitis and that any school absences were due to genuine ill health.

I feel completely futile, as if my life has disintegrated around me. My daughter has been taken, my marriage is over, this house will no doubt be repossessed, and I don't even have a job due to my reputation being in tatters. I don't think I've eaten a morsel for nearly three days and I'm only forcing myself to keep going because of Clover. But even the dog seems subdued, no doubt missing Marnie too and sensing my misery. With our cream-coloured carpets in the upstairs hallway and throughout the bedrooms, she's not allowed upstairs, but the past two nights, I've brought her bed into my bedroom and have been woken up early by her cold, wet nose.

When the doorbell rings shortly before 5 p.m., I wonder if I should answer it, but Clover is barking ferociously, so after the second ring, I walk despondently through the house and swing open the front door.

And there is Marnie. We literally throw ourselves at each other, hugging, wet tears mingling.

'Oh darling, I'm so happy to see you.'

'You too, Mum,' she says, eventually disentangling herself from me. 'I'm sorry.'

'You've got nothing to be sorry for.' I look her up and down but she seems unchanged except for the dark rings under her eyes. It's only then that I realise Connie Mattman is standing next to her.

'We've found nothing to substantiate the claims of abuse,' Connie says, a sheepish look on her face. I want to be angry with her, but Connie is only the spokesperson. 'I'm sure you understand that allegations as serious as these need to be properly investigated, but on a personal level, I'm sorry for the upset that it's caused your family.'

'Can I go now?' Marnie asks. Connie nods and Marnie slips past me into the hall where I can hear her talking to Clover.

'What are you going to do about finding out who started the false rumours?' I ask.

'I'm not sure what we can do,' Connie replies.

'But that's your job, isn't it? Surely the police need to investigate this?'

She squirms slightly. 'Regrettably, the police don't have the resources to investigate something like that. No actual crime has been committed.'

I stare at her in disbelief. Our lives have been decimated, yet nothing will be done about it.

'I'm sorry, Amelia. But I'm just glad that Marnie is home with you as quickly as she is. Sometimes these investigations can go on for months.'

I nod at her, because what else is there to say?

She throws me an awkward smile and turns to leave. I don't wait to watch her get back into her car, but shut the door and hurry into the kitchen where Marnie and Clover are sitting on the floor.

'Where's everything gone, Mum?' Marnie is frowning, her face contorted in confusion. 'The sofa, the paintings? What's going on? Has Dad taken the stuff to Manchester?'

'No. Dad has incurred a lot of debts and is close to bankruptcy. I'm afraid the bailiffs removed our belongings. We will probably have to move house too.'

I expect her to start crying, to be really upset, except she just shrugs. 'I'll be going off to uni in a couple of years anyway.'

Considering all the shocks that Marnie has faced the past few days, she takes it remarkably well.

AFTER MAKING Marnie her favourite supper – burgers and chips followed by ice-cream – we talk through everything that has happened over the past couple of days. She tells me how she walked through the night to Taryn's house, how Paige lied to me when I called her to ask if she knew where Marnie was, and how she eventually notified the police that Marnie was at her house when she realised that the police were involved in the search for Marnie. We discussed the horrible time she spent in the children's home. When we're all talked out, Marnie disappears upstairs to do her homework, and there's a relief in hearing her playing her loud music. I'm clearing up from supper, when Paige's white Polo pulls up on the drive. What the hell is she doing here? I debate ignoring her, but she'll be able to see the lights on in the windows, the old red Fiat parked to the side of the house.

I open the door before she rings the bell.

'Oh, Amelia!' she exclaims, throwing her arms around me. 'I've been so worried about Marnie and about you.'

I stiffen and take a step backwards. Paige stumbles slightly, reaching out for the doorframe to right herself.

'Taryn said that Marnie was at school today. Is she home yet?' she asks.

'Yes,' I say, crossing my arms in front of my chest.

'Goodness, what a relief. Can I come in?'

I widen my stance so I'm blocking her way in and Paige frowns.

'Why did you hide Marnie and then why did you call the police? If you'd told me the truth, that Marnie was at your house, none of the hell of the past two days would have happened. You must have known that I was completely frantic with worry, not knowing where my daughter was.'

'Oh, come on, it's hardly my fault,' Paige says. 'I was doing what I thought was right.'

'But Marnie was taken into care,' I exclaim. 'It was complete hell.'

'Marnie wanted me to hide her,' Paige says. There's a hardness to her face that I haven't seen before. 'And there were all those rumours circulating about you having abused her. You lost your job, after all. What was I meant to do? Hand her back to her abusers or make sure she was safely in the hands of the police? I did what I thought was best.'

I feel rage and injustice surging through me, making me narrow my eyes, wanting to lash out at the woman I thought was my friend. 'Do you really think I'm a child abuser?' I spit.

'Well, not now. Obviously. But–'

I cut her off. 'What kind of a friend could think that?'

'It's not like we know each other that well. I just wanted to do what's right. You're getting very agitated…'

'I'd like you to leave,' I say, my hand on the doorknob. 'The last couple of days have been sheer hell.'

She takes a step backwards and I close the door, but not before I hear her say, 'There's no smoke without fire.'

'Who was that?' Marnie is standing at the top of the stairs. She's changed into a pair of joggers and an old T-shirt and her hair is wet from the shower.

'It was Paige. I don't understand why she lied to me when I called her, when I asked if she'd seen you. And I don't understand why she reported us to the police. None of this would have happened if she'd acted like a normal person.'

'I think that's a bit unfair, Mum. I did ask if I could stay at her house and I was angry with you. I didn't want her to tell you I was there.'

'I'm sorry, Marnie. But I don't want you to be friends with Taryn any more, and I certainly don't want you going around to their house.'

Marnie stares at me with an expression of disbelief. 'But Taryn's my best friend. You can't tell me who I can and can't be friends with. I thought you were happy that I was home.'

'Of course I'm happy,' I say. 'I love you with all my heart and I'm just trying to protect you.'

She scowls at me, turns on her heel and disappears back into her bedroom, letting the door slam behind her. I walk slowly up the stairs and knock on her door. When she doesn't answer, I poke my head around the side of it. Marnie is seated on the bed, clutching her phone.

'You won't run away again, will you?' I ask

She rolls her eyes at me. 'Goodnight, Mum.'

I let Clover sleep in my room again.

CHAPTER TWENTY-FIVE

PAIGE

When the rage comes, there's little I can do to stop it. I have to let it out, to do something that will hurt someone else or myself. I would have taken a knife to Amelia's expensive Volvo except the only car parked in her driveway is a battered Fiat. I climb back into my car and dig my fingernails deep into the flesh of my thighs. It hurts, but not enough. How dare Amelia talk to me like that! To chuck me out of her house when I've only been kind to Marnie. I've been patient for a long time and although I've achieved some of my goals, things haven't moved fast enough. The gloves are coming off now. It's time for Amelia to suffer. Truly suffer.

I look in my car mirror at their lovely big house and I have a great idea. Tonight is going to be the night, and Amelia's last. Amelia mentioned that Marnie is home, so I suppose she might get caught up in my plans too. Taryn will be upset, but so be it. I'll be killing two birds with one stone, quite literally.

I'm impatient for nightfall. Taryn goes to bed, but I am much too wired. I change into all black. Black leggings, black trainers, a black hoodie. I wait until 1 a.m., and then sneak out of our house, tiptoeing quietly so that Taryn doesn't hear me leave. I've parked the car in the next street over so starting the car engine won't wake any of our direct neighbours. And then I'm on my way, a smile on my lips, feeling anticipation and happiness.

I've forgotten how nice it is to be out at night, with the empty roads and the cover of darkness concealing bad things. When I approach Amelia's road, I park up on the main street, turning my car so that it's pointing home, the tyres up on the pavement, the car almost hidden underneath the heavy branches of an oak tree. I sit for a while, taking deep breaths, making sure that no one passes me, thankful that the Myers live in the middle of nowhere, far from the gaze of nosey neighbours.

Slipping out of the car, I wait for my eyes to adjust to the low light. The moon is hazy but it is visible, and I walk along the side of the road before turning into the Myers' drive. The house looms in front of me, dark and full of shadows. I put my hand into my pocket, double-checking I have what I need, making sure that the ringtone of my phone is switched to silent. My feet make no noise on the wet grass and when I approach the house, I open the side gate, holding my breath, worried it might creak. It doesn't. Of course it doesn't. Everything is perfect in Amelia's life. I pad around the side of the house, crouching down underneath the living room windows, darting quickly as I pass in front of the patio doors. A security light comes on and I curse it under my breath. I stand completely still, barely breathing, waiting motionless until it switches off again. And then I'm at the back door, the keys I took from Marnie's bag when we were at the wedding dress shop clutched in my hand. I slide the first key into the lock but nothing happens. For a second I fear I might be thwarted, but then I try the second key, and it slips straight in. I'm smiling as I ease the door open. The idiots don't even bolt their doors at night.

Now is the point when my plan could fall apart. If Clover the dog starts barking or whimpering, she might wake the family up. Then I'd have to run. But Clover knows me and she's a stupid Labrador, led by her stomach. I have a bone in my hand, ready to placate the mutt. I turn my torch on and step inside the utility room. Then I stand completely still, listening. There is silence, just the ticking of a clock from further inside the house.

'Clover,' I whisper. There's nothing. No pitter-patter of paws. I swing the torch around and realise that her bed isn't in the corner of the utility room where it normally is. That's a relief. I suppose Hudson has taken her to Manchester.

I tiptoe through the utility room into the kitchen. It's not as pristine as it normally is. There are dirty plates in the sink and rings left by glasses on the wooden table. But I'm not interested in those. I turn the torch to the windows, making sure they're shut. I close all of the trickle vents and then, very carefully, open the kitchen door which leads into the hallway. Turning back to the oven, I marvel at Amelia's kitchen appliances. It's a big range oven with a six-ring hob on the top. One by one, I turn the handle of each knob so that the gas is on full, hissing noises coming from each. Then I step away and return the way I came. I'm glad that the dog isn't here; at least it won't get hurt when the house blows up. Very carefully and slowly, I close the back door and turn the key in the lock, making sure that it's properly closed and locked. With a wide smile, I walk back the way I came, this time ducking even lower, crouching almost to the ground to avoid setting off the security light. As I tiptoe back down their drive, I turn to look at the house again. I wonder how long it'll take for gas to fill the kitchen, to leak through into the hallway and upstairs. I would love to hang around here, to watch the devastating explosion as the house and everyone within it goes bang and all their belongings shoot high into the night sky. Except I don't know if that will happen in an hour or seven hours, when Amelia comes downstairs to make breakfast or while she's still asleep in her bed. Besides, it would be catastrophic if I was seen anywhere near the Myers' house.

With regret, I stride back to my car, start the engine and return home. I intend to check the local news every hour, so I doubt I'll be getting much sleep tonight. But that's a small price to pay.

CHAPTER TWENTY-SIX

AMELIA

It feels like I have only just dropped off to sleep when something awakens me. There's a faint light coming through the curtains but the birds aren't singing yet, so I assume it's shortly before dawn. I groan. And then I hear a weird scratching noise. I switch on my bedside light and realise it's Clover. She's at my bedroom door, pawing it.

'What are you doing?' I ask.

She turns her head around to look at me but continues to paw at the door.

'Stop that,' I say, with a harsh note to my voice. I don't want scratch marks on the paintwork. Except Clover isn't giving up. I slide my legs from under the duvet and pull on a jumper over my pyjama top, slipping my feet into my sheepskin slippers. It's unlike Clover to need to go out in the middle of the night. She always impresses me with her excellent bladder control. Clover gives a little woof as if to hurry me along.

'Shush,' I say, not wanting her to waken Marnie. I open my bedroom door and Clover scoots out into the corridor, running straight into Marnie's arms, who's wearing an oversized T-shirt and bare legs.

'What are you doing up?' I ask.

'Clover woke me. She was scratching your bedroom door like crazy and then she barked.'

'I'm sorry, love. I think I only drifted off about an hour ago so I must have been in a deep sleep.'

'It's alright. I'll take her out.' Marnie buries her face in Clover's soft neck. 'Come on, you silly billy. How come she's sleeping in your room anyway? You never let her sleep in mine.'

I laugh. 'I was feeling a bit lonely.' I stand up and stretch, looking at my watch. 'It's only 5.40 a.m. Will you go back to sleep for a bit after you've let her out?'

'Yes. I'm just happy to be home.' Marnie stands up and, barefoot, starts walking down the stairs, Clover right at her heels.

It's only then that I notice a strange smell. I sniff harder. The grogginess of sleep and sheer emotional exhaustion is stopping my brain from working properly. I go down a few steps and then it hits me.

That's the smell of gas.

And before I know it, I'm hurtling down the stairs just as Marnie puts her hand over the light switch in the downstairs hall.

'Stop!' I shout. Marnie swings around to face me, her hand falling to her side.

'What's the matter, Mum?'

'That smell. It's gas.'

Marnie sniffs. 'Oh yeah, it's gross. Don't know why I didn't notice it before.'

'Go outside, now,' I say, my voice quivering. 'Immediately.'

Marnie looks at me with big, scared eyes. She's got her hand on Clover's collar. 'Are you coming?'

'Just go, Marnie!'

As Marnie opens the front door, I hurtle around the corner into the kitchen and almost gag. I squeeze my nose and put the palm of my other hand over my mouth. The room is full of gas. I race to the hob and realise that every single knob is turned on, gas billowing out, filling the space. Trying not to inhale, I turn each one off and then run out of the kitchen. My head feels like it's going to explode, and then I realise that there's a possibility that the house might blow up. I've seen the devastating after-effects of domestic gas explosions on the news.

Grabbing the house phone from the console table in the hall, I race out of the open front door. Clover is sniffing around the flower bed and Marnie is standing next to her, too close to the house.

'Go to the end of the drive,' I say.

'But it's only gas!' Marnie frowns. She clearly has no idea of the implications.

'Run,' I say, and watch as Marnie grabs Clover's collar and, in a crouch, runs barefoot across the grass.

I know from experience that I can't get reception for the landline phone down the drive, so I jab in 999.

'We've got a huge gas leak,' I say when the operator asks which emergency service we need. 'Fire brigade, I suppose.' After establishing that the gas was due to the hob levers being left open and not an actual gas leak, which would require the gas board to come out, the operator asks for my name, address and telephone number. He then promises to dispatch a fire engine as quickly as possible. I'm feeling nauseous now, with a headache so severe it feels like my head might split open.

'Should I go back into the house to open the doors and windows?' I ask.

'No, it's safer that you stay away from the house. The fire officers will take care of that.'

We end the call and I hurry towards Marnie, who is crouched down at the end of the drive. She's shivering, and I realise that I'm freezing too. The morning is cold, and we're both outside, with barely any clothes on. Marnie is barefoot.

'Let's huddle together,' I say, wrapping my arms around her. For once, she doesn't pull away.

'What happened?'

'All the knobs were turned on on the gas hob. Did you use it last night?'

Marnie knots her eyebrows together. 'No. I didn't do any cooking. Of course not. It must have been you.'

I'm quiet. I think back to last night. I made us supper, Paige turned up, but I didn't let her into the house. I argued with Marnie but she was in her bedroom. I went to bed early, taking Clover with me. I didn't even clean up the kitchen properly. We ate burgers and chips which I made in the oven, and I only used one of the gas rings to heat up water for peas. There's no way I used all six gas rings. And even when I'm most exhausted, I wouldn't have left the gas on. It doesn't make any sense.

It's not long before we hear the sound of sirens. We stand up, still clutching each other and shivering as the fire engine turns into our drive.

'Stay here, sweetheart. I'll go and talk to them.'

Four fire officers jump down from the truck, fixing masks

to their faces. Three of them rush in through the open front door, and even from here, I can smell the gas.

'What happened?' The officer is dressed in uniform, but he has a kindly face, conker-brown hair poking from under his helmet, and deeply creased eyes.

'All of the knobs were left on on the hob and the house is full of gas,' I explain.

'Right. Stay away from the house, please, and we'll double-check everything and open all the windows and doors. Where are the keys?'

'Hanging up behind the utility room door.'

He nods at me and hurries inside.

Five minutes later, he returns. 'We've opened everything up and double-checked that the gas is off. The trickle vents on your windows were closed. Do you normally have them closed?'

I frown. We always have them open to let fresh air into the house. 'No.'

'Who else has been in the property other than you and your daughter?'

'No one,' I say.

'The doors were locked and all the windows were properly closed. Could anyone else have come in during the night?'

I frown. 'The only person who has a key to the house is my husband.'

'And where is he?'

'I think he's in Manchester.'

The officer frowns.

'He's not in Manchester,' Marnie says. 'He's staying at Uncle Bill's house. I'm going to call him to come and get me.'

I want to stop Marnie from ringing him, wondering if

Hudson could have entered the house and turned on the gas. If he thought I was alone in the house, would he have done that? He may be a liar but would Hudson really do that?

'Does Dad know that you're back home?' I ask Marnie.

'Yeah. I was messaging him last night.'

The fire officer looks confused but I'm not going to start explaining the horror of the last few days to him. If Hudson knew that Marnie was at home, there is absolutely no way that he would put her life at risk. My life, maybe, but Marnie's certainly not. Marnie looks at the phone which I'm still holding.

'Can I use that?'

I hand it to her and she walks away from me, still holding onto Clover. 'Hey, Dad,' I hear her say. 'Yeah, I know it's early. Can you come and get me?'

The other fire officers come out of the house and one of them walks over to where I'm standing with his colleague, my arms clutched tightly around my torso. 'All safe to go back inside now,' he says. 'But you need to be more careful with the gas.'

'I didn't leave it on,' I say.

'So what happened? We didn't find a leak.'

'The knobs were all turned on on the hob.'

'So someone turned them on?' he asks. 'Your daughter? A teenage prank? Anyone else living with you? An elderly person perhaps?'

'No.' I shake my head vigorously. 'It's just Marnie and me.'

'No memory lapses or anything?' I see where he's going with this conversation, wondering perhaps if I've got early onset dementia.

'No. I think someone did it deliberately.'

The two officers glance at each other and a look passes between them.

'We didn't see any sign of a break-in, but perhaps you'd like to have a look yourself. See if anything is out of place. We found all the external doors and windows locked.'

'I'll walk around,' I say. The senior officer accompanies me whilst the others lean against the fire truck, talking quietly between themselves.

We walk in through the open front door. I grab a coat from the hall cupboard to try to warm up and stop my violent shivering. Together, we stride around the whole house and nothing seems out of place. There are no broken windows. Everything is exactly where I would expect it to be. Everything except the trickle vents that apparently were closed, and the gas burners that were switched on. It doesn't make sense, and that prickle of unease crawls across my skin.

As I look out of the window, I see that Hudson has arrived. He's fully dressed, unlike Marnie and me, and after kissing Marnie on the forehead he's pacing towards the house.

'If you think this was a deliberate act, would you like us to call the police and report it as a crime?' the officer asks.

Suddenly, I feel an utter exhaustion, the lack of sleep, the shock, the emotions of the past few days, all walloping me. My brain feels like it's in a fog and my limbs are so heavy, I'm not sure I can muster the energy to walk. He's staring at me, waiting for an answer, just as Hudson appears alongside us. 'I'll decide later in the morning,' I say. 'I don't want to take up any more of your time.' I also don't want to have an argument with Hudson in front of the fire officers.

He nods, tells me to take care, and they all get back into the truck.

'WHAT THE HELL HAPPENED?' Hudson asks, as I watch the fire engine reverse out of our drive. And then it hits me. Hudson is staying nearby. He has a key. He wants custody of Marnie, and an insurance claim on the house would solve all of his money problems. On top of that, Clover didn't bark, so it can't have been a stranger entering our house at night. It must have been Hudson. But then I change my mind. No, it can't have been Hudson. He knew Marnie was staying here and he would never hurt her.

'What happened, Amelia?' Hudson is shouting at me now.

'We had a gas leak,' I say.

'So why aren't the gas board here, fixing it?'

Marnie is giving me a strange look and I realise I'm not going to be able to keep this from Hudson. 'Someone turned the gas hob on full.'

'Someone? You mean you did!' he exclaims, clenching and unclenching his fists.

'I didn't, and Marnie didn't,' I say, quietly.

'So a ghost did it, did they, or perhaps you're going to blame it on the dog? You are so bloody irresponsible, Amelia. First Marnie runs away from you and now you leave the gas on overnight. And you're blaming me for screwing up!'

'Stop it!' Marnie says. There are tears welling in her eyes. 'Please, stop arguing, both of you.'

Hudson's jaw is sticking forward, his knuckles white at his sides. 'Go and get your stuff, Marnie. We're leaving.'

'No, please,' I say.

Except Marnie is already running up the stairs, Clover at her heels.

Hudson shakes his head at me as if in exasperation and stalks back to his car. He opens the driver's door, climbs inside and slams the door shut. I watch as he leans his head back against the headrest and closes his eyes. How could I have loved this man? Now all I feel is fury and hate. I turn at the sound of footsteps. Marnie is running down the stairs, her clothes pulled on rather haphazardly, her rucksack flung over a shoulder.

'You don't have to go,' I say, lamely.

'See you later, Mum,' she says and edges out of the door before running towards her father's car. It isn't until they've pulled away that I realise that Hudson's Mercedes wasn't repossessed, just my Volvo. Did he plan that?

CHAPTER TWENTY-SEVEN

MARNIE

It was nice to have breakfast at Uncle Bill's with Dad. He's got a much younger wife called Po, a Thai lady who barely speaks any English. But she made us all a delicious meal full of sweet stuff that Mum doesn't let me have in the mornings. And I'm relieved that Dad dropped me off at school. He told me to message him if I need him to collect me later.

I spot Taryn walking ahead of me, so I run to catch her up. There is no way that I'm going to drop my best friend just because Mum tells me to.

'Hiya. You're not going to believe what happened early this morning!'

I tell Taryn all about the gas leak and the fire brigade, and how Mum is completely losing it. I mean, who in their right mind switches on all the knobs on the hob – and it has to be her because it most definitely wasn't me. And if, as the fire officers said, the house was all locked up from the inside, it has to be Mum. I'm wittering away, still on a bit of a high from the excitement of it all, so it takes me a while to realise that Taryn isn't being her normal chatty self.

'Hey, what's up?' I ask, noting her rounded shoulders and glum face.

'My mum is losing it too. When Dean was around it was bearable because he was so level-headed and he told her to shut up, but without him, she's like this crazy whirlwind of highs and lows. It's really doing my head in.'

'What is it with our mums?' I ask. But we don't get the chance to discuss it further because the bell rings.

'I've got an idea,' Taryn says. 'Are you free after school?'

'I can be,' I say. I'll tell Dad that I'm with Mum and Mum that I'm with Dad. As they're not speaking to each other, I should be able to get away with it.

'Alright. Catch you later.'

Miss Eisner asks me to go and see her after lunch, so I don't have the chance to catch up with Taryn. Miss Eisner seems to know that I'm back with Mum and that the investigation was dropped, and I wonder if she had something to do with sorting the situation. I promise myself I'm going to try harder at maths because she's such a nice teacher. Anyway, she gives me forty minutes of one-to-one tuition and I think at long last, I actually understand some of the concepts.

As agreed, Taryn is waiting for me after school.

'So what are we doing?' I ask.

'I've been investigating Dean's disappearance and I've found out the last place he was working at. I'm going to go there and see if I can find him. Will you come with me?'

'But he's been gone for ages. He won't still be there, will he?'

She pulls a face. 'He might be camping out there for all I know.'

This isn't the exciting adventure that I thought we might be having but I'll be there for Taryn if she needs me.

'The thing is, he would never have just left me, not after Jasper died. Dean always treated me like his real daughter even though I wasn't.'

'Who's Jasper?' I ask.

'He was my little brother. My half-brother. Mum and Dean's son.'

I come to a halt on the school path and get bashed into by some younger kids. Hurrying to catch up with Taryn, I say, feeling shocked, 'I didn't know you had a brother.'

'I did mention him to you, but you probably forgot.'

I try to rack my brains to remember but if she did, it must have been shortly after we met because I really don't remember. There are no photos of him at Taryn's house and she and her mum have never mentioned him since. That's weird, isn't it? 'Where is he now?' I ask.

Taryn sighs as she shuffles her rucksack higher on her back. We turn out of the school gate and onto the pavement, surrounded by hundreds of other kids. 'He got sick and died in hospital.'

'God, that's terrible,' I say.

'The thing is, Dean was my dad, and even more so after Jasper died. I really can't believe he would have upped sticks and left me. If he was okay, Dean would make contact, even if he didn't want to be with Mum. I know it.'

'And Jasper? How old was he when he died?'

'Six. But I don't want to talk about it, alright?'

'Okay,' I say, although I really, really want to know more. 'Where are we going then?'

'Dean was working in a derelict factory on the edge of town, a place that's going to be pulled down and rebuilt for houses. We'll need to take the bus.'

'Alright,' I say, although I'm feeling a little bit uneasy.

I've already sent Mum a message to say I'm with Dad and I sent Dad a message that I'm with Mum. They both messaged back with acknowledgements, although Mum said, 'I hope he'll bring you home later.' I didn't reply.

We walk down the road to the nearest bus stop. Taryn has worked out which one we need to get. I'm not happy that there are a bunch of kids from school there, waiting too. I spot Ryan, who has his arm around Olivia. My heart sinks.

'Here come the lesbos,' he says. Olivia sniggers and I hate her for it. And then Taryn reaches up and places her hand across the back of my head, bringing my head down to meet hers, and she actually kisses me, her lips smashing against mine. I'm in such shock that I don't pull away immediately and, to my dismay, feel her tongue probing my closed lips.

There are loud whoops, claps and laughter and I feel shame and disgust pass through me. I tug away from Taryn, wiping my mouth with the back of my hand. She turns around to Ryan and sticks a middle finger up at him, while I just want to disappear into the ground. To my huge relief, the bus arrives, noisy and belching fumes. I let the others climb onto it first, but Taryn grasps my hand and pulls me behind her. What was she thinking? I'm not gay. I like Taryn, but as a friend only.

We take the last two seats, which are near the front of the bus. I find myself edging away a little from Taryn. I don't want to hurt her feelings, but when we talked about being gay, I didn't actually mean it.

'Enjoy the kiss?' she asks, giving me a nudge in the ribs.

I don't know what to say and just sit there, feeling a blush creep up my neck.

'Only joking, Marnie. I know you're not gay really, but if you ever decide you want to be with a girl, I'm ready and waiting.'

'Sorry, it's just—' I bluster.'

'It's fine, really.'

We sit in silence for the next fifteen minutes, during which time Ryan and Olivia get off the bus, and I turn my head the other direction to avoid them. Taryn types rapidly into her phone, as she always does when she has free time.

'Next stop is ours,' Taryn says.

I have literally no idea where we are. It's a part of Beacham I've never been to, full of industrial units, big metal buildings with articulated lorries parked up front. But Taryn seems confident, so I follow her off the bus. She's looking at her phone. 'It's somewhere up here,' she says. We walk for what seems like ages, past business parks that have closed up for the evening, past an open area of scrub where a feral cat jumps in front of us and scares the living daylights out of me. And then further still, I see a cluster of falling-down buildings. They're brick with lots of windows, most of which are broken.

'This place gives me the creeps,' I say.

'Yeah, me too. Thanks for coming with me.'

There are hoardings up alongside the road with lots of signs saying, 'Danger. Do not enter,' and 'Trespassers will be prosecuted'. We don't belong here and I feel my heart thumping in my chest.

'Don't be scared,' Taryn says, as if she can sense my nervousness. 'There won't be anyone here. Dean was disconnecting the pipes before this place is demolished.'

'How do you know?' I ask.

'I looked through his notebook and his order book. He listed all the work he was doing. He was good like that, organised.'

Taryn finds a place in the metal fence that isn't attached properly to a post and it looks like it's been pulled back slightly. She wrenches the metal back, creating a hole just large enough to take a small human body. 'Go through,' she says.

I hesitate. It's tight and it's obvious that we're trespassing. I glance around but there's nobody in sight. Even the birds and the airplanes seem quiet out here. I shove my backpack through first and then wriggle under the fence, scratching my hand.

'Hold it up for me,' Taryn says.

I do as she asks and she's quickly by my side.

'Do you know where to go?' I ask, looking around at the derelict building, wooden pallets left discarded along with plastic rubbish bins lying on their sides. There are dandelions everywhere, poking up alongside piles of bricks.

'I think so. Follow me.'

I feel so exposed here and glance around from side to side as we hurry across the scrub to a large tarmac area, now full of potholes and more self-seeded weeds. What if there's a caretaker or someone and we get arrested for trespassing? I've already been in trouble with the police and I'm terrified of doing something wrong again.

Taryn is running now, surprisingly fast and light on her feet, and I'm panting as I try to keep up with her. And then we reach the side of the building and she slows down. 'I think the door is over there,' she says.

'How are we going to get in if it's locked?' I ask.

She reaches into her rucksack and produces a hammer.

'Shit, Taryn!' I say, both scared and a little in awe.

'I took it from Dean's toolkit.'

She's right, and there is a door, but Taryn doesn't need to use the hammer. Blue paint is peeling off it, and a padlock hangs loosely, the door ajar by a couple of inches. She curls her fingers around the side of it, and the door opens with a loud groan. If I was scared before, I'm terrified now. This place completely creeps me out. I follow Taryn inside and into a huge open space. Other than some old oil drums, there's nothing in here. She swivels around and points towards a concrete staircase.

'Dean!' she yells. Her voice bounces off the walls, echoing in this cavernous space. 'Dean, are you here?'

I'm thinking that this is a wild goose chase. Of course Dean isn't going to be here, living in this derelict wreck. Why would he have to? He's a plumber and Dad is always saying that plumbers are never out of work. He'll be able to afford to rent a flat or even stay in a hotel somewhere. But before I can say any more, Taryn is jogging up the concrete staircase and there's no way I want to be left down here by myself. I follow at her heels.

On the next floor, there's a corridor and a few rooms coming off it. The rooms are small, probably used as offices, and other than some broken plastic and metal chairs, they're empty. Taryn stops and takes her phone out of her jacket pocket. 'He was working in the northeast corner of the building,' she murmurs. And then opens a compass app on her phone. I wouldn't have a clue how to use it, but Taryn knows. She points. 'That way.'

Ahead of us is a space where the floorboards have been lifted, exposing old, rusty pipes. Taryn walks carefully, navigating the planks, sticking her arms out for balance, hopping from one floorboard to the next. I don't follow her. My sense of balance is rubbish and I'm scared of falling and hurting myself. But then I catch the whiff of a putrid, sickening smell that makes me want to gag.

And Taryn screams.

CHAPTER TWENTY-EIGHT

AMELIA

I get Marnie's message saying she's going to be staying with Hudson at Uncle Bill's place. Initially, I'm furious. Hudson thinks he can just swoop in and act the caring father when in reality he's ruined Marnie and my lives. And then there's the fact that I don't trust him. Could he really have turned the gas on? If so, Marnie isn't safe with him. After mulling it over for a while, I send Hudson a message.

> I'd be grateful if you could bring Marnie home. I've made her supper.

I remember his words, how he promised to fight me for custody, and perhaps this is the beginning of that game, our daughter the football that we're going to kick between us. At least she's nearly sixteen, so she'll be able to choose which parent she wants to live with. My heart aches at the possibility she might choose Hudson.

A moment later, Hudson texts me back.

> She's not with me. She messaged to say that you were collecting her from school and she'd be staying with you tonight. Everything ok?

No. Everything is not okay. Firstly, Marnie is playing Hudson and me off against each other. I glance at my watch. She'll have been out of school for about thirty minutes and she could be anywhere. Has she run away again? A shiver runs through me, like a premonition, the sensation that something is wrong. That this is more than just a teenage prank or a harmless playing one parent off against the other, more than a silly running away from home. Marnie was so shaken up by having to spend time in the children's home, I really doubt she'll run away again. I pace the house for a couple of minutes and then remember the tracking app that Paige suggested I install on Marnie's phone. It takes me long seconds to remember what the app is called and to open it up. But then I see a little figure on a map. It doesn't make sense. Marnie – or at least Marnie's phone – is in an industrial park on the edge of town.

I try calling her, but it goes to voicemail. 'Please call me, Marnie,' I say, unable to conceal the panic in my voice. What the hell is Marnie doing there? I go onto Google Maps and navigate to where she is, and then bring up the 3D imagery. She's in a building that looks as if the address is 2, Foundry North Lane. I can't work out what the building is, so I search for the address. There's been a few articles written about it, locals in uproar about the proposed demolition and rebuilding of 120 houses. Angry comments online about understanding the need for housing but where are the schools, the hospitals, the doctors' surgeries to support the new development? What is Marnie doing in a building that is due to be pulled down? I think of raves, hundreds of drunk and high young people pushing drugs, forcing her to do goodness knows what. But it's late afternoon on a weekday. Do raves happen at such a time? And after what happened at Olivia's party, which I still haven't got to the bottom of, and how she was running away, would Marnie really be attending a rave?

And then I wonder whom she's with. Taryn. She must be with Taryn, which is why she's not answering my calls. The last person I want to speak to is Paige, but I decide I'll have to grit my teeth and do it. After trying Marnie again, I let out a puff of air and dial Paige's number.

'Hello, Amelia,' she says brightly, as if we didn't have a row the last time we spoke and I didn't tell her to never contact us again. 'This is a surprise.'

'Hello,' I say tightly. 'Is Marnie with Taryn?'

'I don't know. Taryn isn't home. To be fair, I was actually wondering where she was.'

'I've used the app you suggested I put on Marnie's phone and I can see she's in a warehouse at 2 Foundry North Lane.'

There's a very long pause and I wonder if Paige is still on the line.

'Are you there?' I ask.

'Hold on,' Paige says eventually. 'I'll check the app too.'

I can hear her heavy breathing in the background and then she's back on the line. 'Yes. Taryn is also there.'

'Do you have any idea why?' I ask. 'Could it be the venue for a rave or an illegal party?'

Paige snorts. 'Taryn doesn't go to things like that. Can't even get the little madam to have a glass of wine.'

I'm a bit taken aback by the bitterness in Paige's voice.

'I'm going to head over there now,' I say.

'I'll go too. Do you want me to pick you up?' she asks.

'No. We're coming from opposite sides of town. Let's meet there.'

Paige hangs up.

I drive like a lunatic, which is hard in the little Fiat, although it does enable me to nip in and out of tight spaces. I wouldn't be surprised if I get a speeding ticket; another expense we can't afford. Using the sat nav on my phone, I get to Foundry North Lane in precisely twelve minutes. Using the tracking app, I can see that Marnie is inside the building. In the northeast corner. She's moving, and then she's static. I pull up in front of a barrier to the building and park the car. I duck underneath the barrier and run full pelt across a potholed carpark towards a blue door. I had assumed I might see young people milling about, spliffs in their hands, beer bottles scattered across the ground, but the place is like a mausoleum. It's completely empty, eerily quiet, and there are no cars or other vehicles. Not even Paige.

The blue door is slightly ajar, so I heave it open and step inside the building.

'Marnie!' I shout. I walk into the large empty space and my voice echoes as I call her name again. But then I hear something coming from upstairs. I glance around and run up the concrete staircase taking two steps at a time.

'Marnie!' I shout, and this time I'm sure I can hear a high-pitched wail. I race along the corridor and skid into an open space.

'I'm here!' I say.

Marnie and Taryn are crouched over, their arms around each other, sobbing. What the hell? I hurry towards them but lose my footing, my right foot slipping into the recess where a floorboard once lay. I tug my leg out, ignoring the pain in my ankle, and hobble towards the girls.

'What's happened?' I ask, trying to keep my voice level and my panic concealed. 'What are you doing here?'

Taryn is crying so loudly, her body is shaking, but it's when Marnie looks up at me, her eyes wide, her cheeks the colour of parchment paper, that my stomach feels like it's tumbling away. 'Over there, Mum,' she whispers, one arm still around Taryn, the other hand pointing, but she's not looking, instead keeping her eyes on me, imploring. I step forward and that's when I see it.

The body of a man, lying face down, legs at a strange angle and black sludge all around him. The stench is overwhelming. I step backwards, once again losing my footing and letting out an involuntary moan.

'It's Dean,' Taryn sobs.

'We need to get out of here, girls. Now. I'll call the police.' I hold my hands out, ready to reach them, except I'm startled by a voice coming from behind me.

'What's going on?' Paige asks. I turn to look at her, as she strides a lot more nimbly over the broken floorboards than I did. And then Taryn has disentangled herself from Marnie's arms and she's jumped up, her face red and tear-stained, and she's jabbing her finger at Paige.

'You did this, didn't you? You killed Dean and just left him here to rot!' Taryn cries.

Marnie freezes. We both turn to look at Paige and that's when I realise that Taryn is telling the truth. Paige actually smiles. It's not a wide smile, but sardonic, as if she's pleased that her daughter has finally come to the conclusion that she's known all along. Except her words don't match the expression on her face. 'Don't be silly, Taryn. What are you talking about?'

Paige carries on walking towards us. Taryn runs towards her mother, except she loses her footing and falls to her knees. 'You did it, didn't you?' she shouts, tears pouring down her cheeks.

Paige stops still and shakes her head. 'Some things are for the best.'

I catch Marnie's eye and beckon for her to come to me. Except Paige is too quick. It happens so quickly. Taryn is trying to get up. Marnie darts towards me but somehow Paige manages to grab Marnie, her arm circling her neck, tugging Marnie backwards. Marnie screams.

'Shut up!' Paige shouts.

'Stop it, Mum. Stop it!' Taryn cries.

It takes me a long moment to absorb what is happening. What has happened. That Paige is admitting that she killed Dean.

'Why are you holding Marnie?' I ask. I'm trembling from head to toe, uncomprehending. 'You need to let her go.'

Taryn is still on the ground, rubbing her ankle.

'Because I want you to suffer in the way that I did.'

It's then that I see the glint of a knife in Paige's hand and my stomach clenches so badly, I double over. 'I don't understand,' I say, pulling myself back into an upright position, frantically looking around for something, anything that I might be able to defend us with.

'Because you're a fool, Amelia Myers. Jasper died because of you and now I'm going to take your child so you know what it feels like.'

'No, Mum! You're being crazy. It wasn't like that. It was

just one of those things,' Taryn yells as she gets up from the filthy floor.

'Shut up, Taryn. I don't want to have to hurt you too.'

'I don't understand.' My voice sounds so distant and unfamiliar. 'Who's Jasper?'

Marnie starts struggling, but Paige brings the knife up to her face, the blade glinting in the low light.

'Stay still, Marnie,' I say.

'Jasper was only six,' Paige says, her voice quiet now. 'My little boy, just six years old, who died in hospital with meningitis the same day that Marnie was brought in. We were all in the waiting room together, but you don't remember us, do you, Amelia? You were so self-centred, focused on your little darling, you didn't give a moment's thought to the suffering of anyone else. The doctors saved Marnie, but our Jasper died.' She positions the point of the knife on Marnie's neck. 'Here you are, no hint of any effects of the disease, taking your life for granted.'

'Mum, it's not like that.' Taryn's voice has an edge of desperation. She takes a cautious step towards her mother.

Paige waves the knife in the air and Marnie flinches.

'Jasper died because you have money and we don't. Hudson was all indignant, boasting how you had private health insurance, demanding that Marnie be treated right away. That she get the very best medicines the hospital had to offer. If they hadn't put all their resources into saving Marnie's life, then my beautiful boy would be alive today.'

Taryn is moving towards Paige and Marnie now, wobbling slightly, the palms of her hands straight out in front of her. 'Come on, Mum. That's not true. You didn't take Jasper to the hospital soon enough. If you'd acted faster, when we knew he had a high temperature and that rash started to show, he might have survived.'

'No!' Paige yells. Her eyes are flashing and there's spittle at the edges of her lips. 'Shut the fuck up, Taryn.'

'Please, Paige,' I say. I know I need to stay calm for Marnie's sake, but all I want to do is run towards her, take my daughter in my arms, exchange her life for mine. 'I'm so sorry that your son died, but it's not our fault.'

'Of course it is! You and your entitled ways. I'm going to prison anyway for killing Dean so I'm going to make it worthwhile. Marnie can die too and then you will suffer for the rest of your life like I have. I want you to know the pain of losing your child, the desperation in every waking moment that you'll never see him again.'

Out of the corner of my eye, I see Taryn moving slowly. Ever so slowly. Stealthily, like a cat treading carefully, moving so that she's behind her mother. Paige's eyes are flashing, her face contorted so that I barely recognise her.

'Say goodbye to your daughter, Amelia,' she says, baring her teeth like a wild animal. She lifts the knife up into the air and I see with horror the serrated edge, the size of the thing. Our screams all mingle together. Mine. Marnie's. Paige's and then, in a flash, Taryn is behind her mother and she brings something down on her head. It's only as Paige falls and loosens her grip on Marnie, and when Marnie throws herself at me, that I realise Taryn is holding a hammer. A hammer that she has just used to bring down on her mother's head.

CHAPTER TWENTY-NINE

MARNIE - FOUR MONTHS LATER

'How did the exam go?' Taryn asks me. We're walking down the school path. Mum will be waiting in the car on the next road over.

'As badly as expected.' I grimace.

'That's not going to reflect very well on me or Miss Eisner, so I hope you're wrong.'

To be fair, the maths GCSE paper wasn't as tough as I feared it would be. Hopefully I'll pass. Taryn on the other hand sat the Further Maths exam because she's so clever. I've no doubt that she'll get eights and nines across the board.

It seems like much longer ago than four months, except that's all it is since Paige tried to kill me. She's in prison now, waiting for her trial. When she hit her mother with the hammer, Taryn gave her concussion but there wasn't any lasting damage. Paige is denying killing Dean but she's also being accused of trying to murder me. That charge might be reduced to manslaughter, but we're waiting to see. The police explained to me and Mum that the justice system goes so slowly, goodness knows when she'll actually be brought to court. The trouble is, the case against her isn't that strong. The police haven't found the weapon she used to kill Dean with, and without it, well, it might just be circumstantial. I'm terrified that she could be let off and that Paige might come after me again in the future. But for now, I can sleep because she's banged up.

Social services got involved again because Taryn had no one to live with. But as she's sixteen, she was able to choose where she wanted to go. With no grandparents and Dean's brother living in France – who isn't her relative anyway – she was due to be sent to a young person's home. Taryn doesn't deserve that, so when I asked Mum if she could come and live with us, Mum said yes, if that's what Taryn wanted. And Taryn did want to come to ours.

Mum and Dad are still barely talking and I think they're going to get divorced. They're trying to work out their finances but Mum has warned me that they'll be selling our house. I don't mind. Not really.

'How are my girls?' Mum asks as we get into the car. Taryn grins widely. To be honest, it's beginning to grate a bit on me. I know Mum is trying to over-compensate because she feels sorry for Taryn, but honestly, she's the golden girl now. Taryn has already chosen her A Level subjects: Maths, Further Maths, Physics, Biology and English. Five A levels. It's crazy. I'm not even sure I'll be allowed to take three. I read somewhere that the side-effects of meningitis might have affected my brain and its development, but I don't really think that's got anything to do with it. It's simple: Taryn is super-clever and I'm not. When Mum went to talk to the teachers about Taryn, they said that she's Oxbridge material and is likely to be fast-tracked. Mum seemed so proud of her, I had to remind her that Taryn isn't actually her daughter.

'Would you like me to help cook supper tonight?' Taryn asks. She's sitting in the front seat next to Mum, while I'm relegated to the back. I wish Taryn would stop sucking up so much. I made a sarcastic comment about her the other night and Mum chastised me, saying that it's probably the first time that Taryn has been living in a functional family. I snorted at that.

Don't get me wrong. We're still best friends, and Taryn hasn't tried it on with me again, which is just as well because I really don't fancy her. Besides, we're sisters now, so it would be completely wrong. I'm staying far away from all the boys, even though there's a boy in Lower Sixth called Hugo whom I really like. But I'm not going to risk it. The rumours and the bitching have all died down now and I can't bear the thought of them starting again. Next week it's the school dance to mark the end of GCSEs. Mum took us both shopping last week. Because money is tight, neither Taryn nor I had much to spend, but Taryn chose a tuxedo jacket and trousers and I got a red satin dress with spaghetti straps. We stood in the shop together, in adjacent changing rooms, and when I came out of mine, Taryn let out a whistle. 'Look at you, girl. You've got so much rizz!' I wasn't sure about the dress, but Taryn said I absolutely had to wear it. I'd be prettier than the prom queen.

Back at home, Taryn stays in the kitchen cooking with Mum. I take the red dress out of my wardrobe and hold it up against me. I'm worried that it's a bit too daring, too fitted. I look for a little black shrug that I've had for a while and rifle through my drawers pulling out my jumpers. Except I can't find it. And then I remember that Taryn borrowed it a couple of weeks back.

Taryn has the guest room, which actually is a bigger room than mine, but it's a bit soulless, and although Mum said she could put up pictures and make it her own, she's done nothing to the room. She hasn't even got a photo of Dean or her little brother, Jasper, which I think is a bit weird, but I daren't say anything to her, because what do I know about grief? I wander into her room, which is immaculately tidy, unlike my bedroom, which is a permanent tip despite Mum's nagging. The duvet is pulled up and over the pillow, and smoothed out like in a hotel. She's lined up a few bottles and tubes of makeup on the chest of drawers, all in a straight line, with the tallest bottle on the left and the shortest on the right. I walk over to the chest of drawers and pull open the top drawer. It's filled with Taryn's clothes, neatly folded T-shirts and jumpers. The second drawer has her underwear in it. Taryn must be the only person in the world who folds their knickers into neat little parcels. I joked about her tidiness, but Mum bit my head off, saying that it must be one of the few areas of her life that Taryn feels is within her control. Actually, I felt a bit bad after that, because Mum is probably right. I can't find the black shrug, so I pull out the top drawer again, where she keeps her jumpers. I hope she won't mind that I'm going through her things. I slide my hands underneath the pile of jumpers and my fingers curl around something cold and solid. I pull it out.

It glitters in my hand.

What the hell is Taryn doing with Mum's bracelet?

The bracelet that I sent to Jax in return for not posting my nude photos.

I stare at it, not understanding, but then I hear footsteps

on the stairs and I shove it into my pocket, and close her chest of drawers. I'm striding out of her room when she appears in front of me.

'What are you doing?' she asks.

I tug her by the sleeve and pull her into the spare bedroom, closing the door behind me.

'Why have you got Mum's bracelet?' I ask in a low whisper, because I can't let Mum know we've got it.

She frowns.

'The bracelet that I sent to Jax, that I thought was lost forever. I found it underneath your jumpers.'

'What were you doing going through my stuff?' she asks, narrowing her eyes at me.

'Not the point, Taryn. Why have *you* got it?'

She lets out a huff and sits down on the edge of the bed. 'I found it amongst Paige's things. I wasn't to know it was your mum's. I just thought Paige had nicked it from somewhere.' Taryn doesn't call her mum *Mum* anymore.

I turn to stare out of the window. It's a dull summer's day, overcast and muggy.

'Why do you think she had it?' I ask. And then it dawns on me. 'OMG,' I say. 'Was your Mum really Jax? Do you think she was pretending to be Jax, that she was the blackmailer?'

Taryn sighs and lies back on her bed, closing her eyes. 'Honestly, Marnie,' she says. 'it's just the warped sort of thing Paige would do. I told you she's a complete psycho, and now you know the full extent of it. She wanted to create hell for you and your parents and I guess she thought that was funny.'

'But it's not,' I say, rather futilely.

Taryn sits up. 'Of course it's not funny. It's sick. You

know Paige was in prison before, for fraud. She was good with computers and technology and she used to swindle cash out of unsuspecting men. She pretended to me that she was staying with a sick friend for a few months, but I knew the truth. She was in prison. And during that time, in fact all the time, Dean looked after me like a real dad.'

I didn't know that Paige had been sent to prison before, but I assume the police know. I wonder if Mum does.

'I suppose it's a relief that Jax wasn't a real person,' I say, taking out my phone and navigating to his Instagram profile. The real Jax continues to post but the personal profile of Jax, or the one that I believed to be his personal profile, seems to have disappeared. I wonder when Paige took it down. It must have been before she was arrested, and I've had no reason to check on it recently.

'Yeah. At least the photos won't ever be leaked,' Taryn says. 'What are you going to do with the bracelet?'

'Dunno. Need to think about it.'

'Maybe shove it back into the drawer for now,' Taryn suggests.

'Taryn, Marnie! Supper's ready,' Mum shouts up the stairs.

'I need to pee. You go ahead,' Taryn says.

Mum smiles at me when I walk into the kitchen and I feel bad all over again about what I did with the bracelet. I'm thinking about how I can return it to her without it seeming suspicious when Taryn strides into the kitchen, the bracelet lying in the palm of her outstretched hand, sparkling underneath the downlighters.

'Amelia,' Taryn says, her voice saccharine-sweet. 'I was tidying up my things in the wardrobe in the spare room when I found this. Is it yours?'

Mum's eyes widen and her face lights up. 'Oh my goodness, yes! I thought I'd lost it.'

Taryn passes it to Mum, and Mum throws her arms around Taryn, enveloping her in the hug she should have given me. 'I can't tell you how delighted I am!'

'I thought you didn't like things that Dad gave you,' I snipe, markedly looking at her bare ring finger where she used to wear her engagement ring and wedding band.

'This is different,' Mum says. 'It reminds me of how lucky we are to have you.' And then she lets go of Taryn and reddens. 'Sorry, Taryn. That was thoughtless of me.'

Taryn steps away and shrugs. 'It's not your fault that Jasper died. I never thought it was your fault. That was just Paige's warped way of thinking, trying to pass the blame onto someone else. She's delulu. Anyway, I'm stoked that I found the bracelet for you.'

I try to catch Taryn's eye, but she deftly ignores me and helps Mum carry the dishes over to the table.

Taryn takes a big spoonful of the bolognese and groans with pleasure. 'Amelia, your food really is the best,' she says. 'This is bussin.'

'Bussin?' Mum asks, tilting her head to one side.

'Tastes delicious,' Taryn explains.

'It's my pleasure,' Mum says. 'And the fact you found my bracelet, you really are a wonder.' I feel a surge of jealousy because Mum never talks to me like that. It's as if Clover can sense my neediness, because she trots over to me and sits down on my feet. At least I'm still the dog's favourite person.

I can't sleep. I'm tossing and turning and can't stop thinking about Jax, or at least how Paige pretended to be Jax. It's a weird thing for an adult to do, isn't it? I mean, it's not like she got much out of me money-wise, and why didn't she sell the bracelet? It's valuable and she could have got a load of money for it. And it's not like I was to blame for her son's death. In fact, my memory of those days in hospital is all blurred. I think of the messages that she / Jax sent me, and how they seemed so realistic. Even the lingo was right, the sort of phrases that a twenty-something might use, not the sort of language that a forty-year-old woman might know. Mum never uses words like that and I'm pretty sure Paige didn't either, or at least not in my presence. And then it hits me with a wallop. I sit bolt-upright in bed and switch the bedside lamp on. This evening, at supper, Taryn used the word 'bussin' and Mum didn't know what it meant. And Taryn uses words like rizz, and stoked, and delulu, all the urban slang that Jax used in his messages. They're not words that Paige or Mum would use, let alone know. I bash my knuckle into the side of my head as the thought takes hold. Could Taryn have been the blackmailer and not her mother? I don't understand why, but it makes more sense, and it would explain why she had Mum's bracelet.

My mind is racing now. Taryn is in the next-door room. I could ask her, except I doubt she'd tell me the truth. Taryn is clever and she'll twist my words, make it look somehow as if I'm the crazy one. I wonder if I can get hold of her phone, see if she's got anything incriminating on it. I swing my feet out of bed, tiptoe to the door and open it. It's dark in the house and I feel a kernel of nerves, a bit like the horrible sensation in my stomach when the house got gassed. Using my phone as a torch, I step into the corridor and hesitate outside her room. I can see a line under the door, and it's black. Not surprising, since it's about two o'clock in the morning. With my heart in my mouth, I turn the door handle to the spare room. It opens easily without making a sound. I wait for a long moment in the doorway, to be sure that Taryn is asleep. Then I shine my phone towards the bed. Fortunately, she's buried under the duvet, facing away from me, a motionless bundle under the bed covers. I tiptoe into the room, silently praying that she'll stay asleep. I can see her phone on the bedside table, the screen facing downwards. I grab it. Taryn turns over in bed, making a quiet groan as she does so, and I freeze, turning off the light on my phone. But then she settles and her breathing becomes steady and slow again. I tiptoe back out of the room, close the door and hurry back to my bedroom. I sink onto my bed with a feeling of great relief, her phone and mine on my lap.

The next issue I have is working out how to get into Taryn's phone. I've seen her plug in her pin time and time again, except I've never taken any notice. Why would I? It's not like I thought she was hiding anything from me. The only thing I know is that the first digit is a two. I lean my head back against the headboard and think. Taryn's too street-smart to use an obvious code such as her birthday. Besides, it doesn't start with a two. There's a girl that Taryn fancies in our year. They're called Robyn and they use the *they* pronoun. I know that Taryn has been plucking up the courage to ask them out and I'm hopeful that they'll get together at the school dance. I go onto Robyn's socials and search for her birthday. It's the 18th of October. I put in her birthdate but that doesn't work. What else?

Jasper. Her dead brother. A six-year-old was hardly going to be on social media. I scour Taryn's socials, going right back to a few years ago, but there is literally nothing about her brother. I try to recall that horrendous day when I was taken to hospital. It was Clover's birthday and we'd invited a few friends over, telling them to bring their dogs too. Except the party never happened. I woke up and collapsed at the side of the bed. Mum and Dad rushed me to hospital and I felt so sick, I thought I was dying. It was the 2nd of March, Clover's birthday. Poor little Jasper was sick too that day but he didn't make it. Could 2nd of March be Taryn's pin? My fingers tremble as I plug the date into Taryn's phone.

I'm in.

It's a bit sick in the head using the date of your brother's death as a pin, isn't it?

I stare at Taryn's screen, all the apps that are there ready for me to explore. The first thing I do is go onto Instagram, but the only account I find is Taryn's. Of course it is. If she has a fake Instagram account, it'll be connected to another phone, another mobile number. I come out of it and navigate to her photos. The first few are of Robyn, taken at a distance, obviously without her knowing. That's creepy. Then there are a couple of me, including one of me wearing the red evening dress. I navigate back a bit further and the phone slips through my fingers onto the duvet. My breath is coming fast now as I pick it up again.

There are all my naked photos. All the photos I sent to Jax of me in the mirror, posing, exposing. So humiliating. I let out a little whimper. Why would Taryn have my photos? Jax must have been her; she must have been Jax. And I guess she used a burner phone to set up the account and send me all of those horrible messages.

I feel tears prick my eyes as I try to work out what she was playing at. I come out of pictures and go into her notes. She's really organised, with lots of different folders. They're labelled: school; mum; jx; t; uni applications.

Jx. It must be Jax. I swallow hard before I click on the

folder and there it all is. Copies of the messages that she sent me, all dated. Oh God. I thought Taryn was my friend. My best friend. Except friends don't do that. They don't pretend to be a stranger and blackmail each other. I can't stop myself from crying now because I just don't understand. I wonder if it's because Taryn fancied me and I didn't reciprocate, except even that doesn't make sense.

I look through the rest of her notes but there's nothing of interest there, so I come out of notes and look through her other apps. There's one called My Diary.

I feel completely sick when I click on it. So this is what Taryn does when she's forever typing into her phone, her fingers and thumbs moving at lightning speed. Every day she's written what she's done that day along with her thoughts. I go back several months and my eye is caught by a diary entry that is so much longer than most of the others. My chest feels tight as I read.

So it worked. My plan actually worked!!! Dean was a nice enough person, mainly because he was so weak. He let me do anything I wanted, unlike Mum, who creates the biggest fuss over the smallest stuff. So why the fuck did he want to ruin EVERYTHING???? They were so stupid talking about their plans for the future when I could hear what they were saying. Did they ever stop and think for one tiny second how I might feel about it? No. Because they're so fucking self-centred. No one ever thinks about me. What the hell was Dean thinking suggesting we move to the north of Scotland? I mean our lives are here in the south. School is here. Robyn is here. OMG that girl has so much rizz. Everything is here. Maybe I wouldn't feel so bad if I hadn't overheard Dean asking Mum to stop taking the pill. How could he think that he could replace Jasper just like that with another baby? You can't replace a person. Your own fricking son, for God's sake. That just killed me. Completely killed me. And then there was his reaction to me telling him I'm gay. He acted like he was repulsed, almost like he was glad I'm not his real daughter. The thing is, I didn't mean for it to happen because I'm not a psycho like Mum. I left it until today, the day before the wedding. I sneaked out of school at lunchtime and told them I had a dentist's appointment. No one suspects the good girl, do they? Anyway, I knew where Dean was working because he leaves his work diary and stuff lying around. I meant to tell him that I wasn't going to move up north with them, that their plans weren't fair. I knew Dean would listen to me when Mum would just tell me where to stuff it. What I wasn't expecting was for Mum to be there. That was quite the surprise. I stood just behind the door and listened to everything she said and then I couldn't believe it when she hit him over the head with a piece of pipe. Well, actually, I could believe it because Mum's a psycho. Then she left. She just left. I wasn't sure what to do at first. I hurried over to check up on Dean. He still had a pulse, was still breathing. I could have called an ambulance or helped him. And I so nearly did. But then I realised. If Dean died and his body was discovered at a later date, Mum would be the prime suspect. She'd be banged up in jail and I would inherit their money and be able to live the life I actually want to live. Maybe I'd go live in Marnie's fancy house, perhaps get rid of her too and become Amelia's daughter. Maybe I'd just live alone. The more I thought about it, the more it made sense. I'd finish off what Mum started and no one would be any the wiser. I left the piece of pipe that Mum used and found another piece. I brought it down on Dean's head with all my strength. Then...

I can't read any more. Holding the phone, I race into my en-suite and throw up into the toilet pan. I'm shaking uncontrollably as I drink water directly from the tap. I need to go to Mum and we need to call the police. I step out of my bathroom and turn towards my bedroom door and walk straight into Taryn.

'Why have you got my phone?' Taryn asks.

I try to hold it away from her, but she's too quick and grabs it straight out of my hand. Taryn's eyes are dark and she's staring at me with such coldness and hatred, it makes me gasp.

'Why do you hate me so much?' I ask her.

She laughs. It's not her normal laugh, but something more akin to a snort.

'I hate you for the same reason that Mum hates you. You lived and Jasper died. The difference between Paige and me is that she's weak. She should have just burned your house down and everyone in it, not turn the gas on and hope for the best.'

I stare at Taryn, trying to absorb what she's saying. 'Is that what you intend to do?' I ask, my voice sounding croaky and strange.

'Maybe,' Taryn says.

'Why haven't you done it yet?' I ask. 'You've had plenty of opportunity.'

She sneers. 'I'm not my mum. I don't do things on the spur of the moment and fuck up. Look where that got her.'

'But I read your diary. I know that you killed Dean.'

'My diary!' She chortles. 'It's fiction, Marnie. All made up. I'm writing a book.'

'I don't believe you. I'm going to tell Mum and we'll go to the police.'

Taryn laughs again. 'You're so stupid. It's your word against mine, and besides, I'll just delete everything on my phone.'

She's standing there in her long T-shirt looking smug, so pleased with herself. Something snaps inside me and I launch myself at Taryn. I try to prise her fingers off the phone and when that doesn't work, I pull at her hair. But she fights back, stronger and quicker than me. Fingernails gouging at my cheeks, knees knocking the air out of my chest. We're on the floor, scratching, hitting and then, out of the corner of my eyes, I see Taryn pulling at something. The soft pink towelling of my dressing gown. Then, suddenly, I feel something around my neck. It gets tighter and tighter. I can't breathe. I try to force my fingers between the cord and my neck but she's pulling so hard now. The pain is horrendous, the breath leaving my body. I sense my mind shutting down and the bedroom fades into black.

CHAPTER THIRTY

AMELIA

I'm in a deep sleep, but something arouses me. I lie in the darkened bedroom for a long moment trying to come to, wondering what the noises are. And then I sit up in bed. There's banging and screeches and before I know it, I'm out of bed, the light on, and racing out of my bedroom down the corridor. The noises are coming from Marnie's room and terrible images of a stranger dressed all in black, attacking – or even worse, raping – Marnie and Taryn flood my brain. I rush into Marnie's room and to my confusion see Marnie and Taryn. Marnie is on the ground; Taryn is kneeling up, the cord of Marnie's dressing gown around Marnie's neck, and Taryn's pulling, tugging.

'Stop!' I shout.

Taryn releases the cord and immediately jumps up. She's sobbing as she speaks. 'Marnie tried to kill me. She took my phone and then she attacked me. She actually said she was going to kill me, that she hated me because you like me more than her, that I'm cleverer than her and she's so jealous of me, Amelia. I had to stop her. I didn't want to hurt her, but she was trying to kill me.'

I stare at the two girls and then I'm down on my knees, trying to get Marnie to sit up. She's coughing and choking as I rub her back.

'Mum,' she says. Her voice sounds hoarse and sore. 'Get Taryn's phone. Everything's on there.'

The room falls completely silent. The two girls are both staring at me. Waiting for me to do something. Two sets of imploring eyes. Two differing stories. My daughter, still rubbing her neck. Taryn still staring at me, the strangest expression on her face. And in that moment, I realise I have a choice. Taryn or Marnie. Marnie or Taryn. And it's my daughter I must protect. Taryn is a stranger, a girl I barely know.

'Give me your phone, Taryn,' I say, trying to keep my voice level and calm.

'No.' She holds the phone behind her back.

There's a long beat of silence. 'Please, Taryn. Give me your phone.'

'Why should I?'

'Because you're living in my home and I'm asking you for it.'

'Get the phone, Mum,' Marnie croaks. My daughter is shaking with fear and shock. I glance back at Taryn. There must be something incriminating on Taryn's phone, otherwise why would she hide it from me? Why would Marnie be so desperate for me to see it?

I get up and walk towards Taryn, who is standing at the end of Marnie's bed. In that moment, I recall how she hit her own mother over the head with a hammer and a shiver of fear passes through me. I need to take control, to be strategic.

Taryn will have to pass me in order to leave the room. I hold my hand out for the phone, but Taryn tries to dart past, as I thought she might. Except I'm quicker than her, and I stick out my right leg. She topples over it, falling to the ground, her phone skidding out of her hand.

'Stop her, Mum!' Marnie yells as she crawls across the floor and grabs the phone.

I pounce on Taryn, sitting on her back. She struggles, but Marnie joins me and together we're strong enough to pin her to the floor. 'I'll sue you for assault!' she shouts as she tries to wriggle free from us.

'You need to read this,' Marnie says as she opens Taryn's phone.

'It's not true!' Taryn yells. 'Marnie wrote all of that shit to incriminate me. I didn't write it. She's been jealous of me ever since I came to live with you. Haven't you noticed how she's been trying to get rid of me?'

Taryn stops struggling for a moment and there's a long beat of silence. A beat of silence in which I must decide. The decision is easy. I choose my daughter.

'Give me the phone,' I say to Marnie. 'And stay sitting on her.'

Taryn tries to buck upwards, but between us, Marnie and I keep her pinned to the carpet.

Marnie hands me Taryn's phone and I dial 999.

CHAPTER THIRTY-ONE

AMELIA - SIX MONTHS LATER

The last six months have been a whirlwind. Hudson and I are divorcing. The house has been sold. He was desperate to save our marriage and we did sit down and talk, right the way through the night as it turned out. We've both made mistakes. I for being so quick to believe that he was having an affair. He for entertaining the possibility, for trying to cover up his debts, for all those lies. He admitted that Paige came to see him in Manchester, that he took her for supper on the proviso that she had a business proposition to put to him. Except she never did. He woke up the next morning with literally no memory of what had happened that night. To begin with I didn't believe Hudson when he said that she drugged him. I saw the photo of him naked. But the more I got to understand Paige, the more I think he's probably right. Paige left clues for me; the lipstick on the wine glass, the makeup pad in the bathroom. Taryn may claim her mother was impulsive, but she also knew how to plan.

I wish I hadn't 'lost' my savings, but what Hudson did was way worse. It was misplaced pride that stopped him from admitting how bad things had got financially. I can never forgive him for allowing the bailiffs to turn up without giving me any warning. With hindsight, I worked out that it was most likely that Paige stole the money from me, especially when I discovered that she had been convicted of fraud and served time in prison. Romy reminded me how strangely drunk I was that evening we all went out, how I got a phone call from the bank. I feel like such an idiot for never suspecting her. I'm pretty sure that Paige drugged me, and if she drugged me, then she probably drugged Hudson too. So perhaps he didn't have a fling with Paige, or perhaps the woman he was in bed with had nothing to do with Paige. I guess I'll never know for sure. I have told the police about all of this and they promise me that they're actively trying to trace the money, scouring Paige's finances. Even if they do discover that Paige stole my money, I doubt I'll ever get it back.

We will never know for sure if it was Paige who started the rumours about us abusing Marnie. I don't need surety on that; our lives were already unravelling and all Paige did was pull hard on the thread.

At least Hudson and I are on regular speaking terms now. Marnie and I had long chats and we decided that a new start would do us all good. I'm renting a small apartment a few streets away from Hudson in Manchester. Marnie is at sixth form college and is able to relax, away from Taryn, away from Ryan and all the kids who made her life hell. Her GCSE grades weren't the best, but she did well enough to allow her to study A Levels in psychology and biology. She's already made new friends and has settled into our new way of life remarkably well. I'm so proud of my daughter, who has said that she would like to perhaps become a child psychologist one day. Our relationship is much improved, and we share our hopes for the future.

As for me, I'm teaching yoga full-time at a studio in the centre of town. Perhaps one day I will have my own studio, but for now that seems like a distant dream.

Taryn has been charged with Dean's manslaughter. The police found the second piece of pipe that she used to hit Dean with. She'd hidden it in the derelict factory. As expected, it had just her prints on it along with Dean's blood, hair and fragments of bone. She's being held in a young offender's institution. She's also been charged with attempted murder for trying to strangle Marnie. It's a terrible tragedy, because Taryn had such a bright future. The girl literally had everything going for her, except she'd inherited her mother's anger and psychopathic traits. Paige is being assessed in a secure facility. She's facing several charges, including fraud and attempted murder. Before we put the house on the market, the police opened up an investigation into the gas leak in our home, and Paige's prints were all over the hob. Our house key, that she must have taken from Marnie, was found in her home. She was obviously so sure that the house would blow up that she didn't even bother to wear gloves. There's also talk about investigating the death of Paige's mother many years ago, who apparently died of emphysema, although there were also suspicious circumstances.

A couple of weeks ago, I set up a fundraiser for the leading meningitis charity. I've called it, *In Memory of Jasper*. Hudson, Marnie and I are training to run a marathon and I've got lots of other ideas in the pipeline to raise money. I'm setting up a Yogathon, and even Vanessa has promised to promote it and get her staff and clients involved. Money is already coming in online, helped of course by the reams of publicity and column inches over the "Devil Duo" that the press is dubbing Paige and Taryn.

Marnie and I are eating breakfast when the post arrives. Normally, it's bills, so the post isn't something I look forward to. However, in amongst the leaflets advertising double-glazing and orthopaedic shoes, there's a handwritten envelope addressed to me. I don't think too much of it as I tear it open. But when I remove the piece of paper and glance down at the signature, my heart feels as if it is going to leap out of my chest. It's from Taryn.

Marnie looks up at me with a querulous expression. 'What is it?' she asks.

I've promised Marnie and Hudson that we will always tell each other the truth. That secrets will only hurt us. Except it's my job to protect my daughter and, right now, I can't tell her the truth.

'Just a letter from the estate agent,' I say, walking out of the room and into the bathroom. I lock the door and perch on the edge of the bath.

Amelia,

It's been brought to my attention that you've established a fundraiser in Jasper's name. Jasper is MY brother. He was and is nothing to do with you. How dare you use his name without my or Mum's permission! You're exploiting us and we will never forgive you for it.

I can promise you one thing. When I'm free – and I will be free sooner rather than later, by the way – I will come after you. I will come after Marnie. And I will finish off what my mother started. I hope you and Marnie are scared because you should be.

Taryn

My hand is shaking when I finish reading it. This was written by a seventeen-year-old young woman. It's articulate and to the point. And even though I know she can't touch me or Marnie, I'm fearful. I call DC Singh.

That's the trouble with fear. Once it's touched you, when something bad has happened once, you know at a visceral level that it can happen again. Except fear is so destructive. It stops you from living your life to the full. I will never tell Marnie about Taryn's threats, because it's my job to ensure that my daughter lives her life to the full. I will hold the fear close to me forever, I will do whatever I need to, so long as I can set my daughter free.

A LETTER FROM MIRANDA

Thank you so much for reading *You Can Trust Me*.

This book began with a scam. I'm quite a cynical person (perhaps that's why I write psychological thrillers!) and like to think that I can spot a scam. Except I fell for this one hook, line and sinker. An advert popped up on my Facebook feed for a London-based shop that was closing down. The clothes looked excellent and I ordered a number of items.

Yup, you guessed. When I realised I had been sent a Chinese tracking number, I contacted the shop and said I didn't want to receive the goods. They said, tough luck, too late. Of course when the parcel arrived, the clothes were hideous and bore no resemblance to the photos on the website. I requested a refund and to return the goods, at which point I was told I would be charged for every item I wanted to refund and I had to send them back to China.

I had scores of emails with the website, pointing out that they were breaching UK consumer goods laws and were acting fraudulently. I got sob stories and lies and standard responses in return. But ultimately, I was one of the lucky ones. I had paid with my credit card and could prove that fraud had been committed and was subsequently refunded. Nevertheless, it got me thinking. And into my head popped Paige! As normal, the story developed from there and became all about friendships.

Meningitis is a terrible illness and hopefully less prevalent these days, as awareness has grown and vaccinations become available. I had meningitis just before my fifth birthday. In those days, little was known about it. Fortunately, our family GP had seen it in another patient a couple of years earlier, so I was correctly diagnosed and treated. All the same, the repercussions have been life-long.

If you receive my newsletter or are in my Facebook Group, you'll know that I give my followers the opportunity to name characters in my books. Thank you to the following people who requested the names that I've used in *You Can Trust Me*: Taryn Thacker; Cheang Wai Kuen; Natalie @The Spoonie Mummy; Jackie May; Melanie Pleat; Anita Lewis Russell, Melissa Suslowicz Bartz; Amy Louise Hawkins; Romy Wheeler; Vanessa Harrelson Keck, and Teala Higgins who suggested the name Clover for the dog.

As I've mentioned in my previous books, I am so grateful to the book blogging community and the wonderful bloggers who take the time to review my psychological thrillers, share my cover reveals and talk about my books on social media.

A LETTER FROM MIRANDA

Of course a huge thank you to everyone at Inkubator Books. It's such fun working with Brian Lynch, Garret Ryan, Stephen Ryan, Jan Smith, Alice Latchford, Claire Milto, Elizabeth Bayliss, Ella Medler and the rest of the team.

Most importantly, thank *you*. If you have a moment to leave a review on Amazon and Goodreads, I'd be massively grateful. It helps other people find my books.

If you would like a **FREE** copy of my novella, The Cheat, and the chance to name characters in my future books, please sign up to my newsletter at: **https://bit.ly/The-Cheat-Signup**

You'll also get exclusive access to new releases, giveaways and more!

My warmest wishes,

Miranda

PS – Here's that FREE thriller for you: https://bit.ly/The-Cheat-Signup

www.mirandarijks.com

ALSO BY MIRANDA RIJKS

Inkubator Books Titles
<u>Psychological Thrillers</u>
THE VISITORS
THE ARRANGEMENT
THE INFLUENCER
WHAT SHE KNEW
THE ONLY CHILD
THE NEW NEIGHBOUR
THE SECOND WIFE
THE INSOMNIAC
FORGET ME NOT
THE CONCIERGE
THE OTHER MOTHER
THE LODGE
THE HOMEMAKER
MAKE HER PAY
THE GODCHILD
EVERY BREATH YOU TAKE
THE HOUSE SWAP
VIOLETS ARE BLUE
YOU CAN TRUST ME

The Dr Pippa Durrant Mystery Series

FATAL FORTUNE

(Book 1)

FATAL FLOWERS

(Book 2)

FATAL FINALE

(Book 3)

FATAL SERIES BOX SET

Titles Published by the Author

GASPS

I WANT YOU GONE

DESERVE TO DIE

YOU ARE MINE

ROSES ARE RED

Made in the USA
Monee, IL
25 July 2025